cyan sky

BY
rane eden

Thank you for reading my work!

RANEEDEN·INK

THE CAPTAIN

Nikita Venko had commanded the Rhineland for sixteen years. Pushing sixty-three with a bad limp and increasingly painful arthritis, he knew this would be his last tour – but space was his life; giving it up was not something he was ready to face. The thought of it sent his mind reeling. Losing himself in the minutia of life onboard was his only respite.

Even though it had ended decades ago, everything still seemed to involve the war. All the promise behind exploring more of the void had died the moment someone realized they could profit off the deplorable situation they left on the colonies. Mining heavy metals and ice for the reclamation effort was the dominant industry these days. It was the only reason the mining corps came so far out.

Bleary-eyed, he stumbled over to his desk, collapsing in the cracked leather chair. He had accepted that Torv would take his place. Up until now, the younger man had never been given command of a ship this size. Repurposed frigates with twenty or so people, sure – but not two hundred. It was the curse of inexperience, which was all too common in the mining corps. Too few ships.

Dispatch was putting them under a lot of pressure – going so far as to include Torv on the crew roster as second in command. It was plain they wanted him in charge. Which meant, as much as he wanted to relax on this tour, he couldn't – he had to focus. Not just for Torv...but for all the people counting on him for their tour bonus, not to mention their jobs. All of this was just...maddening.

He reached his hand over, steadying it as he powered on the terminal. Cole was worried about the new equipment straining the reactors, but he had given him as much of the budget as possible to keep them online. Naturally they needed more. Only five stops this tour. Reluctantly, he told him to wait.

Thankfully the galleys were stocked. Food was cheap. Metal. Fuel. Tech. Those weren't. At least the crew would be fed until the ship broke down and they were forced to file for unemployment, provided they could make it home in a reasonable time. He ran through the rest of his messages, making quick replies and reminders for tomorrow...or rather later today.

Exhausted, he pulled off his worn jacket and slid back on his bed, flipping on the monitor to an old show. One thing you could always count on, he smiled weakly, was that there would never be a lack of entertainment. It took a lot of effort to push all the Rhineland's worries to the back of his mind, but it had become his norm as he watched the fictional story unfold, lulling him to sleep with its blissful escape from reality.

Morning came too early. He showered and dressed quickly, then fired off a couple messages for the more critical issues. He took the outer loop to the front of the ship, being quickest despite its longer distance. The inner loop had more frequent stops, with miners and departmental crew shuffling in and out. As the tour drew on, he might use it more, but not this near the beginning.

A couple of deck officers exited the door to his left, throwing a slight nod his way. He ambled out, kneading his leg as the doors shut behind him and the automated train slid back down the track. This near the front, the walls were mostly made of metal and vacuum-tempered glass, stained by dust and chemical wash.

Just behind the bridge was a compact room they often used for staff meetings and small breaks. He ducked inside, careful not to hit his head on the door frame. The rest of the roster had already gathered. Sebastian Cole, head of engineering. Nathanial Royce, responsible for networking and records. Akiko Rai, ship's primary doctor and medical supervisor. Zain Rhali, quartermaster. The only one absent was Mikhail Torv, serving as commander for this tour.

"Sir," everyone nodded, as he entered. No one stood. They had abandoned that early on. Very awkward. Lots of bruises.

"Mostly just a summary today," he exhaled, "since not much has changed, based on this morning's messages. Mikhail handled all the pressing ones during the night." A slight grumble escaped Sebastian and a casual grimace from Zain. He knew they weren't accustomed to his taking charge. Not yet.

"Judging by the regular stats and the crew loadout for this tour, we're fine on supplies. All the same, we're getting close to the starting line, so keep a close eye on the tail, Zain, as always," Nik nodded to her. Zain had a very light tattoo around one eye, composed of miniscule blue chain links. Another peeked up through her corps jacket beneath her silver-blond hair, just short enough to glimpse it. The edge of a dolphin.

Zain nodded, "Still restocking all the hot spares we used up on our mining parts, but we should be clear by the time we leave port."

"Good to hear. Nath, I approved as many requests as I could, but I had to give Cole the priority. A couple pallets of net cards should be waiting for us at the last stop tomorrow."

"I'll make do," Nath answered. He never liked his full name. He had served the longest, having been on the Rhineland for every tour. His calloused hands were cradled around his head, matting his wavy red hair. "Can always use rotary dialers. Or tin cans," he winked at Akiko. She smiled slightly.

"I assume you're keeping us free of sickness, Rai?" Nik queried, ticking the dial on his wrist, flicking the display to her report.

"The usual storm colds. Nothing too serious out of the gate. Exposure stats are within acceptable range for the starting leg. I'll let you know of any changes as we progress." Akiko had jet black hair, graying slightly, with blue eyes that bled into purple contacts. She was not a mining corps doctor – she was from the medical corps – they had served together during the war before they went their separate ways. She had signed on for this tour at his request.

"Bloody storm colds. You lot haven't cured them yet?" Nath piped up, rousing a chuckle from the others.

"My *lot* usually works in clean rooms. If you want to live in one, come down to my office and I'll strap you in," she offered playfully. That quieted them. Nath coughed before he stayed quiet.

"Cole," Nik continued, "you and my engines have the full support of the corps credit line...what's left of it at least – I would appreciate it if you didn't waste it." He was only a few years younger than Nik himself, but he was still fit, physically and mentally. His hair was close shaven, alternating between gray and brown.

"Just keep the obstacles out of my way and we'll have a safe trip," Cole nodded, his tone a tightrope of tension.

"Alright," Nik sighed, finally taking his seat, "enough." His coffee mug nearly tipped, his hand shaking as it gripped the table's edge.

"This is my last tour. Naturally, like any captain, I would prefer not to be shadowed – but what I would *prefer* and what the corps *wants* are not in agreement. Mikhail needs the experience, so for this tour, his orders are my orders. I know it's difficult – but we all need to figure out how to make this work. Give him a chance. It's all any of us can do."

"Nik, I didn't mean..." Cole started, but Nik's eyes told him to stop.

"I have to take care of the rest of the deck staffing before we get in. Is there anything else?" he looked around the small room. None volunteered. He stood up, picking up his coffee, "Dismissed."

They all nodded, standing to leave. Cole stayed behind.

"The corps needs captains, Sebastian – make peace," Nik put his hand on his shoulder. Cole again opened his mouth to speak, but stopped.

"I know," Nik nodded, pausing, "but trust goes both ways. Let him figure this out on his own. He'll get there."

"We'll see," Cole agreed reluctantly, leaving with a stifled sigh.

Nik tapped through the rest of the reports, drinking the rest of his coffee. Satisfied, he kneaded his knee again before he stood and left. Nath and Akiko were waiting for him just outside the door.

"I know I haven't been here long, but I thought they would be over this by now," Akiko sighed as the others left the corridor.

"Torv's pushing his limits, Nik," Nath said after a moment. He wasn't used to having Akiko in on their casual conversation – but he knew that Nik trusted her to keep anything to herself. She was in the medical profession after all. Confidentiality was drilled into her.

"That's just it. As far as the corps is concerned, Torv has no limits. He might as well *be* captain," Akiko pointed out.

"Doc, even the corps has its definition of leniency. If not, Nik would be on the docks begging for a job on the passenger liners."

"He's right," Nik sighed, "They don't think Torv's ready."

"Why does Cole have a problem with him, anyway?" she asked.

"Depends on what side of the trench he had a foot in," Nath chuckled morbidly, "I'm guessing Torv must have said something to get to him."

"Any idea what?" Nik asked, bringing up the report from the night before – the ship had lost main power in a couple areas. According to Cole, he patched it. According to Torv, he had made it worse. The report gave credence to both conflicting viewpoints.

"You're the expert there, Nik...guess you are, too Doc. I wasn't part of the first draft. I wasn't in any trenches."

"Oh, I'm sure they could have been in the same trench shooting the same people and Cole would still find a problem with him. It really doesn't matter," Nik shook his head, "because either way, they're liable to end up in *your* office before mine," he looked at Akiko. She smirked and nodded in agreement.

"I've got drugs, but they don't cure egos," she shook her head, fidgeting with the arms of her white-accented jacket. Still fresh.

"You two let me know if anything escalates. For now, I need to have a chat with the miners. Their terms have changed."

"Again? Seriously?" Nath called after him.

"Yeah," he grumbled, starting to walk away.

"Hey, I was being half serious about those storm colds. I think I might have picked something up..." Nath's voice trailed off, followed by Akiko's laugh. He missed that laugh. He missed a lot of things from his old life.

"Captain?" a timid voice asked him, just before he got on the inner loop. He stopped, looking back. It was a girl. The name escaped him – it was one of the deck officer's children.

"Yes?" he answered, summoning a smile. He didn't have time for this.

"I can't find my mom," she said, voice quivering. She could only be seven. Maybe eight. Nadia. That was her name. Couldn't find her mom? The ship was big to a child. He stepped back from the door, leaning down to her level so he could look her in the eyes. He flicked the dial on his wrist. His staff were already on the loop. Nadia's mother was not at her post.

"Let's find her, then," he smiled, suppressing a groan as he stood on his knee. "Where did you get lost?"

"I was trying to count the stops on the tram, but they went by so fast."

He nodded in understanding and the girl took his hand.

There were nine children on this tour. A handful would be adults by the time it was over. Due to age restrictions, they were confined to the outer loop, living quarters, and recreation. That way, they would stay out of the way, but clearly the girl had gone too far. They couldn't afford biometrics everywhere...her mother might need a reminder.

They stepped off a couple minutes later, crossing through the substructure. Nadia's mother worked in hydroponics. A wide array of plants and the smell of fresh flora poured over them as they walked through the aperture. He helped Nadia over the small rise so she wouldn't trip. A man was waiting around the corner.

"Captain? What can I do for you, sir?" he asked.

"Do you know where Junie Lowe is?" Nik asked, slowly pulling Nadia over. The man quickly guessed the problem.

"Nadia, your mom told you not to get off that end of the loop," he scolded slightly, before turning back to him, "Junie is not on duty today, sir. Haven't had time to set the roster. Too busy inventorying for the last stop. I can take Nadia to her quarters."

"But she's not there," Nadia cried. She squeezed Nik's hand, looking between the two of them.

"Do you know where she might be?" Nik asked.

"Yes," he hesitated.

Nik cocked his head and raised his eyebrows, waiting.

"Oliver Tam's quarters, sir."

"I see," he said simply, a slight grin on his lips.

"Please tell her I'm sorry, sir," he said sheepishly.

"I'll let her know," Nik smiled weakly, turning to the girl. "Come on Nadia. Let's get you to your mom."

They left the hydroponics section and crossed back onto the outer loop. After a couple stops, they ended in the bridge officer quarters. The little girl was looking around, wide-eyed at the different way the common room was furnished. It wasn't his choice – corps regulation dictated the higher quality. Perks, they had told him once. He had better battles to fight than lounge furniture.

A few officers nodded to him as they headed out, throwing a glare at Nadia before they quickly looked away. The two of them stopped in front of door marked with "Tam, Oliver" and his corps number etched next to it. He could hear voices, very faint. Music, too. He hated having to do this…but he wasn't Nadia's parent.

Nik pressed the door chime. Oliver answered.

"Captain? Sir, I, uh – what…" he faltered, seeing Nadia. He turned around and said a fast whisper to someone behind him. There was a lot of shuffling before a woman emerged.

"Nadia got a little lost," Nik flashed another weak smile.

Junie pulled her child into the room. "I told you, two stops. Just two, Nadia! Go sit down over there," she huffed, before turning back to him. "Captain Venko, I'm so sorry. I…I'm sure she was hungry. I thought she might sleep more, but with this ship and the…anyway, thank you, sir. But how did you…?" she trailed off.

"We made a stop at hydroponics," Nik explained.

She swore under her breath, "Axel. I'll kill him."

"He said to tell you he was sorry," he added quickly.

"He meant well," she nodded, smoothing her hair. "Oliver and I are registered, sir," she added suddenly, a cold look of realization having crossed her face. "You might need to sync—"

"No need to explain," he cut her off. "Just get the girl some breakfast," he grinned, turning to leave.

"Thank you, Captain!" Nadia's playful voice shouted after him. He could hear her Junie's harsh tone and Nadia's voice rise in defense as the door shut. One crisis down, he laughed softly. If only terms renegotiation was as easy as returning a lost child.

He took the interchange to the inner loop, emerging into the processing center of the ship. The noise of the machines deafened him, barely dampened by the protective barriers. He took the active cancellation buds and stuck them in his ears. Instant relief. A lot of the current activity was just machine testing – if they had any kind of ore inside, the noise would be far less shrill.

"Lisle!" he yelled as he neared the end of the line of machines.

"Venko. Wondering when you'd show up," a grease-stained face answered, pulling his head out of a smoking panel.

"Your office?!" he yelled. The man nodded. They retreated to a small enclosure, ducking inside.

"Don't tell me—" Lisle started.

"They changed the terms," Nik said bluntly.

"—they changed the bloody terms," he finished.

"You knew they would. You saw the price dip."

"Consortium induced inflation. Or is it the coalition. Sometimes I forget which one of us won the war. Seems we're all paying for it."

"Feel free to shoot the messenger. I moved the dials as much as I could. Tour pay remains unchanged. Bonus is entirely yield dependent now. They wouldn't move on that."

"These people have families, Nik!" Lisle shouted.

"And those families are getting advance pay. I made sure of that. I did all I could – they want me out, after all."

"Yeah...heard about that. Sticking you with Torv. I may leave after this tour. Not dealing with that."

"He's learning."

"He better learn faster. Cole is up and ready to kill him. I saw the power drain – pure equipment failure."

"Backups don't turn themselves off on their own," Nik said coldly, "but we're not talking about this. Tell your miners. If the corps had their way, they would have told you after the last stop, not before. The Tigris is in dock and they still have open positions."

"Ice mining don't pay the same way as ore mining, Nik. You know that," he shook his head, already flicking the dial on his wrist, bringing up the mining roster for the trip.

"I did—"

"All you could. I know. I know," Lisle finished for him.

"It's still solid work," Nik sighed.

"Thanks for the heads up, Cap. They may not like it, but I'm sure they'll appreciate it."

"Let me know the damage before we leave the dock," Nik ordered, turning to leave. Lisle grunted in response.

The noise cancellation resumed as soon as the noise hit his ears, leaving him in a strange silence as he stared at the dark array of machines, crunching the remnants of the last tour in their bays. He had remembered working them when he was a kid, watching his dad at the controls. It was a strange art. Compositional analysis could only tell you so much until you cracked it open.

One of the miners had stopped to look at him, pointing his finger behind him. Nik turned to see the machine moving into place. He followed the lift's natural arc as he dodged, groaning as his knee twisted unnaturally. It moved back into place but left him with an aching pain.

Seeing that he seemed to be hurt, the miner came up next to him, signing to ask if he needed help. He seemed impressed that he had dodged it. No, Nik signed back. He was fine. The miner asked one more time before he nodded in understanding, moving on with his work, guiding the lift driver.

He left the processing center behind, taking the interchange back to the outer loop, then back to the bridge. There, he settled into the station near the back. With a small click, he removed the pad on his wrist and connected its hardpoints to the terminal.

The Rhineland's real-time operating system popped up on its display. Everything he cared to know was highlighted in a cascade report on the right. His mail was bunched up on the left. In the center was a free space for writing or archive lookups. His last entry showed the data blocks he'd requested before they moved outside of the common network. They were still filling.

Bandwidth was a precious resource. So was his time, if he cared to admit it. He spent the next few hours rolling through the requests that needed his approval. Departmental shifts. Officer schedules. Mikhail had begun to take on many of them, but they were still shared with him as captain. Nath messaged him every so often to check in – he was getting ready for the last stop, too.

They had asked for the same block of shows. So had some of the deck officers and even a few of the miners. Nath had to filter the requests, so it made sense he could see who was asking for them. Everyone had different tastes. It made him wonder who liked the same hundred-year-old comedies.

Lunch came and went – he skipped it. Torv eventually ended up back on the bridge, offering him some food he had grabbed on his way back up. He ate a few bites before they met to discuss the deck officer staffing. They were a few short, but they'd be able to pick them up from the last stop. Offers were drawn up. Some were accepted before the day was out.

Finally, the night shift had started. Torv had begun to move his hours toward later in the day so they could be staggered. He took over and bid him good night. Nik hesitated before he left the bridge. He had taken his station, clicking his own mobile into place. It didn't feel right, he decided. But it was out of his hands, now.

Crossing the loops during the night was oddly peaceful. The lights were artificially darkened, following a cadence for the ship's clock sync. He took the inner loop into the rear of the ship, where the medical section had been sandwiched between ore processing and living quarters.

"Rai, you finished?" he asked, making her look up from her desk. She was wearing glasses now. Her eyes still had a small wisp of purple without her contacts, otherwise a deep blue.

"I thought I was when I messaged you. I'm not used to people filing a request for every little cut and bruise. Understandable, I guess. Scary thing, getting infected out here."

"So, you lot haven't cured storm colds yet?" he asked playfully. She smirked at him, taking off her glasses. Her eyes grew more brilliant the longer he looked.

"Royce has a case of hypochondria. Probably breathing dust off those ancient net cards in his quarters."

"Did he show you those?" Nik cringed. Royce was a collector. He was trying to get an in with Akiko. Very early in the trip to start, though. They had a few years to warm up to each other.

"No, thank god. Just came up in conversation. He's too friendly, that one. Spent too much time in space," she answered, toggling the switch on her terminal.

"What do you want for dinner?" he asked.

"They make it there. Why do we need to choose?" she turned her head, folding her glasses and slipping them into her pocket.

"Well there's more than one kitchen and they don't all have the same food. For instance, there's a potato spice sandwich that only the mining kitchen makes. Plov and Thai are best from the common kitchen. Or if you're homesick, sushi is Lancing's specialty down in the labs. He might make some old world tempura if you ask. He only opens for a few hours every other night. You have to be on his list."

"And you're on his list?"

"I'm the captain. I'm always on his list," he smiled.

"What's quieter?" she asked, turning off the lights as they left her office. She nodded at one of the other doctors she left in charge.

"Lancing's."

"I'm in the mood for something fried. Is he open tonight?"

"Pretty sure. I'll let him know."

They headed past the loop and down below hydroponics. The smell of the fryer was already in the air by the time they walked into the lab. Workbenches had been cleared and populated with a few trays of food. A couple miners still in their floor jackets were in the corner, trading bets on something they were eating. A handful of uniformed officers were huddled around another. Only a couple single crew members ate on their own, in plainclothes. All of them recognized him immediately, with an almost simultaneous nod before he took a seat.

"Nikita, where have you been hiding her?" an excitable man asked, holding his hand out to shake Akiko's.

"Justice Lancing, Akiko Rai," Nik introduced.

"Filling that vacant post left by Getty, no doubt. Pleasure to have you aboard." He leaned in conspiratorially, whispering, "Getty was getting... stir crazy."

"If his notes are any indication," she nodded, taking the first drink he offered and savoring the first sip before downing the rest. "Can we get sushi and tempura? Nik said to ask."

"Sushi and tempura, coming right up. Feel free to have some of the hors d'oeuvres. Lime concentrate with pepper blends." She thanked him as she tried one. Nik tried the same. Lancing left them alone. They chatted for a bit before she finally stopped the conversation.

"So, is this a friendly dinner?" she asked quietly.

"It's a catch-up dinner," Nik said simply. "Old friends can do that, can't they? That's...friendly, isn't it?"

"I just can't help but think you've lured me into being on your ship for the next five years," she chuckled.

"You said yes," he pointed at her.

"Maybe that's why it felt like a marriage proposal."

"No. The Rhineland is my mistress. Obviously."

"Do the other captains tease you, being Russian on a ship named after a German river?"

"Only the ones who are as smart as you," he laughed, looking into her eyes. She held his gaze for a moment, but Lancing interrupted with a couple plates, filled with sushi rolls and still-smoking tempura.

"Polard gave me his wasabi modification," he pointed toward the small dollop of green sauce.

Nik had a little laugh to himself.

"What?" Akiko asked, a piece of sushi almost to her lips.

"Something I had to do this morning. Axel Polard in hydroponics. Forgot his name at the time," he laughed again, letting it fade out.

"You're worried," she said finally, nibbling at the roll.

"Maybe," he shook his head, dipping a piece of the roll in wasabi and swallowing it whole.

His mouth turned hot and he quickly took a drink of water straight from the carafe.

"His mod has a bit of a kick," Lancing noted, fixing another plate on the other side of the room.

"Yeah. A bit," Nik coughed.

"You're not ready to be off this ship, are you?" she whispered, biting a piece of the tempura. "This is great. I mean, really great. Mama would be impressed."

"How is she?" Nik asked, dodging the question.

"Old. Senile. Nearly blind. Plays too much mahjong with her friends, gambling away her dinner fare. Khiti keeps her company, though. She knows I can't." Khiti was her sister, Nik remembered. Very different personalities.

"We can't all stay on the ground," Nik agreed.

"Is that your way of answering my question?" she smiled.

"I have this tour to figure it out. No matter what, I know my knee is going to kill me if I have to be under real gravity."

"Still hurting?" she frowned.

"Never stopped," he winced, shifting in the chair.

"Getty left your prescription – said you never took it."

"I can take the pain," he smiled with difficulty.

"Stress will make it worse."

"Oh, don't worry, the corps is relieving me of all my stress. Mikhail will have it all soon enough."

"The others don't seem too keen on him."

"Zain will be the one letting me have it soon – Mikhail was both engineer and quartermaster in his previous assignments. Smaller ship. I'm sure he'll have some ideas for 'efficiency' she won't like."

"Rhali. Is she related to—"

"Yes," Nik said quickly, "and she won't talk about it."

"Oh. Cause she's—"

"Not a man. Yeah."

"You would think even runners would make an exception. They've got to be running low on bodies just like everybody else," Akiko drew back, scrunching up her forehead from the last bite.

"I think she'd rather be out of the family business. Ask her when you find the time. She might open up to you. I operate under the impression that she likes me because I *don't* ask."

"I'll leave it alone, then," Akiko nodded to herself, grabbing the last piece of tempura. Nik was glad – he only liked the chicken. She was still fond of shrimp.

They talked a little more as they finished up. He filled in the few gaps where they had not messaged each other over the years – mostly due to his periods spent exploring and scavenging for the corps off the beaten path. She had completed her medical thesis on the effects of zero gravity in medicinal plants – far from the first one on the subject, but by far the most comprehensive.

"I better get going. Tomorrow will be busy. You should too – you need some sleep," Akiko glared at him. He sighed in agreement.

They waved goodbye to Lancing and headed out to the substructure, passing through the recreation section before they ended in the officer's quarters. Akiko's were setup in the ring beside the other department heads. Nik's were sequestered. He stopped at her door. Nearly an hour past midnight, the floor was deserted.

"Why did you say yes?" he finally asked.

Akiko sighed, "It was a lot of things, really...but one in particular. You mentioned your dad. I know you only bring him up when you're struggling with a decision. I didn't want you to struggle. You'll always be my friend. I wasn't doing anything special and you needed me. The timing worked out well enough."

"Read me that well, huh?" he smiled.

"It's not *that* easy," she squinted and narrowed her eyes at him, laughing slightly. His head lit up with other memories of that laugh.

"Come here," she held out her arms, giving him a hug. She was shorter than he was, leaving her head cradled on his chest. He held her for a few more moments, closing his eyes.

"Thanks for coming with me, Akiko," he whispered, then broke the embrace, "Good night."

"Good night, Nik," she nodded with a yawn, opening her door.

Nik left as it closed, heading to his own cabin on the next floor up. The lights slowly brightened as he neared his door. The hidden biometric scanners read him and let him inside. He slid into the chair, leaning back and stretching his leg under the desk. He toggled the terminal and quickly went through the last remaining messages.

Was he worried about the tour? No. This crew would be fine. Was he anxious about giving up the Rhineland? Certainly. If he wanted to relinquish his command tomorrow, they would have no choice but to promote Torv to captain. He briefly imagined what kind of trial by fire would befall this ship if he left it on the docks.

The fantasy ended there. He had nowhere he wanted to go. The only refuge he knew was here. And the corps was ready to take it away from him. He scrolled down to his saved messages, picking out the memo. The text glowed beneath the screen's ink.

DATE: 2248-03-17 EC
TO: Consortium Registrar; Coalition Registrar; Transfer Registrar
CC: Nikita Kristian Venko; Mikhail Alexei Torv

FROM: Dispatch, Mining Corps Operations
SUBJECT: MCV Rhineland

Nikita Venko has captained the MCV Rhineland for three successful tours. Along with his previous 22 years of service under the Consortium transfer regime, his benefits have been maximized to their post-war values per the cross-class agreement.

While Venko's service record has been exemplary, his extended time in low gravity environments puts him and future tours under his command at increased risk. In the interest of his crew and by the authorization of the Mining Corps management, the captain is to be retired following the completion of his fourth tour.

Effective 2248-06-01 EC, Mikhail Torv will oversee day-to-day operations aboard the Rhineland, with Captain Venko delegated to a support role, retaining final judgment on personnel and command decisions. Per the attached authorization, we request the Registrars sync Commander Torv with the appropriate opcodes for buoy, dark and scuttle protocols.

Deckard Fisher
Director of Dispatch, Mining Corps Operations

That was it then. The clock on the terminal was synced, reading 2248-06-01, 01:23 hours. Torv was in command. He took a half empty bottle out of his desk drawer, twisting to see the label. He shook his head, putting it back in the drawer. Maybe he would get an extra hour of sleep today.

He sighed and slumped back in bed, stretching his aching leg.

Ryan Mainer liked the Rhineland at night, when the ship's heating was turned down and most of the crew was asleep. Deep mining tours were usually boring and finding time by himself was next to impossible. Pulling the folds of his jacket tighter, he left the barracks, his footsteps quiet while he left his snoring bunkmates. A small *clank* let him the know the door had shut behind him.

A large ore processing factory made up the midsection of the Rhineland, running through its smelting phase to keep the sound down. Only one shift ran the smelting hours and they usually weren't the most amicable people. Avoiding the noise was a long walk, but Mainer was happy to. It was 02:37 ship time, according to the clock sync on his arm.

Officer quarters, medical, and recreation were all situated near the back, as was the only kitchen still open at this hour, all woven into the hexagonal cylinder framework of the ship's superstructure. Hydroponics and the mining barracks, where he had just left, were hiding in the substructure in the ship's center. Engineering was connected all along the length of the ship, controlling the thrusters laced to the outer hull.

Muscle memory led him straight to the inner loop, where easy access corridors led to most parts of the ship, aided by the magnetic lifts. This late, they ran on demand. He hit the kitchen section then slid down into a seat. The blank substructure and the mining lights slid by in a kaleidoscope.

Four 12-hour shifts made up the rotation – 06:00, 09:00, 12:00, and 18:00. Each miner was given two days off a week rather than a set weekend, so productivity was always smooth. He was in the shift that ended at midnight. After taking a quick shower, he usually took his walk to the common. His meal schedule had always been messed up – most ate near the end of the shift during their break, though he preferred to be done working when he was eating.

Slowly the lift decelerated, and a soft green light told him he had arrived. A handful of people walked by outside, wearing exercise clothes, towels around their necks. A couple. Must be some of the officers, he decided. He was wearing his usual set of casuals, black jeans, dark blue t-shirt and a light jacket. He stepped out, watching the couple pass by the corner up ahead. Something one had said to the other...it was in German, which he didn't know.

Most people aboard spoke the colonial dialects, but he quickly found that most of the officers knew English or Mandarin, which was the only thing spoken in the trade lanes. He was born to Earth migrants on Proxima. People from all worlds had joined the mining corps when intersystem spaceflight was commercialized. It was a regular melting pot of personalities, with all the simmer and bite.

Only a few others were in the common with him, its soft lighting appropriate for the late hour. He took a seat at one of the tables near the kitchen. He had put in his order before he left the barracks and one of the two people in the kitchen crew was already bringing it out. Her name was Iris. They had gone out a few times since the tour started, but nothing came of it. She smiled on seeing him. He smiled back.

"Rough shift?" she asked, her German accent heavy, "Your eyes look darker than usual."

"Nothing out of the ordinary," he deflected, returning the smile. She had to break away as a couple others stepped in, and it took him a second to realize why. It was the captain and the new tour commander, Torv.

A conversation took place between them, mostly in Russian, lasting for several minutes. He understood very little. Iris delivered a couple plates with steaks, which the captain quickly thanked her for while offering up a quick joke. Mainer ate his burger, trying to discern what they were talking about through context. Captain Venko was a public figure on the ship. Though he was getting on in years, his personality was relatively warm. He had often been through the mining section on surprise visits.

Something was wrong. Something in the captain's expression had changed subtly. His normally plucky demeanor had taken a solemn turn. As soon as the pair finished their meals they left, still trading comments, though they had grown much quieter. Iris eventually made her way over to him and sat down. She was trying to hold back tears, forcing him to forget about the captain.

"What's wrong?" Mainer asked quickly, her transformation from earlier not lost on him.

"I...I'm pregnant," she whispered softly.

It's not mine, was his gut reaction. Couldn't be. But he had learned to hold back comments like that, "How far along?" he asked quietly, leaning forward. She didn't look like she had gained much weight yet. That probably wouldn't last for too long.

"Two months," she replied, "but I can't afford it. I can't, Ryan."

The tour just started two months ago. It wouldn't end for five years. A trip back to Sol would cost way more than the corps was giving her as part of the kitchen crew. In other words, she was going to have it here regardless. Government regulation was explicit on abortion periods...as well as fines and punishment. Had been since the war ended. She had broken down in front of him, her eyes sullen.

"Who's is it?" he asked, against his better judgment.

"He doesn't know," she paused, sniffling, "but he's back in Sol."

"Can you get a ticket back?" he asked, knowing the answer.

"No...there's no work there, Ryan. There's nothing. He...he doesn't deserve this."

"Neither do you," Mainer said quickly.

"It doesn't matter. He doesn't have money anyway," she shook her head, wiping her tears with the edge of her jacket. Mainer looked into her eyes, which were scared and afraid. There were a few other children aboard – but they were all the officers' kids. Miners and the civilian crew weren't classed for them. Against corps policy.

"Whatever you need," Mainer started slowly, swallowing hard against his throat, "I'm here for you." He grabbed her hand and held it for a long handful of moments. Between the gradual flow of diners, he talked to her, catching up with what had happened. She told him how they had met. Apparently, the man was a first-year military university student and it would destroy them both if it was reported. Undocumented children would land him in prison. In the end, he knew she wouldn't tell him, no matter what.

Iris eventually ended her shift at 06:00, and Mainer walked her back to the auxiliary crew quarters. She was feeling better, which made him feel better about leaving her alone. He didn't think she would do anything too rash...but she sounded desperate.

A lot of people were getting out and about on his way back to the barracks. Luckily everyone in his section was still asleep as he hit the bunk. Most wouldn't get up for another couple hours. He threw his jacket to the side on top of his footlocker. He struggled to keep his eyes open as he pulled the blanket over his face, blocking out at the ambient light, thinking about Iris.

He woke up for his shift a little later than he liked, forcing him to wait for an unoccupied shower. The night before weighed on him while he got ready, lingering in his thoughts. Iris was in for some trouble. Minimizing it was the only hope she had...and the only way to do that was to throw himself in the way of the politics. He laughed to himself as he dried off, thinking about what his sister would think about him having a kid.

But it wasn't his kid, he reminded himself. No. It was some idiot who had gotten his girl pregnant. He just wasn't here to pay for his part in it. She could try to pretend otherwise but how else was it going to happen? They knew the risks. Why were they both so...stupid? He half wanted to look him up and report him just for that – but it would also hurt Iris. That kind of cruelty wasn't in him.

It stayed in the back of his mind as he went into his shift. As he passed by the foreman's window, he saw Lisle talking with Torv, both yelling. *Probably the lack of miners*, he thought grimly. They had left the dock with a few too short of regulation and despite Lisle's assurances, they all knew it was going to be a problem. That was why there were four shifts rather than three. As if rotation was going to solve the issue.

This was his second mining tour but only his first on the Rhineland. It was a decent enough ship. A bit old – but all of them were a bit old. The corps preferred to use up the fuel rods before commissioning new ships. At least, that's what his last ship's chief engineer had told him. Cole was a different breed. Never saw him outside of engineering – he always seemed to be working.

While the machine was threading the large rock into its waiting socket, he took a couple minutes to eat a last-minute breakfast made up of juice and a protein bar. He took bites absently, accidentally taking a hard chew on the wrapper after he had already eaten the last piece. Swearing in frustration, he swallowed the juice and picked up his headset, slipping it down until it clicked on his suit.

In front of him, the rock had been seated in the socket, lighting up with thin crisscrossing lights, gridding it out so he could pick where the compositional analysis pointed him. He took a deep breath and walked in, letting the ship's inner gravity wash away and leave him weightless. The vacuum seal on his suit tightened, cinching the form fitting harness around him.

He aimed his mining laser at the first grid spot he could reach, a small cube of exactly 10 cm. Nothing. He moved to the next, then the next, then the next. The hours passed, yielding a handful of useful dense metals but none of the real prize – nuclear concentrate. Thorium, usually, but other metals seemed to pop up from time to time. Mining it was a careful undertaking. The ore processor did most of the preliminary work, breaking up large rocks and leaving the chunks for manual processing.

Of course, it was all toxic. All the miners, himself included, had been given the K9 anti-rad panel before the tour started. Most of the crew already had the older K8 from their previous tenure. The inoculation was just a front line precaution, however – the ship's filters were extremely efficient at scrubbing and expelling larger than average amounts of radioactive metals before they made it into the rest of the ship.

After a long twelve hours, he finished up and punched out. He hurried back to the barracks, showering and throwing his casuals back on. He made his way to the common, where Iris was serving a large group of officers. Someone's birthday, apparently. She waved at him and he waved back. After a few minutes, she came to give him his tray, saying she would meet him later. He told her about his current shift hours, and she frowned.

"My next day off is tomorrow. I'll come by then. I think there's a game day in one of the labs...if you want to go."

"Ok, sounds fun," she said after a moment, smiling before she left him.

He left his tray after he finished eating, heading over to the row of terminals in the common. The sync on his arm was just a fancy space radio that read what the inside of the ship was broadcasting, not a full-fledged computer. It told the ship time and some event notices, but not much else. Full mobile links were expensive to make and maintain, usually only requisitioned to the senior officers.

There was a small terminal on the wall of his bunk, but he didn't feel like heading back there just yet. He looked up the basics on birthing. All the different trimesters and the signs. There was no way Iris could hide it. Not without ending it, and even if she could stomach that, regulation-wise it was out of the question.

The risk to the child was too great to ignore, too. If she didn't get checked up, the centrifugal tensors – the things keeping the ship spinning so they could feel some semblance of gravity – they could be hurting the baby. Blood clotting in the wrong places. His face went a little white while he stared at the images. Having read everything he cared to, he turned the terminal off with disgust. He suddenly felt a surge of regret.

Was this right? In truth, he didn't love her. She just had no one else. What would the captain think – or worse, the new commander, Torv? He got the sense from the other miners that had been on the Rhineland longer that he didn't seem as forgiving as Captain Venko – at least not in their yield results. Could be different for the civilian crew. Some people were like that...treating miners with no respect.

He took a walk around the outer loop, thinking about what he could say – what *could* he say? If he said it was his, the fine would be on both of them... but at least it wouldn't all be on her. All the same, any DNA comparison would out him. They weren't going to radio home, not until the first legitimate stop at 30 months.

Nothing had gone as planned, he decided, sidling up to a window to watch the stars streak by. He wondered how fast they were going. They were still building acceleration, technically. Cole may have been absent around the ship, but he certainly wasn't sleeping on the job. Catching comet debris and asteroids was the hardest part. The lasers were the most violent and beautiful thing he had witnessed.

He remembered the first time he had seen one of these ships. His dad had walked on out on his mom when he was thirteen. She had died a couple years later. Draft work was easy to come by when you were younger. He absentmindedly rubbed his shoulder where the injector had gone into the muscle. Space was dangerous – almost everyone out here was on a pharmacopoeia of vaccines.

His old ship, the Yangtze, was almost as big as the Rhineland. Both were asteroid catchers. He closed his eyes and imagined the near-invisible lasers, slicing through the vacuum and shearing the rocks. You could almost make out the whisper of blue and violet light as it stopped, its wake haloed in the space dust.

A loud noise interrupted his stream of thought. A kid was wailing as his parent carried him by the neck. No more than ten or eleven, he was fighting his father with everything he could, shouting at his dad to let him go – that he hadn't done anything wrong.

"It was Nadia. She told me there was—"

"I don't care what she told you – I care what *I* told you. The bridge is off limits to children, period. If I see you or your friends up there again, I'll lock you out of the terminal for a month."

"A *month?*" the child screamed, trying to wrestle away.

"Want to start right now?!" the father yelled.

Ryan tried not to look but the officer caught his eye, giving him a half smirk as he passed, shrugging his shoulders as the child gave up in defeat. He nodded and the officer nodded back, hurrying away and almost dragging the kid. Was this what he had to look forward to? He laughed softly, hoping the man hadn't heard him.

There were other girls – other *women* – he corrected, that he had been with as he drifted between ships. Some were younger, some were older. Always ended the same. Once the tour was over, so was the relationship. He had tried the same old formula with Iris. She didn't want that kind of relationship. Now he knew why.

So why was he doing this? He didn't know, he decided, looking at his fingernails. They were clean but they didn't feel clean. He knew they were – the showers in the barracks were bled with a lot of abrasive salts and melted ices that wouldn't kill their skin but rid his pores of virtually anything else. No. He was a miner. It wasn't what he had *wanted* to be... but it was what he was.

This child. This kid. This *person*, he corrected, was going to grow up on this ship for at least four years of their life. It made his heart turn over in his chest. He couldn't be their father. What had they gone out on? Four dates, he counted. Three, the one where he left early didn't count. What was he thinking?

"I'm here for you," he whispered his own words to himself, "what were you thinking, Ryan?" He watched the vapor fog up the dark glass on the inner hull of the ship. He was leaning all the way over, breathing heavily. His heart danced to its own tune and he felt weak. It got colder.

"Hey, you alright?" a voice asked after a while. He lifted his head, swallowing hard and trying to find his voice. The panic attack had slowly subsided. He looked over to find a woman sidling up to the railing with him. She was the quartermaster. He couldn't remember her name.

"Yeah," he said after a while, "I like your tattoo," he added spontaneously. The circle of chain-link ink was intriguing.

"Thanks. You're one of the miners, right?" she asked. He looked at her eyes. They were very green, like tiny emeralds. Her silver-blond hair was matted against her head. She had been running.

"Yeah," he managed, "Ryan. Ryan Mainer."

"Zain. Zain Rhali," she mimicked, putting the mobile link she was carrying back on her arm then holding out her gloved hand. He shook it, his hands clammy. Lisle was usually the only one who talked with her. She seemed kind enough.

"You sure you're alright?" she asked, "You were doubled over the rail there like you were storm sick. Cold's going 'round – had one last tour. Not a fun time."

"No, I'm not sick," he shook his head, "just tired."

"Lisle is working you guys to death. I could move some more of the livelier coffee down to the floor for you, if that would help."

"I don't drink it – the others do. I'm sure they'd appreciate it."

"I'll get the order in. Lancing's been wanting to push his blend. The magicians in hydroponics are interested too," she laughed. He chuckled.

"Well, I've got some missing crates to find – get some sleep, Mainer," she half-yelled, starting off again.

"I will," he nodded as she disappeared down the corridor.

He looked at his sync. 05:38. He had a shift in six hours, then a day off. A day he really needed. With a heavy sigh, he started back to the barracks. His eyes barely stayed open long enough for him to collapse in the bunk. When he woke up, his shift was in less than ten minutes. He rushed to the shower. Thankfully one was empty.

With little time to spare, he pulled his suit on and entered the chamber. A carved-out rock had already been loaded, leaving the last section to him.

He worked as fast as his hands could manage, clearing the yield and leaving the chamber so he could start the ejection process.

The clamps released, gently nudging the sliced and diced rock out in sheets, carved by invisible lasers and ejected through the tunnel that led to the ship's rear and ultimately into space. Another rock loaded but his shift was over. The next miner shook his hand as he exited the chamber, face hidden behind the helmet. He knew who it was. Kipp Euler. First tour.

After a shower, he collapsed back on the bunk and turned to face the terminal on the ceiling, grabbing the earpiece tagged to it. He pulled down the keyboard and keyed in the series he had been watching a few days ago. It was a period drama from the late 2080s, when exploration was first starting out. The first season had been so-so, but the second picked up quickly enough, ending in the cliffhanger that there were spies in the terraforming corporations working to keep the colonists on Earth.

The two spatial governments didn't exist at that point in time. No Consortium. No Coalition. No complex post-war transfer regime. The writers had decided on an organization called UNA, which stood for United Nations Autonomy – every character had their own way of pronouncing it. The show was an acronym soup. UNA's job was to protect the expansion of the colonists.

It painted a pretty picture. Heroic individuals banding together to keep people safe from the power-hungry space barons. He supposed that was why he was drawn to it – the parody had become reality. In the real world, the Mining Corps had started as a combination of several asteroid cracking companies from those first years.

Independent corporations couldn't run things forever. By the mid-2100s, the Earth-founded Consortium had leveraged its regulatory power to settle disputes and created the legal oligopoly. Not to be outdone, the extra-planetary city-states under the Coalition took issue with this and established their own oligopolies to control the rest of resource distribution. The war came next.

But the war was now history – and more *story* than anything else. Unlike the wars of the past, this one left no legends. Devastating nuclear weapons and hard radiation obliterated populations. The war was the reason he never knew his grandparents. The teacher that had taught him all this was only a kid themselves when everything had finally quieted down.

He knew very few people who had come away alive. They were like the captain, grey-haired and damaged in one way or another. The old man had a limp that became painfully obvious if you stared long enough. No one dared mess with him, however. The rumors he had heard among the miners painted the otherwise kind old man as a vicious killer. Trained as a pilot and a shock trooper. How else would he still be alive?

The truth was somewhere in between. Always was. History was a mild curiosity for him. When the rocks were loading or unloading and he could spare some time, he would read articles and books on the war he'd loaded on his static pad. Reading was his secondary hobby, after terminal shows.

The show eventually stopped on its own and he was too tired to keep going. He folded the terminal back up and pulled the cover over his shoulders, falling asleep in the quiet darkness. His sync woke him up at 11:00. He felt much more rested than he had the last few days, ready for a day off.

Iris was waiting for him at the common. She was wearing her dark blue petticoat jacket and a thick white sweater underneath. It was usually a bit cold at ambient temperature in the labs, so it was sensible. He was wearing his, too. From what few clothes he owned, it was his favorite. He had bought it with the payout from his first tour. It was dark with cobalt blue accents. Light, but warm.

"What do you like to play most?" she asked.

"Anything where we're on a team," he replied quickly.

"You don't like to compete?" she laughed.

"If someone loses, we all lose. If we win, we all win. I like it better that way. Makes you help rather than try to ruin each other."

"Sounds like you're forcing people to help – is that fun?"

"Well, I can play competitive if you want," he smiled.

"I just like to play what's fun," she said innocently.

"Then let's play what's fun," he agreed as they walked into the lab. Several tables were setup with terminals.

"Let's play against the computer. That's not really competing, is it?" she asked, turning her head to face him.

"Depends on what the computer thinks," Ryan snickered.

"If it starts thinking, you're in trouble, Mainer," Euler said next to him. He must have just got off his shift.

"Same rules as last week," the lab technician explained as the tables filled with others, "no new game variants. We scrubbed the model data, so it won't know who you are this time around. Let me know if it errors out and I'll check its net connection."

"Kipp, this is Iris. Don't know if you two have met," Ryan introduced. Kipp shook her hand.

"Think I saw you in the common – you work the kitchen, right?"

Iris nodded, then closed her eyes, "Chicken salad, bean and crutons?"

"Yes," he laughed, "that's me."

"How do they keep that meat fresh?" he asked.

"Do you really want to know?" Ryan eyed him, furrowing his eyebrows. Kipp nodded that yes, he did.

"It's a really serious plant-based preservative. We have to take it out before serving – you don't actually eat it," Iris said quickly, watching Kipp's expression change and his face turn a little green.

"Welcome to space," Ryan laughed.

"What do you think they do with what they learn out here?" Kipp had recovered, taking a seat with Iris and Ryan.

"What the computer learns? Sell it for something, I'm sure," Ryan guessed. They started the program on the terminal.

The flat screens on the table went black, then lit up with several tiles and cards. After a tutorial round, the three of them figured out what they had to do – the computer was building a product of some kind. They had to match it by making trades between each other so that it would run out before it could produce the end-product. Learning who and what to trade was simple, but hard to get right in order to beat the computer to market.

"This is a bit boring," Kipp said as they finished.

"You should try the simulator," Ryan told him.

"What simulator?"

"The auxiliary navigation simulator. They use it for training navigators should the network go down," the technician explained. "They also use it for more...recreational purposes."

"One of the network team loaded it with combat sims," Ryan said, raising his eyebrows.

"With guns and everything?" Kipp perked up.

"Yup. All you need to do is ask to be put on the list and promise not to break anything – do that and you're never getting back on that list," the technician warned.

"Sounds like they're just inviting someone to break something," Iris grimaced at the thought.

"Well it needs to be tested, too, just like the hardware for these games – that's what these game days are for, to make sure the net links are error free. Finding ways to repurpose downtime into recreation is part of the fun, honestly."

"I guess that makes sense," she nodded, shrugging at Ryan.

They left after that to get dinner at the mining kitchen, since Iris didn't want to make her friends at the common kitchen work more just for her. After that, they headed toward the movie night that was hosted in the rec ring theater.

Two bags of popcorn and a large soda later, the movie was over. It was one of the new ones from the Benjamin Actors Guild – the only high-production value group left – so it was probably licensed. Most of the time they had indie films. It was pretty thrilling though. Lots of action. The complex projection mirrors gave the people on screen a lot of depth.

Together they took a walk to wind the night down. They came to the farthest part of the outer loop, where a small view opened on a spot beneath the railing, showing the rest of the ring above them. Looking too long made your head spin.

"You don't have to help me," Iris finally whispered.

"It's alright," Ryan replied in kind.

"No, it's not. I shouldn't have told you. It's just..." she stopped, unsure of what to say.

"It's alright," Ryan repeated, wrapping his arm around her, lowering them both down next to the railing so they could look up without getting sick.

"What am I going to do?" she asked, fighting back tears.

"We'll figure it out – together," he promised.

"I can't do this to you," she shook her head, pulling away from him, "this is my mistake. I won't make it yours, too."

"And I won't let you go through this alone," he said resolutely, putting his arm back around her. After a few moments, she gave a large sigh and slowly nuzzled her head on his shoulder, looking up.

"Thank you," she whispered.

Ryan looked over to see her closing her eyes. He hadn't really noticed during the day, but she was clearly exhausted. Her breathing slowed and he knew she had fallen asleep. He gently brushed some of the dark hair out of her face, watching her rest.

Two months ago, he had considered leaving when the terms changed. If he had, he wouldn't have to deal with this, but Iris would be alone. Was this the right decision? Was this what he wanted? There were other ships he could have found. Other jobs that paid higher. But there would always be other paths to take. There would only ever be one path *taken*. Now that path was with her.

I'm here for you, he thought, closing his eyes.

THE DOCTOR

Akiko Rai was a light sleeper, which helped her to deal with the odd hours aboard ship. She was the only real medical officer onboard. The mining corps had tried to send another candidate to be trained as a permanent replacement, but he had canceled his posting before they left – space was not his calling. Ever since the first time she left Earth's atmosphere...it just felt right to be out of gravity. Even if it was in orbit – even if it was on an old mining ship. It was the only way to see something other than the inside of an operating room.

Like Nik, she had been enlisted when the war started. Those dark moments had served to solidify her feelings rather than dim them. Safety wasn't found in hiding. It was found in freedom. And nothing was freer than space. That was a nice thought, she told herself, filling out the rest of the forms for the day, filing them digitally in the ship's archive server. It helped to distract her from the way Torv had been running them the past few months.

Her thoughts turned to the young woman in the civilian crew, Iris Friedrich. She had an undocumented pregnancy. On Earth that wasn't too abnormal...but the mining corps had strict rules on medical supplements – which included a timed birth control. The chances of circumvention were at least 100000 to 1. She had beat those odds...or somehow skipped the birth control. It didn't matter anyway. Abortion was only recommended in the first few weeks. After that, regulation was clear that the child had to be surrendered to the state.

Of course, what the "state" was on a five-year tour was a very interesting question. They wouldn't book her a ticket to Sol, so how to handle this was a difficult question. Iris likely didn't know they knew yet. Best to get this settled as soon as possible. She brought up Nik and Torv's schedule, found a slot for fifteen minutes the next day, then slotted her own time to go and collect the girl.

One more set of reports left. Miners complaining about the early stages of radiation sickness. Or more correctly, miners watching too many movies and reading too much medical advice. Unfortunately for them, they all had the same wheat poisoning from identical non-traditional alcohols. Akiko sent a note to their supervisor to warn them subtly, unless they want a real report with all the official markup. No point in upsetting the status quo down there...they had more than enough to deal with already. If they would stop making rotgut like a bunch of idiots, the problem would solve itself, anyway.

She powered down the terminal and left the two orderlies alone, who were stitching up a broken arm on a man who came in an hour earlier. He also had a few unusual bruises which had not quite gained their natural color back, as if he had applied quick healing gel a little too liberally. Could have been any number of things – maybe he was accident prone. She wasn't sure if he was an officer or a miner – she'd yet to memorize them all. Maybe he came at night to avoid a closer look. She'd follow up tomorrow.

"Torv and Nik are busy again, I take it," she said, slightly annoyed to find Nath was waiting for her in the corridor. He had made it a goal of his to get to know her, either for personal or professional reasons – they were both Nik's friends, after all, and should get to know each other. It wasn't the worst idea.

"Yeah, the commander is still getting his bearings. Three months in, I figured he'd have it down, but I guess it's the people aspect he hasn't quite grasped yet. Expects a lot more of out the regulars than they're used to. Even Cole is saying he should take a break – and that man barely sleeps."

"And what about you? It's past midnight – shouldn't you be in bed?" she mused, turning the corner with Nath catching up behind her. She hadn't bothered to stop for him.

"I don't start shoving until midday. Most of my job is better done at night, when no one's using the critical systems. Natural downtime. Figured you'd have noticed that by now," he lamented.

"I guess I haven't. So, are you going to follow me to my door?" Akiko laughed, half-heartedly. He stopped. Slowly she did as well, turning to see just how much she'd hurt his feelings. He did not *seem* phased, but she could tell he knew what was coming, all the same.

"I just noticed that you keep the same hours during the week and I wanted to ask if you might want to sync up a little more often. Now that it's finally quieted down the last few weeks. You know. For a date. Or two."

Akiko sighed softly. "I'm usually a private person. I still have a lot of things to catch up on. All of this – being on a ship – it's still new to me, and adding more on top of that isn't what I want to do right now. I'll let you know when that changes, ok?" Most of what she said was true.

"Alright. Another time," Nath nodded, heading off in the opposite direction. She watched him go, hoping she hadn't hurt him too much. Finally, she turned and headed toward the common. Her order should be finished by now. She was right – it was waiting on the heating pads. While she picked it up, she looked back into the small kitchen.

Iris was off to the side, running the processing units. She was a short girl, under a meter and three quarters, dark haired with a round face and hazel eyes. She was attractive and had a nice smile – Akiko watched as she laughed at her coworker's joke. Her eyes shifted down to her stomach, where the smallest bump was showing. Part of her didn't want to ruin her equilibrium, but the professional in her knew she had a duty.

The drugs she and her boyfriend in the mining barracks had been requesting were the most telling – they were both clever, but not too clever. Drugs could only prolong the inevitable. That was the main reason she needed to out this problem now – not given more direct treatment, the artificial gravity would start harming the child in the next few weeks.

Everyone had physicals days before the mission started, and they didn't anticipate this thing happening so soon – first onboard physicals were in six months. According to those initial results, she was on the monitored birth control, so chance seemed to have favored her. It wasn't her fault, Akiko decided. It had been a long time since she'd had to deal with this sort of thing...but leniency always seemed to be the right option when children were involved.

Akiko left the common and went to her quarters. They were spacious, like the other senior officers. Three rooms. Regular officers had two, civilians had one. All came with a full bath. Miners were crammed together four to a barracks, due to regulation...with the high-content decontamination showers better to handle the latent radiation and other cross-contamination. It was a small price to pay for guaranteed income, food and recreation for the trip. Still, it could get cramped in there...she'd had to visit on a few occasions.

She grabbed a drink out of her fridge and found herself staring at the few pictures magnetized to the front. A few of her sister and her mother. Others taken from moments she liked to remember – graduation day, the day she was discharged with full honors, the day she had defended her thesis, and last...the day the war had ended.

"There you are, Nik," she touched the photo. His young face – void of the beard he sported now – smiling and laughing as the two of them and others from their unit finished drinking in celebration of the official announcement. Her own face stared back at her – it didn't look like her anymore. She had been through much since that time. Much that couldn't be shared in one "catch-up" dinner.

That was the real reason she had blown off Nath. She could forgive him coming on so strong. Nik had found little time in the last few months to talk to her. What dinners and lunches they had were in spare minutes, sprinkled only with token conversation. He was exhausted – and so was she – but, she reminded herself, that was why she was here. He needed her. If only he could stop and understand...she needed him, too.

She ate her dinner in silence, not bothering to turn on the monitor. Nothing from the common kitchen had yet to live up to Lancing's, but by all measures it was still hearty and flavorful. After she finished, she read from a book out of the trunk of real books she had brought with her. Though her static pad was loaded with all the content she could cram into it, the pages of a real book still gave her comfort. It was how she had learned to read. For times like these, it was what made her feel at ease.

The sync ticked past 04:30 by the time she fell asleep. When she woke up it read 10:26. She left her quarters before noon to get Iris, who should be off work. Nik and Torv had replied in the night to say they would meet her at the medical section as suggested, which would be in thirty minutes. She sent off one more message before she left, just in case.

She pressed the door chime and waited. Iris eventually came to the door, wearing her nightclothes under a robe. Her eyes went wide when she saw who it was.

"May I come in?" Akiko asked pleasantly.

"Yes…of course," Iris answered amicably, hesitating slightly.

She stepped into her quarters. It was a single room, somewhat messy but nothing out of the ordinary. A shirt that was obviously not hers lay on the other side of the bed. Iris quickly cleaned up, throwing her clothes in the corner closet and slamming it shut.

"Sorry it's a mess," she said absently, grabbing a few items of clothing and heading into the bath, where she shut the door behind her. Akiko looked around. The tiny fridge and sink in the corner were smaller due to the accommodations, next to an equally tiny pantry and controlled reheater unit embedded in the wall.

The pad on her desk was still open to a page she must have pulled from the archives. It was a long-form article on recommendations she should follow for handling the pregnancy. Luckily it was sourced from one of the recent medical corps manuals, according to its citations. Articles from the old colonist almanacs were filled with terrible advice.

"Is something wrong, Dr.…" Iris asked through the semi-transparent barrier. They had technically never met, Akiko realized. They had always made requisitions for non-subscription remedies.

"Dr. Rai," Akiko said loudly, so she could hear. Iris finally opened the door. She was shaking.

"You know, don't you?" she whispered, starting to cry.

"Yes, I know and no, nothing is wrong," Akiko said gently, "nothing that can't be helped. Can you come with me to medical? I promise not to make this any more difficult than it has to be."

"Are you going to…take it away?" she croaked.

"No, no, nothing like that. I need to make sure you and the baby are alright – that's my chief concern. All the paperwork can be sorted after that's done. Ok?"

"Ok," Iris nodded, picking up her jacket. "Can I...can I send someone a message?" she said sheepishly.

"To Ryan Mainer?" Akiko guessed. Iris nodded.

"I've already asked for him. He should be there soon. Are you ready to go?" she asked, putting her arm on the girl's shoulder.

"Yes," she nodded, tears starting down her cheeks.

"It's ok, Iris. Everything will be fine, I promise," she tried to soothe her, but she remained as jittery as ever. They left her quarters and started down for the medical wing. Nik and Torv were clearly having a loud discussion in her office. She knocked to let them know they were there.

"Doctor," Torv nodded, "we were just discussing..." he trailed off when he saw Iris. His expression remained neutral – thankfully it wasn't aggressive...though she was prepared to deal with that.

"Take a seat, Iris," Akiko motioned her toward the corner of the room. A bank of medical equipment and monitors were embedded in the wall next to a padded chair. Slowly, the girl took a seat. The two men stood on the opposite side of the room, still whispering, loudly.

"Can you two take it outside?" Akiko ordered, filling her voice with as much authority as she could muster. They did as she asked, leaving her alone with Iris.

After taking some samples, both from Iris and her unborn child, she positioned the scanners and let them process for a few minutes, holding the shaking girl's hand, which was cold and clammy, trying to reassure her. The results flooded the screen.

"Overall, not bad for self-medicating. Though I'm going recommend you stop," she laughed, turning Iris to see the results. The markers were all in the appropriate ranges. Nutrition seemed to be lacking a little.

"Is that...is that it?" Iris asked, her eyes widening as she pointed at the scan imagery.

"That's her heartbeat," Akiko smiled. The girl's jittering had finally eased, and her hand grew less cold.

"A girl..." Iris exhaled.

"Where's Iris?" a voice asked from just outside the door. The miner had arrived. He was still in his vacuum suit's bottom layer.

"In here, Mr. Mainer," Akiko motioned. He came in, his harried expression evaporating on seeing her. His eyes drifted to the scans next, as he walked over.

"Is it...ok?" he asked finally, taking in the scan information. "It looks like it is, from what I read. Did you check—"

"Yes, I checked. Yes, it's ok. Now...my next question is going to be delicate, mainly because the two men outside will be waiting on my judgment. Ryan, from these scans I know you are not the father...but you are complicit with hiding this information from us. Iris, I can forgive – but you, what's your excuse? You obviously knew the long-term damage that could happen. Did you honestly think we don't monitor cross-requests for pattern drug use?"

"I'm a miner...she's kitchen staff. I wanted to come forward, but she was worried you'd take it away. I've seen that happen – my own mom...she had an undocumented kid on the colonies. I...I never knew them. I know there's no excuse—"

"But you did as Iris asked. That...I can understand. And to be honest, you didn't do too badly with monitoring her condition."

"If you're going to punish anyone, take my wages. Garnish everything. Just let her keep it. Please."

"That's out of my hands, Ryan. Now...one of my techs needs to work out a treatment and checkup schedule for Iris. Keep her company while I talk with the Captain and Commander Torv. Beka is waiting for you outside. If she finishes, don't leave until I have a chance to speak with you.

Most of all – don't do anything foolish. Under the circumstances, you've done the best you can. No need to change that now," Akiko smiled, hiding her sense of worry. The pair of them left and the two men came in after.

"Shut the door," she said as they walked in, immediately raising their tones again. Torv shut the door.

"What is wrong with you two?" she asked angrily. "She could hear everything you were saying."

"Us? I think the insubordinate couple having a child out there has the problem," Torv replied hotly.

"And openly arguing about it is going to make it better?" she shook her head.

"No. It's not," Nik agreed. Torv opened his mouth to say something but slowly closed it.

"She is scared out of her mind – having a child she didn't plan for on a ship she can't practically leave for another four and a half years. Perspective, gentlemen, if you please."

"It's not about—anyway, how did it happen?" Torv asked, breaking from his first thought before she could shoot it down.

"Well, the usual way. The birth control failed...or they started her too late. The dosage timing between her last tour on the Nile and the start of this one is too close to be sure. Just know that Mainer is not the father. That much I can tell from the scans."

"Then who is it?" Nik asked, leaning against the wall and kneading his leg. She caught a glimpse of the brace's outline under his clothes. He saw her looking and stopped.

"Unregistered. Nothing matched the data sync we have on file. Unless she feels like telling us – and I doubt that she will, in any case – that will probably stay a mystery."

"We have to report it," Torv said resolutely.

"No, we don't," Nik said after a few moments. She and Torv both gave him a questioning look.

"And why not?" Torv asked. "This is a breach of protocol – we're not setup with a neonatal unit. There are no precautions – she's incurring cost from having this child, Venko."

"She is a member of this crew and last I checked, I have final say on crew and command decisions. And besides, even if do we report this, her child will be born by the time we make it to the first stop. State surrender law has its limits."

"Up to five years old, I checked. They'll take her as soon as we dock at tour's end. Why prolong the woman's agony?" Torv shook his head, looking to Akiko for support. She kept her face neutral, waiting for Nik to respond.

"Because you're suggesting she let the child go at one of the stops and wait for judgment later."

"It's policy," Torv replied, adamant.

"It's wrong," Nik said, his expression changing slightly. Akiko looked down at his fist. It was shaking, just slightly.

"You risk something either way, Commander," Akiko took up the explanation, "if we leave the child with state services at the first stop, Iris would have to go with them, which is a cost in and of itself – or she would have to stay on the Rhineland, with the very real loss and clinical depression that accompanies separation. She would be a danger to the crew – or a *cost* as you put it – on or off the ship."

"It's not what I would do, but it's your call, Nik," Torv said finally, lowering his head to brood on the situation.

"Write the exemption and log it," Nik said aloud. Akiko could barely hear him mumble, "...can take it out of my 'maxed-out' benefits for all I care."

"Yes, sir," Torv nodded, leaving the office after a glance at Akiko told him she needed to talk to Nik alone. Once the door shut, he almost fell over.

"Sit down," she hurried to him, pulling him into the chair. He grimaced with every step. She rolled up his pant leg and looked at the brace. It was clearly constricting blood flow and its small readout had several warnings already listed, most actively ignored.

"Nikita," she whispered softly, clenching her teeth.

"Just take it off," he said through clenched teeth, "don't drug me. I can't...not now."

"Ok," she agreed, hitting the necessary combination. It slowly released and he sighed heavily. Normal color returned to his leg, but the scar tissue and bruising still warped around where his kneecap should have been. A pang of empathy and guilt shot through her.

"You have to take *something*," she shook her head, grabbing an injector and filling it with a small dose of direct application gel. Before he could disagree, she shoved it into the wound. It bled into the veins there and gradually made his muscles relax.

"That's it. No more," he said, breathing heavy. She let him sit there for a few minutes in silence, his eyes mostly closed.

"Put it back on," he ordered. She didn't want to, but she knew it would probably be unwise to disagree. As gingerly as possible, she reset the brace and let it grasp his leg. He made one last grimace before his expression relaxed. Ignoring her help, he stood up and walked to the door.

"You can't have children, can you?" Akiko asked.

He stopped. "No," he whispered.

"I'm sorry, Nikita. Really," she lowered her eyes, regretting asking the question. He stood there, with his hand on the lock pad.

"Is the baby alright?" he asked, before he opened the door.

"Yes...she is," Akiko confirmed.

For a moment, she could see him smile, just before he opened the door and left. The urge to go after him, to sit and just talk with him, was almost overpowering – and it hurt. She stared back at the corner, where he had nearly collapsed. He was hurting too...and from more than physical pain. The corps had taken much more than they knew when they asked for his ship, and she hated them for that.

"Rai, I have the schedule for Iris. She's asking to see you," Beka spoke through her desk comm.

"I'll be right out," she said, turning off the scanners in the corner and heading outside to the main clinic. Ryan and Iris were seated on one of the beds. He had his arm over her shoulder, his other touching her chest.

"The commander said I'm exempted?" Iris asked.

"What exactly does that mean?" Ryan added, their bewildered expressions telling of the little information Torv had given them.

"The mining corps will not be officially informed of your pregnancy. The state surrender law can be enforced for up to five years, but only if informed, which Captain Venko – acting on behalf of the state aboard the Rhineland – has opted not to pursue. It means," she paused, taking Ryan's hand and positioning it nearest the baby, "that you will keep your child."

"You're serious?" he asked.

"Yes," Akiko nodded, "the exemption has been logged. It can't be challenged in court even if you leave the Rhineland."

"Oh my god," Iris cried, getting up to hug her, "thank you." Akiko was taken aback, but gradually embraced the younger woman.

"It's not me you should thank," she said quickly, "this is Captain Venko's decision."

"He hurried off so fast...I thought the worst," she explained.

"He head to check on something urgent," Akiko covered.

"Your schedule is here," the technician Beka explained. "We'll have the right equipment printed before your next visit. Try your best not to miss – come late rather than not at all, ok?" Ryan and Iris watched her point out the visitation added to both of their calendars.

"Ok," Iris smiled, "I will, thank you."

"This will help in the meantime," Akiko motioned to her arm. Iris looked at Ryan, who nodded in approval. "It's a primer for the tensor resistance treatment. You won't get as sick from *her* getting sick," Akiko explained, placing the injector Beka handed her.

"Her?" Ryan paused, looking at Iris.

"It's a girl," she told him, her bubbly smile managing to lift Akiko's spirits, which she was thankful for after the harrowing experience with Nik.

"Come and see me in two weeks, ok?" Akiko helped her off the bed and waved them out. They left, with Ryan's arm around her shoulders and his other still excitedly pointing at her stomach.

"Expectant parents. Never thought I'd be dealing with them out here," Beka mused.

"Stranger things have happened," Akiko agreed.

"You have any kids?" Beka asked.

"No. Never found the time," Akiko lied.

Nik stood outside Akiko's quarters, hand hovering over the door chime, as he had done many nights over the past few months. Each time he had talked himself out of it. Each time he had come close to pressing it...but each time he resisted. She never came to him. Was it him? Was it her? It was nearing the middle of the first year into the tour and the stir-crazy atmosphere had slowly crept in – many in the crew had paired off, mostly to stave off the monotony.

When he was younger, he didn't have the luxury of that kind of monotony...not with the dull roar of war happening all around him. Even with that chaotic life, he believed he was happier then than he was now. He knew what he was going to do, even if it meant getting on a gunboat and sailing to defend parts unknown. Afterward, the military psychiatrist had told him it was natural to feel like this. He accepted that convenient lie, but it took a long time to learn how to deal with life afterward.

Sometimes he just looked at the door and kept walking. He pulled his hand away; today wasn't going to be any different. The way back to his quarters was dimly lit and uninviting, so he turned and walked toward the inner loop. His sync showed 22:17. Still plenty of time left in the evening to ignore his gut-wrenching knot of emotions and bury them away.

Lancing wasn't open, so he headed to the common and ordered a quick meal from the standing fry cook on staff. The young girl Iris was working behind the counter, waving at him when she saw him. He smiled at her as he took in her swollen abdomen. She came over to hand him his meal and say hello.

"Do you always stay up late, Captain?" she asked.

"Part of the job," he admitted, taking the meal from her.

"You always look tired. I was just worried you don't sleep," she said innocently, handing him a bottle of his usual, low-alcohol mix.

"I sleep, don't you worry about that," he smiled, giving her a curt nod in goodbye. Her expression told him she didn't believe that, but he knew she wouldn't call her captain a liar to his face.

After a quick decision, he decided to head down the inner loop and exit near the bridge, detouring down to the auxiliary deck. Nath was working on the navigational simulator, pulling a mess of optics out of a large box behind one wall. Three terminals were plugged in series next to it, with light and color floating across them.

"You're out late," he nodded, pushing his eye protection back up the ridge of his nose as he soldered a loose connector.

Nik slowly kneeled and leaned back against one of the inactive panels, breathing a heavy sigh. "Torv's sewn everything up quicker than I thought he would today. First time I left my terminal without fearing I'll get a message in the morning when something goes wrong. Strange feeling, that."

"Yeah, he's a late bloomer, was all. Cole was ready to jump ship there for a little bit. Which – speak of the devil," he raised his head up and adjusted his optic-filtering glasses.

"Let me have some of that," Cole begged, flopping down next to Nik, who smirked and slid the bottle over to him. He gulped down a good half pint. His chest heaved, causing Nik to take a closer look at him. He was sweating profusely, with several fresh cuts and abrasions along the lengths of his arms.

"You guys talking about Alexei?" he asked.

"Yeah," Nath nodded, lowering his eyes in a conspiratorial glance toward Nik, "we were talking about *Alexei*."

"Well, I take back what I said when we started out – I made a comment about him not wanting to do the dirty work around here and he wasn't having it. I didn't expect him to actually go *deal* with it himself, ha."

"Where exactly is our commander right now?" Nath laughed, soldering another connection before he switched to the optic lathe.

"In the cooling ducts, dislodging the stuck valves. Powerful fumes down there...but he's almost gotten them all open. I figured he was doing it out of spite, but I don't care – got me out of doing it."

"He better come back out," Nik grinned, tipping the bottle back and draining the rest of it after he polished off his sandwich. "I'm getting too old for all of this."

"Leg botherin' you again?" Cole asked, nodding at the brace Nik was subconsciously kneading.

"Worse than last tour. Must have been the stop at the main office that did it. Real gravity really makes it hurt."

"I reckon they knew that," Cole shook his head in disgust. He was a large man, with muscles to match. Scars littered his forearms, and some pockmarked his face. His eyes were a bright teal, lost under the brim of his engineering hat hanging over his face.

"They knew it alright," Nath agreed, sharing the look of disgust before switching his glasses to a dark filter and lasing the optic point. Nik wouldn't admit it to them, but he was touched by the shared disgust of his friends. They clearly didn't want him to go – they still had a couple more tours left in them, easy. Cole could probably do another four or five, with his daily regimen.

"What are they playing tonight at the theater?" Nik asked.

"Deadrunner or Threatrunner. Something like that, I swear," Cole thought, scratching his arms.

"Now, now, just let me finish up and I'll show you something better than a movie," Nath promised, almost affronted. The other two sat there in silence, watching him finish up the repair and slowly slide the box back into its control panel. He got up and dragged and the terminals out, motioning for them to get off the panel.

"This had better be good if you're making the old man stand," Cole laughed, helping Nik up. Once he was on his feet, the simulator went dark and they were all huddled, waiting.

"Bought this off a Coalition dealer. Latest shared beta of the combat sims scheduled for the 2250 wargames. It's a work of art, the amount of detail they put into these things."

Nik had to blink when the lights exploded. The edge of the panels morphed together, and he couldn't tell where one ended and the floor began. It was a simulation of a Juno cluster, a small habitat that housed a thousand or so farmers in range of a sun. The edge was on fire, with ships landing in waves. Nath lifted a dummy weapon and the colors morphed on its surface to match the lighting of the scene unfolding around them.

Enemy soldiers flooded in, firing ion bolts and spent cartridges, forcing their way into the foxhole. Nath held them off, letting Cole take the weapon and fire off his own set. It showed precision angles, displaying the terrible stats they both shared. When he offered it to him, Nik turned it down, staring in amazement at the detail.

"Oh, come on," Nath begged, "just once."

"You know his rule," Cole warned lightheartedly.

"It's not even real!" he shouted, firing off wildly, dragging the statistics further down.

"It is, though," Nik whispered, walking up to the screen's edge, reaching out to the fire on the edge. The voxels were so tightly packed inside the glass screen the light was coming out at him like a real fire.

"If we need to nav through one of those fields again like we did in '37, this will get us through it," Nath explained, "While we were in port, I made sure to grab the hardware *and* software upgrades – granted it took some doing without my usual budget – but I did it. Not only will navigation see the rocks coming, so will you. I told you...it's a work of art." The simulation ended when his numbers dropped below acceptable.

"Makes me almost regret taking all the money this trip," Cole slapped him on the shoulder. He winced but stayed smiling.

"Good work, Nath," Nik smiled. He meant it.

"It still needs some fine-tuning. Let's face it, it always needs some fine tuning...but it'll be ready before the year's over. Been letting a selective part of the crew have a run at it. Some get a little too aggressive and rush the screens. Good thing those panels are cheap – it's replacing them that takes all the labor time."

"You'll get it there," Cole agreed, "if it's worth doing, it's worth doing right. No need to rush art. Anyway...I'm out. See you tomorrow."

"Night," Nath nodded. Cole clapped Nik on the shoulder then left.

"I believe the film is Darkrunner, if you're interested in the after-midnight screening," Nath said absently, packing up the rest of his tools and stowing them in the locker behind the panels.

"Sure, why not," Nik decided.

"Where's your lady friend? Or have you two given up?" Nath asked, motioning the way out. They headed to the inner loop.

"It's not like that," Nik shook his head.

"I've asked her out a few times. Either she doesn't like me...or she's still into you," Nath laughed, dripping with sarcasm.

"Leave her alone. She's always been that way. You need to remember; she's not used to being on a ship where she can't escape. This is still a new experience for her. If she's interested in you, she'll tell you."

"Well, she's on this ship for another fifty-five months, give or take. It would do her some good to loosen up."

"Yeah, I can see why she's turning you down."

"Oh, come on," Nath punched his shoulder, "I'm not that bad, am I?"

They drifted into the back of the theater just as it started. The movie was an indie film, its cinematography subtly unfocused, paired with a thin, but elegant plot. A neo-noire setting in post-space Earth where all the power stations are going dark, leaving the postal service to couriers dubbed 'darkrunners'. One of them has to deliver critical information unaware of its importance, chased by thieves and assassins alike.

"Not bad for a Benjamin special. Ran out of popcorn in the first ten minutes," Nath judged, chewing on the last of the popcorn kernels left in the bag they'd scored midway through the movie.

"Earth settings and parkour – it hurts my knee just watching," Nik cringed, though he agreed with Nath's thoughts. It was a fun little film. Nath was obligated to like it, of course – he chose to pull it down from the system nets before the tour started.

"Well, good night. Hope it settles down," he nodded at his knee.

"Thanks. You, too," Nik waved him off as they reached the fork in the senior officer wing. His quarters welcomed him on approach. He threw off his jacket and collapsed on his bed, trying not to focus on the throbbing ache in his knee. Sleep came slowly.

He woke up to his sync vibrating madly and his extra alarm ringing in his ears. The pain in his leg was unbearable. He stumbled out of bed, crawling to the terminal. Swallowing hard, he found the daily meeting and noted he was delegating it to Torv. It had become a convenient excuse lately. With the message acknowledged by his senior staff, he returned to bed and tried to ignore the pain.

The door chime interrupted his pain-filled reverie. His mobile link lay on the edge of the bed. He hit the shortest sequence to show him the biometrics on the door to his quarters. It was Akiko. He was angry with himself – she had gotten worried about him.

"Come in," he messaged her directly, sitting up on his bed and placing his foot on the floor. He was half-dressed. He grabbed his jacket and threw it around his shoulders, running his hand through his hair to smooth it over. Taking a deep breath, he stood up and headed to the doorway, leaning into it while she entered.

"Hey, you've been missing the daily a lot," she said loudly as she entered, looking around. Her eyes eventually landed on him, looking him over.

"Torv needs the experience," he said, almost clenching his teeth.

"The others know something's wrong," she explained.

"No, the others *know* what's wrong," he confirmed.

"Then tell *me*," she urged.

"It's nothing," he shook his head.

"If it was nothing, then I wouldn't be on the Rhineland. Try again," Akiko tightened her tone.

"The nerve pain is spreading," Nik swallowed, "and there's no drug that's going to stop it."

"You're no stranger to pain," Akiko said evenly, keeping the same tone as before. She knew there was more.

"If they ground me...I might as well just die," he said finally, "because what I feel when I'm down there...it all comes back. Like it's still fresh. Physically and mentally."

"Look at yourself. You're barely holding it together out here – their decision isn't wrong. It may be cruel, but it's in the interest of this ship and its crew. You know that."

"You sound like them."

"I *was* them, remember? I played the game. Look where it got me. All of the good we did and what do we have to show for it?" Akiko was almost shouting, and Nik found the pain getting worse.

"Then what's the plan?" he asked abruptly. "They didn't ask, they didn't get second opinions. They just made their judgment. I should be happy they gave me *this* tour."

"Would you rather they left you on the docks to rot? If you're ready to give up, then I really do regret coming on this trip," Akiko shook her head. "You ask me onboard, do one 'catch-up' dinner and that's it? You've left me alone out here, Nik! Is that what you wanted," she yelled, "for us to both be alone?!"

"I didn't tell you to say yes!" Nik bellowed. "You want to know what I want? I want to be useful. I want to be wanted. Not drained, useless and discarded. They took what we had to give and used every ounce of us. That's what they do, Akiko – they take and they take and they *take*. There's no amount of money, medals and benefits they can 'give' us that will make up for what we've lost. Not for either of us...I stood by your door. I wanted to say all this...wanted to say I was sorry for inviting you." He stopped, breathing hard, "What I want is to live out what's left of my life without feeling like a victim of a war no one even really remembers."

"I want that, too," Akiko whispered after a long pause, catching her own breath. He had gripped his leg and staggered to the couch, collapsing into it and looking up at her. She took a seat next to him, looking him in the eyes. "Understanding that I know all of this – that *we together* know all of this – what do you want me to do to fix it?"

"I want the pain to stop," he whispered, "because I have nothing left to give…and I'm starting to forget what it felt like when I did."

Akiko put her hand in his, clenching it tight. "I won't let you give up. Not like I did." Nik stared into her eyes. Bloodshot and as tired as his own. He felt the air change, convinced he was having an episode. He tried to remember the first time he saw them. When they were happy. When the world had not yet become so cruel.

A noise on his link interrupted his thoughts. On both of their links. His terminal died in the corner. Then the ship shook. They both rushed to their feet. When a staggered vibration shook the ship again, he swore as it sent a fresh pain up his leg. He went to his desk, toggling the manual bridge comm and getting a strange static.

"Bridge, what's happening?" he asked. There was no answer.

"Bridge? Report!" he yelled. There was still no answer. He and Akiko shared a glance, fearing the worst. He pulled his mobile link, trying to get the operating system to respond. It was sluggish. He pinged all the senior officers. None answered. Network timeout.

"Captain?" a voice came over the static. It sounded very pained. The ship shook again, accompanied by a whimper of pain.

"Quint, what's happening?" he asked, recognizing the voice.

"Acceleration loss…all of the tensors are compensating. We hit something…I've directed us at the nearest terrestrial body. I think it hit the outer ring…the Rhineland's RTOS is showing red for most of the environmental scans." Nik could hear the wheezing and the pain, not daring to interrupt. The mental image he was forming in his head was straight out of his nightmares.

He and Akiko stared at each other in the horrifying lull.

"Time to crash?" he finally asked, steadying himself against the desk as another vibration buffeted the ship.

For a moment, neither was sure Quint was still breathing.

"Deceleration vectors are still calculating...an hour. Maybe less. Everything's out...I'm bleeding out, Captain. I can barely stay awake..." Quint's voice was getting much weaker.

"We're on our way to you – hold her steady. That's all you need to focus on. I'll take care of the ship," Nik ordered, toggling the comm and motioning Akiko to a cabinet behind his desk. The vibrations began growing in intensity. The look in Akiko's eyes was both a mixture of fear and resolution.

"Is this really happening?" she asked. "I mean...it can't be, can it? Mining ships don't crash. You told me these ships don't crash."

"You need to get to Quint," Nik ignored her delirium. "With the real-time OS down, she's the only thing standing between us and getting spun apart by vacuum. If she bleeds out, that hour will turn to minutes and the body count is going to rise. Get over there, make sure she gets us in atmosphere, then both of you get to one of the escape pods in the outer loop."

"How do I get there – she said the outer ring is out?" Akiko asked, frantically helping him get the cabinet open. It kept getting stuck, but he finally wrenched it open.

"Take this," he gave her a mask and handed her three more bundled together. He put the last one in the cabinet on himself.

"Pressurized breathers. There are vacuum suits in each ring at regular intervals. Find the first junction off the inner loop and trace the rail to the bridge, fast as you can. Don't stop for anyone – you *have* to get to Quint, no matter what."

"And what are you going to do?" she asked, hands shaking as she pulled the pin on the pressure cap, making her voice sound like it was in the bottom of a bottle. He did the same.

"Minimize the damage. Procedure is clear – if everyone's awake, they know what this means and where to go," he pointed at his link, where the warning protocol was spelling it out, bit by bit. "The inner ring houses the connections to the mining platform. If it breaks, that could slide out of the ship's housing and strand anyone inside."

"Why can't we communicate?" she asked, a heightened note of fear creeping into her otherwise calm demeanor.

"I don't know...the network shouldn't be down like this. The radio transceiver is powered to send out these warnings regardless – mobile radio can't pierce the inner hull, so link-to-link comms don't work out here. Anyway – it doesn't matter – get to the bridge. Save Quint. Now, Rai!" he ordered, pushing her toward the door. She just stood there, dumbfounded.

"This *is* happening," he rasped, "Quint is on the bridge. Get to her before she bleeds out. Please, I need you to do this," he urged. The world had turned upside down. Not a handful of moments before she was begging him not to give up...like she had. It hit him, then...he had so many more questions he wanted to ask her. If only he had knocked one of those nights...then he would have had the chance.

"Akiko," he hurried to her, slowing down to pull her fidgeting hand away from the mask, magnetizing the last strap. "Hurry."

"Yes...yes. Ok. Yes. I'm going," she nodded, pulled the latch on the door and left him behind, hurrying away. He could only hope she would be able to reach her in time.

Nik's own frantic thoughts were spinning a million different directions. The first thing he had to do was dull the pain in his leg...he'd be useless if he didn't. He ripped the drawer out of his desk, slamming it down on top of it as another vibration shook the whole section. No time for caution, he grabbed the prescription injector in the corner and deftly jammed it into his knee. The sensation made the brace around it feel icy and untenable, but without pain. He prayed a silent prayer then sped off behind Akiko.

Emergency lighting had taken over when the network operating the lights failed. He could hear a lot of hurried voices and shouting echoing through the corridors. They were slowly heading toward the pods on each ring, murmuring in disbelief.

An alcove near the front of the labs was already ripped open and two of the three vacuum suits removed. Nik grabbed the last and pulled it on, ignoring the dull pain that struck like lightning with each vibration of the ship. Lights winked in and out as the shaking began in earnest. Hopefully Akiko had one of those other suits and was on her way to the bridge.

He slammed the helmet down and connected the hard suit pieces together, checking the seals and fixing the one on his torso before heading toward the inner loop. The display in his helmet showed a string of pressure numbers, steadily decreasing the closer he crept to the substructure. The section door to the mining area was closed when he reached it, the lock's small readout reading no pressure on the other side.

Nik swallowed any pent-up fear and overrode it, decompressing the small area and leaving both sides in vacuum. The other side of the door was no more inviting than he imagined. Machinery and inner tubing strewn throughout the space, floating and flitting about as the mammoth exposed tensor spun wildly in the distance, doing its best to stabilize them.

A few shadows he could make out in the darkness were shaped an awful lot like people and he shook his head in morbid frustration. There was nothing to be done. Those who were left were his priority now. Now that he was inside, he had to assess the damage and what he could possibly do to stop it from progressing.

He could see the crack in the outer ring, where a large object had punched right through it, damaging the connection and unbalancing the tensor network. Of the three core bridges from the ring to the substructure, only two were left. If the Rhineland had any hope of reaching solid ground, the best option was to force a disconnect of the remaining pair and let it drift away.

With no time to waste, he scrambled to the first of the two bridges, struggling to stay tethered to the ground with the hard suit magnetics. They made his legs wobble and tear at tendons he had forgotten. The rest of Getty's prescription was flooding through his veins now, dulling the tears to a slight tingle. Not only could he not feel pain, but he could barely feel himself walking.

The connection panels were already open, and he soon realized why – someone had gone ahead of him, having taken the first hard suit, provided Akiko had taken the second. He turned to face the second bridge, seeing a silhouette opening the same connection boxes on that side. They had turned, waving when they saw him. It took him a few moments to realize they were pointing at the box.

A mobile link had been tapped into the box next to him.

"Together," the link's static text read, next to a diagram of the bridge controls. The disconnection protocol was already loaded. Nik turned and gave him a thumbs up, pressing it. The shaking grew worse this near the spinning tensor. When he placed his hand to the metal, it made his bones tingle up to his shoulder.

A countdown started on the link. When it hit ten, it triggered the disconnection protocol and the resulting vibration knocked him and the link away from the boxes. As he grasped for the nearest hand hold, he watched the tensor slowly drift down the outer hull, fading out of sight into the murky black of space. It tore the rest of the connections with it, but they got caught by the substructure before they could make the leap into space with it.

He fumbled for the holds, trying to steady himself for a few desperate minutes, unsure if he would just...fall away. It would be easy, he thought. Just drift into the dark, never to be seen again. He wouldn't be the first captain to die that kind of death out here. As the drugs finished pervading him, he felt nothing, not even his hands, numb to his failing grasp. The last thing he saw was the dim outline of a horizon, framing the concave globe above him.

It was dark, but it was beautiful.

Akiko could barely breathe, trying desperately to call on her medical and psychological training to calm herself. The hard suit was claustrophobic. Back in the medical research station, she had to wear a hazard suit...but never one with a vacuum seal against space. The substructure had depressurized along the rail, making for the wildest walk she had ever taken on the ship.

Reaching the bridge in a short time had taken a monumental effort on her part, but as Nik had repeatedly told her, it was vital she get there in time. Poor Elyna Quint. She had met most of the crew during their first batch of physicals earlier in the month. The young woman was doing her navigation primer this trip. It hurt to think of her huddled in the simulator, correcting their course.

The pressure picked up as she neared the bridge. It was deserted except for the pained sound of hoarse breathing. She rushed to the forward navigational bank to find the young woman sprawled across the console, one hand tapping the holography controls and the other shifting the map as best she could.

"Elyna, I'm here," she told her, receiving only a slight cough of acknowledgment. Akiko put one of the masks over her pale face, rubbing her back and encouraging her to breathe. Her eyes refocused a bit. The field aid kit was open next to her, emptied of gauze and quick gel, which she had smeared across a large gash in her right side.

Blaire Vauss, the Rhineland's official navigator, lay dead on the ground a few meters away, head gashed open from being thrown into a console a short way from her lifeless body. Akiko positioned herself between Elyna's view of the body and the console.

"I'm going to fix the gauze. How long do you need to keep maintaining our course?"

Elyna grunted in reply, holding up all the fingers in one hand.

"Five minutes?" Akiko asked. She nodded yes.

Akiko pulled the gauze and re-wrapped it with a fresh roll from the kit, applying the gel so it would reach her deeper wound more strategically. She did her best to ignore her cries of pain, knowing that giving her something to dull the pain would make her pass out.

After the fourth minute, Akiko watched her fingers click the keys on the console, directing them in and out of burns that were placing the ship into as graceful a falling orbit as possible. Once the final course was punched in, Elyna let go and pulled away from the console. Her uniform was covered in blood.

"Take a deep breath," Akiko ordered, lifting her up on her shoulders. Elyna's head rolled, losing her balance.

"It's ok. We need to get to the escape pod and I'm going to have to do my best to carry you there, ok?"

"Ok," Elyna croaked, blood dripping down her lips.

Akiko carried her through the shaking ship, dragging her at times. She lost consciousness before they got to the pod. It was one of three left, waiting on the ejection sequence to be keyed at the bulkhead. Four taps later, she dragged the younger woman inside with her, gingerly pulling her up into a crash seat, strapping her in as best she could before taking a seat across from her.

She had barely secured herself in when the rush of momentum threw her head into the side of the seat, leaving a throbbing headache. The vibration had stopped, but soon enough it started again. It heated up quickly as they burned through the atmosphere, growing louder and louder as the air pierced the insides. When the pod's air scoops caught, she was buffeted into the other side, making stars in her vision and leaving her conscious enough to glimpse the panel in the front, streaming calculated altitude. When they hit, she blacked out.

She woke to a dull ache and blaring klaxons. The pod had landed. Elyna was languishing in her seat. Akiko pulled at the straps, feeling the bruises beneath her uniform. A cold sweat hit her as she sat up, forcing her back down. The inside of the pod swam. Distant thoughts of the planetfall manuals streamed through her mind, but the rules were jumbled and she couldn't think.

After a few deep breaths, she got up again, able to withstand it this time. She walked the two steps to Elyna, pushing her fingers into the artery on her neck. There was nothing at first, but her hand was shaking violently. Forcing it to be still, she found a weak pulse, mouthing a silent prayer of thanks.

The panel in the pod was streaming new numbers, showing a weak graph of the surrounding environment. No water, relatively flat land. Arid temperature. It was getting hotter by the minute. She waited for the last analysis to complete, the two ominous dashes hovering next to the O_2 marker.

It was a very high content, but breathable.

"Elyna," she shook her eagerly, "you did it." The battered woman stayed silent. Frowning, Akiko pulled her out of the crash seat and laid her in a position where the wounds would push in on the gauze. The gel was leaking through the webbing, but it had set. The pod's cooling unit was working to counteract the encroaching desert, but it eventually would run out of power. After another cursory exam of her wounds, all she could do for her now was just keep her cool. The consequences of the initial internal bleeding would have to be treated with more than field aid.

Akiko sat still for a few moments, surveying the situation in her mind. There had to be other pods, but they could be separated by several kilometers. Each had a radio, she remembered. She headed to the front panel, looking for the comms status. A small screen in the corner was rippling with blips. Other radios were trying to mesh together, running through the protocols.

"Come on," she bleated, exasperated by its slow time to live. After a few minutes of patiently waiting, she came to the realization that it wasn't going to connect. She sat with her throbbing headache, trying to fight the mental anguish of leaving the cooled pod. After a full minute, she resigned herself to the fact she would have to leave and survey the world outside.

"I'll come back for you," she whispered in Japanese to the silent Elyna, hitting the latch. A blast of warm air gusted through the opening, whipping her sweat-matted hair around her face. Soft blue rays beamed down at her in the darkness as she walked out. It was a desert, as the pod computer predicted. They had made a large dent in the dried rock, smoke still pouring off the burst engine.

She took the field aid kit off the wall and hooked it inside her jacket. Fighting her own worries, she shut the door to keep the cold in, then looked at her wrist where the mobile link was still attached. It had gone dark with no connection to the Rhineland. The thought of the ship made her look up. Her eyes were still adjusting to the dark, but she could make out a glint of reflected blue light on a growing speck in the distance.

Her first thought was one of mourning...there were bound to be others like Vauss who hadn't made it off the ship. Maybe there were some still on it, unable to get out in time. It was starting its burn in the atmosphere, throwing off a very different light. Her very next thought was more morbid than the last – what if it landed on some of the pods? Not knowing what she could do, she tore off at a run.

The ship's mass was falling slowly but steadily, growing larger and larger as she raced across the desert. It was going to hit somewhere beyond it. They had crashed near the edge. A gust of wind nearly threw her off balance when she found the cliff face. A wide plain spread out beneath them, covered in grass that almost perfectly reflected the moon...and the object about to crash into it.

At least two pods were under it, bound to be crushed by the tangle of dense metals. She stood there powerless to help them, watching the large ship begin its final crawl, throwing echoes and further gusts at the cliffs where she stood. Her thoughts turned to Nik...had he found a pod? Would she ever see him again?

The Rhineland crumpled into the ground, spewing sheared metal and screeching echoes across the landscape. It was several minutes before it all stopped. Akiko collapsed to the ground not far from the edge, pulling off her mask. The air was stale, and she could taste the metallic dirt of the desert in her mouth. It was oddly silent.

That was it. They were stuck here. She had remembered one golden rule in the planetfall manual...get comfortable, if you can – no help is coming. Despair overwhelmed her. She cried, wiping her eyes with the torn sleeve of her jacket. Elyna's blood was dried on the cuffs. Stifling her heavy breaths took a long few minutes. Satisfied she had recovered and cried herself out, she got to her feet – there could be people down there, and she was a doctor.

She scanned the cliff face, looking for a way down. Once she found one, she scrambled down its edge, ignoring the aches in her bones as the adrenaline had finally ebbed away. Near the bottom, she started to hear someone screaming for help. The ship's skeletal remains loomed in the distance as she followed the voice.

"Where are you?!" she shouted, causing the voice to stop.

"Over here!" it yelled to her right. She followed it to find a man standing over a woman, who was huddling over a child, holding their hand. *No,* Akiko prayed, *not this first. Please, not the children first.*

"Let me see—" her words hung in her mouth.

"He's dead!" the woman shouted, "he's dead!" She pulled the lifeless child to her chest, clutching his head where the eyes were still open.

"There's a group on the far side," the man whispered, pulling Akiko by the arm, away from the woman. "I don't know if they got out from under before it fell." He seemed to be preparing to ask her to stay with the woman until he got a look at her jacket.

"You're the doctor, aren't you?" he realized.

"Stay with her," Akiko said decisively, "I'll check on the others." He nodded in understanding and she left them behind, making the trek around the outer perimeter of the wreckage, closest to where she imagined the second pod had landed. It took her longer than she cared for to find any trace of them. The pod was buried in the wreckage, totally crushed.

"Is anyone out here?!" she yelled. No answer. She yelled again and again, with no response. Another gust of wind blew through the plain, throwing her hair into her face then whipping up her torn jacket, shredding it further. She held the hair out of her eyes and looked up at the cliff face on this side. A small movement caught her eye, like the foot of someone crawling away from the edge.

Hope ignited in her chest.

She found the way up, breathing hard and heavy by the time she reached the top. Two men were huddled together, looking over the edge. One was laying back, shivering. She hurried over to them.

"Can you help?" the first man asked, seeing her jacket.

"He's in shock," Akiko nodded, dropping to her knees.

A bloody piece of shrapnel lay next to his foot, where his partner had pulled it out. She pulled the kit out of her jacket and opened it on the ground, finding the thick roll of gauze and canister of setting gel. She dipped her fingers in the gel and ran them along the length of the wound. Then she ripped off the right length from the roll, wrapping the wound. It was probably too late to save his foot, since infection was bound to set in, but she couldn't make that judgment just yet.

"Was anyone else with you?" she asked his partner, trying to look him in the eyes. He was focused on his friend, in shock himself.

"No...no one else," he coughed after a few moments.

"Was that your pod down there?" she interrogated him, hopeful that he would say yes. It took a few moments, but he shook his head yes. He had carried him out of the valley.

She hung her head in relief and sighed.

"Did you see any others?" she tried, pushing her luck.

He pointed behind her, at another part of the desert.

"Thank you," she clapped him on the shoulder, causing him to flinch and look at her. "He'll be ok, alright?" The man just nodded, looking away from her as she got up and started for the other pods.

As she hiked into the perpetually gusty landscape, she realized they were miners. Their suits were still on them. Another pang of hope put a little vigor into her steps – if they had made it out, then Nik had been successful. Maybe he was in one of the pods. She started to run, looking for any sign of the small lifeboats.

Her heart was straining by the time she found one. Despite her regular exercise, she couldn't fight age forever...and now she was fighting real gravity, too. The door wasn't open yet. She banged on the outside, hoping they would hear. After a few moments of no response, she banged again.

The door slid open.

"Is the bloody thing open yet?!" a familiar voice yelled within.

"Nathanial, thank god," she ducked inside.

"Only my mum calls me that – though if she was here, I suppose she'd be thanking him, too."

"Are you alright?" she asked. One of his technicians was fiddling with the panel in the front when Nath turned around. He had a bandage across his head already, visible bruising beneath.

"Never better...the others?" he asked, standing up.

"Elyna Quint is in a pod on the other ridge. She's lost a lot of blood. I found a pair of people down in the valley...one of them was holding their son who didn't make it. A couple of the miners are back on this side of the ridge. Don't know their faces to names yet – didn't make it through everyone's physicals."

"You got Quint? What happened to Vauss?" Nath asked, walking out of the ship with her. He had to adjust his eyes, too.

"She's dead. Quint made the course corrections. We owe her a lot, I think," she nodded, ignoring his resistance as she reached up to peak under his bandage. He had applied a liberal amount of gel.

"Considering we're on the ground, I'd say you're right...we hit *something*, but I have no idea what. The network died instantly, so it must have surged the controller circuit. I threw all my techs I could find in the nearest pods and we ejected before the forward section filled with vacuum...less suits. I feel like a coward, leaving the ship early like that," he hung his head, looking at her with a look she had yet to see on him.

"You saved who you could. You're no coward."

"We'll see when we pull everyone together down here. I'll reserve my self-pity until after we do a headcount."

"It's shot," Nath's tech told him, emerging from the pod. Her red hair was striking in the blue light, falling somewhere between indigo and purple. Nath's own seemed to fade to black.

"Rai, Ester Kim," he introduced. She shook her hand. "And what's shot? The transceiver or the mesh?"

"Both. It won't ping and it won't mesh. There are so many echoes it cancels as soon as it leaves the pod."

"Echoes?" Akiko asked.

"Radio ghosts. The Rhineland is throwing off all sorts of them right now. Can't you sort them out?" he berated, like he was talking to a child. She shook her head no.

"They're not from the Rhineland – I ran the signal analysis. It's natural radiation of some kind, and it's everywhere."

"If there's radiation, I need something to test the levels before we all get irreparably poisoned," Akiko interjected.

"Ester, pull the panel...no point in keeping it intact if the radio isn't going to work. We should be able to rig a solution for you to test levels *and* to find the other pods," he nodded at her. She finished stretching then went back in.

"Thanks," Akiko smiled.

"Sure," he shrugged, wrapping his arms around his chest, stretching his shoulder blades. "What are the odds we crash on a planet with breathable atmosphere?" he mused.

"What are the odds of crashing at all?" she turned to him.

"Higher than you'd think," he quipped, raising his eyebrows at the odd look in her eyes and lowering his arms slowly. "The tour path typically follows planetary systems, just in case. Better to be on the ground, even if the air isn't quite up to human standards."

"How are you going to find the other pods?"

"They'll be dead spots in the echoes. Probably narrow it down to within a kilometer or so. Calculating the spread shouldn't be too hard once we map it all out. If Quint was even marginally on the mark with her corrections, we shouldn't be too far away from each other down here."

"She was on the mark," Akiko nodded absently, "she wouldn't leave until she finished."

"Tough girl," Nath agreed.

"How many pods made it down, do you think?" she asked next, deciding to keep her hopes about Nik to herself, in case she was wrong. She knew he had to be wondering about the others, too. Not just Nik, but all his friends. She had to remind herself she was the outsider here.

"Doesn't matter. Whoever did is all that matters now. Like I said...we'll do a headcount later." His voice broke at the last handful of words. She had guessed right.

"We're going to have to figure out the radiation levels coming off the Rhineland so we can camp far enough away," she informed him, trying to move the conversation ahead.

"Right...Ester, how are you coming along?" he asked, ducking back in. Akiko decided to wait for them, staring back at the halo of light thrown into the sky above the valley.

"Alright...just bring them outside," Nath grunted as the two of them reemerged with a stack of metal boxes. He and Ester laid them out separately then started tearing open their seams. They had to share an omnitool between the two of them, but eventually the screws and seals were broken on all of them and a mess of electronic components was strewn about.

"That one," Nath pointed, "and that one. No, the other one." Ester handed him the components then started breaking down some on her own.

"How long will this take?" Akiko asked, growing restless.

"Just give me a few minutes to get the parts together and we'll just start testing on the way."

"Did you remove the environment controls or does your pod still have air conditioning?" Akiko asked.

"No, just the scanning equipment," Ester answered her.

"Ok...I'm going to go back and get the miners. One of them is hurt and needs to get out of the heat."

"Do you need any help?" she asked, standing up.

"Maybe."

"Go on," Nath nodded, "I've got this."

Ester and Akiko walked back toward the ridge, soon coming up on the pair of miners. The one with the injury was still not moving and his friend stayed next to him, absently tracing in the dirt.

"We're going to move him, ok?" Akiko explained. He stood to his feet. "What's your name?" she thought to ask this time.

"Kipp...this is my first tour."

"Mine, too," Ester smiled weakly, "what's his name?"

"Halim," he answered.

"We're going to move Halim to Ester's pod," Akiko directed, "where he can get out of the heat. We need to do it carefully. I need you to make sure his leg doesn't twist too much."

"Ok," Kipp nodded. The two women picked up Halim, whose body was thin and wiry. Common for miners, due to diet and the way they had to squeeze in and around mined out asteroid rock. They slowly carried him back to the pod. Nath looked up briefly from his work to make sure the parts weren't in the way.

"That's better," Akiko smiled, feeling the heat lift as they carried him inside the pod. Even if it could only give him a few hours of relief, it was better than leaving him outside.

"Nath, this is Kipp," Akiko introduced him. "Halim is inside."

"You made it out of the mining section?" Nath asked, juggling the parts in his hands to reach out and shake the young miner's.

"Yeah," he nodded grimly.

"Did anyone else?" the older man narrowed his eyes.

"It happened so fast…I don't know," Kipp shook his head.

"It's alright, son. I'd be lost, too."

"There's another group in the valley plain. I'm going to get them away from the ship. Will you be ready by the time I get back?"

"Yes," Nath promised. Akiko knew he had understood she wanted to go alone. Neither Ester nor Kipp needed to see a dead child and grieving mother. Not yet.

"I'll be back," she nodded, heading off.

Her legs were sorer from walking than her arms, which had taken hits being tossed around the pod on the way down. She ignored the pain as best she could, unsure how to handle the child. Eventually she would have to go get Elyna, too. Hopefully everyone else had landed in the same area.

The man saw her coming, standing up as she drew near. He was an officer, she saw now. The woman had to be an officer too, provided she was the mother of the child she held.

"Did you find them?" he asked.

"Yes," Akiko answered, "and we need to get you away from the ship. It might be bleeding radiation and your anti-rad panel isn't going to protect you for much longer."

"Ok," he answered, nodding to himself. "I'll try to keep her calm," he whispered. "I'm Oliver, by the way. Oliver Tam."

"I remember now," she nodded, "you were one of the next few on my schedule before...all of this happened. My name is Akiko Rai. Most people call me Rai."

"I'm glad you made it, Dr. Rai," Oliver nodded, taking a deep breath before heading over to confront the shaking woman.

"Brit, we need to get out of this valley," he told her. She looked up at him, not wanting to move.

"Then go," she declared stonily.

"It's not safe down here, and I'm not leaving you here."

"I'm not leaving him here," she shook her head.

"I'm not asking you to...but I can carry him for you," Oliver offered. Brit looked at him for a long moment, and slowly nodded her head in agreement.

"Here," Oliver took off his jacket, wrapping her son in it.

"Ty, right?" Akiko asked, drifting closer.

"Yes," Brit sputtered, her expression moving between mortified and distant as Akiko reached into her pack and swabbed some setting gel which she used to close the boy's eyes.

"Now he can sleep," Akiko nodded solemnly at Brit, her eyes still puffy and her face sullen. She nodded in thanks.

"Oliver," Akiko nodded. He took the cue, gingerly picking up the child's body and holding him flat in his arms. The three of them began the walk up out of the valley and up the ridge. It took longer, but none of them spoke until they reached the top.

"Royce and one of his techs crashed up here. He's working on a scanner to find the other pods. They're a little way into the desert, this way," Akiko motioned. They followed her. When they reached their pod, Nath ambled over to them, motioning for Ester and Kipp to stay behind.

"Nath," Oliver nodded.

"Tam," Nath nodded back, looking down at the child. The old man hung his head at the sight of Ty's immobile body. Akiko could see him mouthing something to himself before he raised it again.

"I'm sorry," he said to Brit, who made an empty nod in his direction. She reached over and took her son back, staggering with the added weight but staying upright.

"Is this all you've found?" Oliver asked.

"Yes," Nath replied, "but we'll find the others." He pulled Oliver and Akiko away from Brit. "What do we want to do about her son? I'd suggest putting him in the pod...but that miner Halim is in there unconscious. There's a body bag, of course."

"I'll talk to her about keeping his body out of the open air before decomposition starts. It won't be proper, but I think she'll agree to it," Akiko suggested.

"No, let me talk to her," Oliver disagreed, "she'll take it better from me." He left them and pulled her aside, leaving Akiko and Nath to head back to the pod.

"The scanner's almost ready," Nath told her, looking over his shoulder to see the look of disgust on Brit's face that slowly melted into resignation. Satisfied Oliver had solved that problem, he pulled Akiko over to the open box on the ground. Ester handed him one last component and he paused, making sure to stick it in the right slot. He picked up the plate and sealed it back with the omnitool.

"Ready?" Akiko asked apprehensively.

"Just need to program it," Nath confirmed. He disconnected his mobile link and clicked it into the magnetic alcove on the front of the box. She watched him key through several screens before the box's running lights lit up and its screen showed directions toward dead spots. On one side, the ambient rad levels were spiked. He pulled the link of its socket and clicked it back to his wrist. It was building a set of calculations, narrowing their search field automatically.

"We're not in immediate danger from those levels," Akiko tapped her finger on the numbers, "and that's...six more pods?"

"Or large rocks," Nath explained, "Either way, it's our best bet. Let's go find our people."

Ryan woke up to a light in his eyes. He waved his hand in front of him, hoping to fan away the flashlight in his face. It was a few moments before he understood that the light was *sun*light. The door to their pod was stuck half open. Seated across from him, slumped and unconscious were Iris and one of the officer's kids. He stirred violently, pulling at the straps until they unclicked.

Free, he reached over and felt Iris's neck for a pulse. It was still strong. He grabbed the child's wrist next, finding a pulse there, too. He pulled Iris's wrist out, looking for the tiny wristband that was synced to her baby's vitals, waiting for it to light. When the wristband glowed with the baby's heart rhythm, relief washed over him and he slumped back into the seat, taking a moment to look around the pod.

Lights and warnings were blinking on the front panel and vapor was pouring through the open hole, probably from the pod doing its best to keep them cool. They were on a planet. He hadn't been on one in many years. Real gravity made his body feel strange. Along with the new sensation, he had a dry mouth and his muscles ached.

It was hot – and if the vapor was anything to judge by, humid. He remembered very little on planetfall from the few tour prep courses where he had paid any attention. The pod was little help, since the radio connection was still blank. Other than the tickers for oxygen, which were a shade between green and yellow, nothing else on the screen mattered. He had little memory of anything immediately before the crash, other than it had been night.

He wrenched the door open a little more, clutching his mask and trying not to look directly into the sun. It was a stark blue. All he knew was that meant the sun was "young", whatever that really told him. There was no other noise but the soft rumble of the pod's coolers. Not even crickets.

The sky was a mix of green and blue, a little like Proxima, where he grew up. It briefly occurred to him that Iris's child might be born under a sky – the few planetfall instructions he recalled were quite clear that the chance of rescue was virtually zero. There were no hot communication lines back to the inhabited systems, and there were no craft capable of escape velocity hiding in the corners of the Rhineland...if it had even stayed intact.

Outside the pod was a very strange kind of forest, or at least it reminded him of a forest. Tall columns with the texture and color of white oak bark stretched on for several kilometers around them. There were no leaves, just a strange mess of thin entangled branches near their tops, over ten meters up. No animals he could hear. Nothing but the ominous silence of the forest.

He circled the pod, looking for any sign of flames. Satisfied that it had burned up whatever fuel it had left, he went back inside to find the child stirring. She started to scream but he hurried in, dropping to his knees to calm her down and help her out of her seat.

"It's ok, it's ok, you're safe now," Ryan said in a level voice, looking up into her eyes. She recognized him after a few seconds and her scream died to a whimper as he helped her get out of her straps. Iris had finally woken up next to her.

"Ryan?" she asked feebly, twisting to see the girl. Ryan helped her get her straps off, too. "The baby!" she looked at him in alarm.

"Her heart's still beating," Ryan nodded, realizing he could do more. "Do you still have your static pad? I can't find mine."

"I think so," she said slowly, easing out of the seat.

"Where's my mom?" the girl asked, "where's my mom?!"

"We'll find her," Iris echoed, holding her hand with one arm while handing Ryan her pad. "Nadia, right?" The girl nodded her head nervously. "I'm Iris – that's Ryan."

Ryan tapped through the stored articles, finding the one on field kits that they had bookmarked after an incident in recreation. "Need to check for concussions. Scanner should be..." he trailed off, looking around for the kit. He unhooked the strap and swiped it off the wall, clicking it open.

"Nadia first," Iris said resolutely, looking at the girl. She squirmed and raised her arms in her face as he took out the scanner.

"No!" Nadia yelled. "I want my mom. Where's my mom?" Iris took the small scanner from Ryan, taking hold of the girl's arm.

"We'll find her, Nadia – right now we need to make sure you're not hurt, ok? Your mom wouldn't want you to be hurt."

"Ok..." she dropped her arms. Iris laid the scanner on her head.

"That feels funny," the little girl said, frowning.

"Nothing to worry about," Iris smiled, pulling it away. Looking at it briefly, she passed it back to Ryan. They both saw the little girl did indeed have a concussion.

"You next," Iris said to Ryan directly. He gave her a look but didn't argue. The scanner read a negative for him – he had just blacked out from sudden gravity drop. Iris's scan read the same. The concern was now for Nadia. While Iris continued to console her, he read the advice on concussions in children. They were going to have to watch her...she may simply have lost consciousness from the same gravity drop, but they had no way to tell without better equipment.

"Is your baby ok?" Nadia asked after a while.

"She's fine," Iris smiled, "thanks for asking." Ryan knew she was lying for the child's benefit – they had no way of knowing there, either...but they were going to have to play this by ear and hope someone in the medical wing made it off the Rhineland.

"Can you stay here just a minute?" Iris asked Nadia, "We'll be right outside, ok?" The little girl pulled her legs up, rocking back and forth in the crash seat.

"Can we do anything for her?" Iris asked when she left the pod, whispering so Nadia couldn't hear.

"Not without a doctor. Just have to look for the signs – seizures, eye problems, anything abnormal."

"What do we do then?"

"Give her some isocaine. There are a couple rolls of tablets in the kit. Dose for a kid is a half tab every twelve hours."

"Can we even tell time down here? My sync is dead," Iris pointed at her wrist. The screen had gone blank.

"Mine, too," Ryan realized, looking at his own.

"What about *her*?" Iris asked, nodding to her abdomen.

"We need to find Dr. Rai or Beka. Or one of the techs. Someone had to have made it off...they had to."

"And if they didn't?" Iris asked with a slight tremor.

"We'll figure it out, ok," Ryan smiled, "we've got this." She smiled, too, but they knew it was not a scenario either one of them wanted to dwell on.

"What do we do now?" she asked, "I mean...where are we?"

"We can breathe down here. Wherever we are, we're lucky – and if we made it down, others did, too. I'm going to look for them."

"I'll stay with Nadia...I don't want her to get hurt and we need to watch her anyway. How do we stay in touch?"

"The radio should work," he nodded, heading back inside the pod. Nadia had her head half-submerged in her shirt, her dark eyes watching them with scared fascination.

"No signal," he jammed it with his foot, struggling not to lose his cool. He wanted to do more than kick it. His eyes drifted to the labeled drawers under the pod's crash seats. He bent down and pulled one open, finding more field kits, boxes of rations and a box of metal bricks.

"Here," he unwrapped one of the rations and gave a small piece to Nadia, "eat this." She pulled her shirt down and took it, eating it.

"It tastes like bananas," she grinned. Her laugh brought a smile and a chuckle to both them in turn.

"Take this," Ryan gave one of the bricks to Iris.

"What is it?" she asked, turning it over to find a screen and small keyboard. He hit the power button on his then hers, rubbing the backs together where a small circle icon was engraved.

"Short range transmitter. I think that means they're paired up," he pointed at the green lights popping up on the small screen. He typed a message in one and it lit up on the other. "I don't know how far these will reach and they don't look like they'll carry sound. I'm going to try and get outside the forest. I'll stay in touch."

"Ok..." Iris nodded, "Ryan – be safe."

"I will," he reassured her.

Nadia started asking Iris about the brick as he left.

"It works like your terminal, you just type..." Iris's voice trailed away.

Ryan headed away from the pod, sending a message every couple of minutes. It had a bit of a time lag, but Iris replied each time. Sometimes Nadia replied when Iris let her test it. The silence grew stronger the further he walked away from the pod. There was nothing – not a bug, animal, or soul in sight.

The edge of the forest came up so suddenly he nearly fell off the side of its adjoining cliff. He swung his hand up to his forehead to block the sunlight. A lake in the center of a large valley stretched below him, slowly morphing into a plain. In the distance, he thought he could make out a small metallic glint – another pod!

He messaged Iris, who agreed he should keep going. The cliff was hard to get down, but he managed to find some holds where he could, sliding to the ground near the bottom, ripping his jeans near his foot. He stifled the anger he had for his luck and kept going, pushing past the lake.

Near its edge, he paused to message Iris. It took a few tries before she confirmed with a garbled acknowledgment. The signal was getting worse. He walked back toward the cliff and sent a message saying he would try to be quick. It took a minute for her reply to get translated by the brick, a reiteration that he stay safe.

It took a good twenty minutes or so to make it past the lake and over the hill where he could see the pod. The near he got to it, the more he sensed something was wrong. Finally he could see why – smoke was pouring out of it. Someone was lying unconscious, stuck in the door. He took off at a run and crashed down next to them. It was the quartermaster, Zain.

He kicked the rest of the pod door open with his foot, releasing a plume of smoke into the air. A couple other bodies were still inside, lying flat on the floor. He pulled Zain out, then the others, trying his best not to inhale the acrid smoke. The other two seemed to still be breathing, but their masks had run out of usable air. Zain's mask had fallen off. He pulled his off and pushed it onto her face.

She opened her eyes slowly, looking around. Her hands clawed at the ground, pointing toward the others. Ryan left her and tried to wake them.

They didn't stir. Both had a very weak pulse. He pulled the field kit off his belt and rifled through it, looking for the injector. It was pinned to the corner. He scraped at its metal edge and pulled it out, pushing in the pins for stabilizer drugs.

Zain's eyes went wide as he jabbed it in her thigh. She lifted her hands and pulled the mask down, breathing heavy. He went to the other pair and did the same. They stirred slightly.

"Thank...you," Zain coughed.

"You're welcome," Ryan nodded, helping her to the side of the pod, resting her back against it. He pulled the other two over to the same side, where they were shaded a little from the sun. One was wearing a miner suit and the other was part of the civilian crew.

"I remember you...Ryan. Ryan...Mainer," she chuckled, trying to stop herself from coughing violently.

"Zain," he smiled back at her.

"That's right," she echoed hoarsely. Her eyes were red, and she was drenched with sweat. "They're not waking up," she noted, glancing over at the other two.

"No...but it's not safe to dose them for another few hours."

"You seem to know what you're doing."

"Not really. Just been doing a lot of paranoid reading."

"Paranoid reading?"

"For the baby. Iris Friedrich's."

"Oh...you're the boyfriend. That makes sense, I guess. I'd be paranoid, too," she coughed again, taking a deep breath.

"What happened? We were just—"

"I don't know," Zain cut him off, a look of anger crossing her eyes, masking her relief. "I barely had enough time to secure the core freight before finding a pod."

"Iris and a girl named Nadia are in a forest up on the cliff over there," he pointed way in the distance. "The girl has a concussion."

"We need to radio for—"

"Can't," Ryan cut her off this time, "it's not connecting. I was hoping yours would...but I'm guessing that's not an option."

"It's gone...popped couplers or some other cascade breakdown. Pods are too old...don't think they've ever been serviced."

"We need to keep looking then. We can't be that far spread out," Ryan hoped.

"Depends on our descent...I imagine she's crashed by now. Probably just need to look for the smoke – the pods will be centered around it."

"I'll see who I can find, then. How are you feeling?"

"Can I walk, you mean? Let me see..." she pushed up, then slid back down. "Nope...sorry, won't be help for a bit, I guess."

"Here, this brick is tagged to its pair in our pod. Signal's pretty degraded, but you should be able to get through. Let me write up a message so you can keep retrying for me."

"Sure," Zain nodded. He tapped out a short message saying he found a pod and was going to find more. He paused.

"Do you know if that's the girl's mom?" he pointed at the woman in the civilian crew jacket.

"No...Nadia's mom is Junie Lowe, from hydroponics. That's Camden, one of my asset management techs."

"Ok, 'no sign of her mom'," he said aloud, finishing the message and pressing send. It failed, but he set the retry clock.

"If I can't get it sent from here, I'll be able to walk in a bit – I'll get it to her," Zain promised.

"Alright. Here, the injector," he handed it to her, too. She set it to the side, near the others.

"Good luck, Ryan...and thanks."

He nodded, taking off for the next hill. Another valley dropped off below him, with several caves cut into the sides. Water snaked through them, drying up further downstream. A natural bridge spanned the gap to the other side, connected by the tops of the caves. It took a little while to cross, but he managed it without falling, crossing over the next hill when he made it across.

A cloud of smoke was visible now. It hovered over a few more hills. Before he crossed the last hill, he could see a group of figures walking across another natural bridge a couple kilometers away. He took a detour, yelling at them when he was close enough, waving his arms. They finally saw him, breaking off their own path, meeting in the middle of a hill in between the peaks and valleys.

"Dr. Rai?!" he saw, his heart turning over – Iris would be alright.

"Ryan?!" Akiko called out, finally closing the gap.

"I just came from that way," he pointed back over the hills, "I found Zain Rhali and her tech Camden. Another miner, too – he wasn't awake, and I don't remember his name. Iris and Nadia Lowe are back in my pod in a forest beyond all these hills. Nadia has a concussion...I'm worried about Iris's baby, too."

"Nath, I need to check on them," Akiko turned to the older man with a bandage wrapped around his head.

"Alright...I'll go ahead and keep telling the others to gather at that large lake. Cave should be large enough to hold us in if the weather takes a turn. You remember where it's at?" he asked. Akiko nodded and tapped her temple with her index finger. They separated from their group to join Ryan, crossing the bridge.

"Didn't catch your name?" Nath asked, stretching out his hand.

"Ryan Mainer," he answered, shaking his hand.

"Nath Royce. This is Ester Kim," he pointed at the woman hanging off to the side. She reached out to shake his hand in turn.

"Did any of your pod radios work?" Ryan asked before he and Akiko broke away from the group.

"No. It's some kind of environmental interference," Ester explained. "Not sure what, yet. We've been tracking pods in the dead spots." She lifted the box hanging off her shoulder.

"Ok...we got the message bricks to work in the provisions box. Doesn't seem to work long range, though."

"Yeah, those bricks should have a hundred-kilometer distance with the tighter frequency," Nath shook his head in frustration, "They're suffering from the same spectrum density issue."

"We'll get there as soon as we can," Akiko assured him.

"Don't take any unnecessary risks and don't go anywhere on your own. We need to stay together," Nath cautioned.

"Will do," she promised, turning to Ryan, "lead the way."

They crossed back over the hills, coming up on the pod. Zain was just walking back from the direction of the cliff, looking much better than when he had left her a couple hours before.

"Rai! You made it off!" Zain ran up to her, hugging her before the doctor could resist. Ryan could tell the older woman wasn't used to that kind of greeting.

"Good to see you, too," Akiko beamed.

"Camden and the miner are still out," she said, pointing toward the two slumped people next to the pod.

"Alright, let me check on them first. After that, we need to go get Iris and Nadia off the cliff."

Ryan watched her check their pulse and pick some more medicine out of her own field kit, pressing the drugs into the injector and pushing them in a couple different places on their body. After a few moments they both nodded their heads up, pealing their eyes open. She checked them both.

"Camden, are you ok?" Zain asked. She nodded.

"Hey, I don't think we ever met. I'm a miner, too. What's your name?" Ryan asked, bending down next to the miner while Akiko packed her kit away.

"Greer. I...I don't...how did I get here?" he stuttered.

"We carried you," Zain replied. "You blacked out when you came out of the mining section."

"Burin and Mandell...they were in there with me."

"We didn't see them...I'm sorry," Zain shook her head.

"Where...are we?" she asked, looking at Ryan.

"We don't know," Akiko said quickly, "but for now, Rhali here is going to take care of you while we go get some more people off the cliff up there. After that, we'll head for a lake where the rest of the survivors are gathering."

"Survivors..." Camden whispered. Her voice was scratchy. She and Greer both were struggling to hold back tears.

"I know," Zain put a hand on her shoulder.

"Ryan, let's go," Akiko motioned. He followed, picking up the brick and starting a message, letting Iris know they were coming. For an old woman, she was remarkably agile under gravity. The message finally went through below the cliff. Iris messaged back a few minutes later, asking about Nadia's mother – he had forgotten to ask about her when they met up with Royce.

"No, we haven't seen Junie yet," Akiko nodded gravely. He forwarded the message to Iris, who sent back a note of concern.

"We didn't tell Nadia she has a concussion. Didn't want to scare her any more than we had already."

"You made the right choice. If we can't find her mother...she'll be hard enough to console as it is."

"Do you think the baby is ok? We came down pretty hard."

"Babies are tougher than you think...the only thing I'm concerned about is getting her out of the heat."

"I'm just worried about her...about both them," he mumbled as they crawled deeper into the forest. They came up on the pod soon enough, where Iris and Nadia were waiting, the little girl walking around under the trees.

"Dr. Rai!" Nadia shouted.

"Nadia," Akiko smiled, coming to rest as the child came up to hug her – she was much more comfortable than she had been around Zain. She returned the embrace, rubbing her head.

"Where's my mom?" she asked again.

"We're still looking for her," Akiko told her, dropping to her knees and putting her hands on the child's head, taking out a new scanner to look at her eyes.

"They said that, too," she whimpered.

"They came and found me – don't I count?" Akiko laughed, pulling her in closer as she started to cry. Akiko gave a thumbs up to Ryan and Iris. He took that to mean she didn't suffer anything major on the way down.

"Yes..." Nadia said timidly, "but my mom counts, too."

"Of course she does – and speaking of mothers...I need to look at Iris. Do you want to help?"

"Yeah," Nadia wiped her eyes, walking over to Iris with Akiko.

"Put your hand here," she told Nadia. The little girl did, smiling at Iris when she felt the baby move. Akiko used the same scanner on her abdomen, pulling readings and feeding them into the mobile link on her arm. He hadn't noticed it while she looked at Nadia.

"You're both just fine," Akiko grinned, nodding to Ryan that she meant it. He did his best to hide his relief. That was one worry down in a sea of others. At least Iris and her baby would be ok for now.

"Now...we need to get down this cliff. Are you ok walking? I know it's hot, but we need to get back to the lake where Royce is gathering the other people who landed."

"Yes," Iris said matter-of-factly.

"Is my mom there?" Nadia asked quickly.

"Let's go find out, ok?" Akiko took her hand while Ryan helped Iris up. He then doubled back to the pod to grab some of the supplies. Before leaving, he could have sworn the radio lights had been blinking, like they were connected. He tapped the box, but the lights stayed dark. Figuring he must have imagined it, he shook his head and grabbed the rest of the contents out of the provision drawer, racing to catch up with the others.

Akiko woke up with one arm asleep under her side. She had drifted off sometime before night fell, lying on one of the sleeping bags they had pulled together from the pod provisions. On the other end of the cave, she saw Nath and Zain seated around one of the mobile evaporators they'd pulled from the one of the pods. Half of them had already failed, the others fanning the air in the cave's center.

She crept off the ground, careful not to disturb the others asleep near her. Nadia was snoring softly in Oliver Tam's arms – they had yet to find her mother. Brit Jameson was huddled to herself in the corner of the cave… they had buried her son before everyone had gone to sleep. Iris and Ryan were dozing against a crate, her head on his shoulder. They had gone back for Elyna soon after they searched the dead spots – she was lying unconscious on top of a couple sleeping bags to keep her comfortable.

Only a dozen others were there with them, a mix of deck officers, civilians, and miners…less than an eighth of the crew. Nik, Torv and Cole were all still missing. Nath and Zain were talking about a plan to find them. She could hear them discussing it as she walked closer to that side of the cave. While they were onboard, the two of them seemed amicable enough, but Nath did like to lord his years and experience over others.

"Hey Rai, have a seat," Zain offered, pushing one of the small provision drawers over to her. She sat down, getting closer to the evaporator, trying to catch some of the cool air. Nath had the radio box on the ground, the side with the magnetic alcove facing up at him while he programmed it with his mobile link.

"How long do we have on these rations?" she asked.

"A few months, if we're careful," Zain replied, tapping away on her own mobile link. Nath had helped reset hers.

"Are we going to talk about what happened up there?" Akiko wondered, holding her hands near the evaporator.

"No time to evacuate properly. Whatever hit us tore the connections in the substructure," Nath replied, voice muffled by the omnitool hanging out the side of his mouth.

"Same story. Only had time to clear the core freight housing before the environment went dark. Found one of the miners and jumped in a pod... then nearly died of asphyxiation," Zain shuddered.

Akiko nodded, not sure what to make of it. "I went to see Nik after he missed another one of the dailies. He and I got into a bit of fight...but then the ship shook. He radioed Quint directly. She said we'd been hit, and she was steering us toward a planet."

They all looked over at her unconscious form, in silent thanks.

"The network was out...so Nik told me to get to her as soon as I could before she bled out. I did that, helped her out of navigation and into a pod. I saw the Rhineland crash...no idea how many people were still left on it. He told me everyone knew what to do and where to go...but how did only this many people make it off? There must be more. We can't really be the only ones left," her voice died to a whisper, so only they could hear.

"No one ever expects this kind of thing. Panic makes people careless," Nath muttered. Zain nodded in agreement, eyes glazing over.

"What are you working on?" she pointed at the improvised scanner he and his tech Ester had patched together.

"Trying to source the interference. If we can remove it – or at least isolate its predictive frequency – we may be able to get the radios to mesh and see who else is really out there."

"Do you really think there are any more?" Zain lifted her head from her link. Akiko could see she was making a ration schedule.

"I don't know, but I'm not going to sit here and wait for them to find us. We should start polling the rad rates near the wreckage. We may be stuck here, but if we can patch the comms, we could setup a beacon. Another tour will come along when we don't report back. Might be five, ten years from now – but if we can last that long, we can get off this planet."

"Ten years?!" Zain half-whispered, half-yelled. Akiko didn't know what to do. Zain's attitude had changed dramatically in the last few hours when she saw how few of them had made it. Nath must have guessed she would behave this way, as he had already made plans without her.

"At the very least, we need to focus on finding the other survivors," he stared at her, pulling the omnitool out of his mouth and screwing a card into one of the now-exposed slots.

"You saw the pod's landing patterns. You *know* there are no other survivors!" she hissed. Someone stirred behind them. Zain leaned forward, embarrassed, running her hands down her face.

"We can't know for sure," Akiko put her hand on her shoulder. She was cold and shaking. Zain shrugged her off, throwing her link to the ground and storming off.

"She'll come around," Nath nodded, sticking the omnitool back in his mouth as he adjusted the scanner. "Just give her some time to adjust. Apart from the crash, she's not used to real gravity. Grew up in space like a lot of these people. Not enough oxygen making it to her head."

"You don't seem too phased by all this," Akiko commented, moving her seat closer to him. He had abandoned the original bandage, opting for a large plaster fix on his head wound. It was still crusted in blood.

"Not my first time being stuck. You learn to deal with the isolation. At least she's not alone."

"Stuck how?"

"I used to test prototype comm riggings. Volunteered for the release testing...biggest mistake of my life. Ran aground on a moon, crashed. Took them months to find me. That incident taught me to pursue a different career path. Met Nik soon after. When he was put in charge of the Rhineland with one of the transfer regime programs, I walked onboard with him and haven't left since."

"If you tested riggings, that means you were helping the Coalition. I didn't think they let civilians do that job."

"Right," he confirmed. He did not seem interested in elaborating.

"The Consortium was no different," she shook her head.

"I don't think it matters anymore," he said abruptly, screwing in the last part of the radio. He frowned when the results on his link were not matching with what he wanted.

"He didn't think so, either," Akiko whispered, remembering one of the last things Nik had said to her. "A war no one even really remembers", she said aloud.

"A war no one wants to remember," Nath looked away.

"All this time trying to find common ground with me and the one thing we have in common you don't want to talk about?" she chuckled morbidly.

"It's a real shame," Nath smirked. She knew she had hit a nerve, but she also knew that his flexible personality seemed willing to overlook it. She figured it was better to drop the subject.

"Is Zain right – about the pod landings?" she asked, quietly.

Nath nodded his head slowly, pulling the omnitool out of his teeth and pointing it at her, "But just because she's right doesn't mean there are no survivors. Those pods are rough tested, even if they are ancient. If they made it through the atmosphere, they made it to the ground – and we'll find them."

"And if they didn't make it to the atmosphere?" Akiko narrowed her eyes, watching as he screwed another card in place.

"Let's just say that hydroponics isn't only for the food...and those pods don't have room for grow lights."

"Let's hope they made it," she said gravely. He nodded.

The two of them sat there in silence for a while longer, growing steadily cooler as the mobile units caught up with the cave's volume. It felt much better than the dry heat on the outside. It was a wonder anything grew out there...she'd have to check on that when daylight came back, she decided.

"I'm going to check on Zain," she said, standing up.

"Hey," Nath stopped her, "are *you* going to be ok?"

"It's not my first time either," she said quickly, walking away.

Zain was sitting on a small rock at the edge of the cave, where the vaporous cool from the units was leaking out into the uncovered heat. She was still shaking, and the closer Akiko came, she realized that she had been crying.

"Hey," Akiko sat down next to her, declining to touch her this time. She was startled, pulling away before slowly settling back.

"Hey," Zain said simply, wiping her eyes with her sleeve.

"It's ok to cry," Akiko said after a while, "we all have."

"Doubt that Royce has. Acts like this is just a minor setback – we're stuck out here, Rai. I mean...royally stuck. The truth is that ten years is overly optimistic. I'll never...I'll never see my friends again. Just one more tour, I told them. One more and I'd have the money to get setup."

"I thought this was your career. What do you really want to do?" Akiko asked, careful not to use the past tense.

"What my family does. Just without all the lobbying and smuggling. But, the new bylaws mean direct genetic tracers take possession. I asked my parents for a small divestment. They didn't budge. Why can't they just make an exception? Too much hassle, they said. Over a stupid bio lock."

"If they won't make the exception, what were you going to do with your tour wages?" Akiko wondered.

Zain smiled, "Go independent. No bio locks, protection laws and blood contracts. I know the trade. A couple of my friends are looking into some gaps in the process. Places where we can do some real good and make good money. They're back there now, working to get their thirds together."

"Guess all of that's legal out in space," Akiko mused, "never really thought about it. I wasn't in supply."

"Standard scripts and even exotic ones, yeah. Had it all planned out. They don't bus the lanes – we had a clear line and a whole set of suppliers. I'm ready to...I *was* ready to play that game. I'm good at that. The logistics. Made being a QM easy."

"You can still play that game. It's only the first few days down here – no need to accept it and give up just yet. Losing hope is the easiest way to make sure you stay here."

"Don't accept it? That sounds like bad advice," Zain laughed, "aren't I supposed to follow the five steps of grief or something?"

"I'm not a psychologist – I trained as a field medic. It was 'do no harm' in one hand and my sidearm in the other."

"I just can't picture you fighting," Zain grinned, her eye tattoo outlined in the blue-tinged moonlight. "You are too nice."

"It was a different time – and I was a *lot* younger," Akiko lifted her hands in the light, showing the lines in her skin to Zain. "See, that one's from my first target practice. Missed every shot and caught the reload bar. Bled everywhere."

"What's that one?" she pointed at a deeper crease in her index finger on the left hand.

"First field surgery. Sliced it wide open. Very nervous. Saved her, though. She still writes sometimes."

"And that one?" Zain couldn't stop laughing.

"Oh, that one? I was trying to open a can. They used to ship out these osmium capped bottles in the first couple years of fighting. We called it 'redcapping'. Saved them for good luck. Whole superstition built up around it. I still have a couple in the trunk I brought."

"Why have I never heard about any of this?" she calmed down, quieting her laugh when someone stirred behind them.

"What's there to teach? History didn't help us to avoid it. Guess they just wanted to get people back to work afterword. Plus, I think a lot of the teachers were drafted anyway. Not many came back."

"You lost your friends," Zain paused, ceasing her laugh.

"You always lose in a war. You always lose outside one. That's what life is, Zain – gains and losses. How we deal with it matters. How *you* deal with it matters. We lost a ship...we lost our friends. But we're still here."

"And we're just sitting here talking about my fantasy future while...while all those other people are just gone," Zain dropped her head, tears in her eyes again. "I could have saved more. Maybe there were other people around the corner. I thought there would be more down here. I...I know we're still here. But they're not."

"No, they're not. But *you* are. I am. Nath is. All those people over there are," she waved her hand at the corner, "There may still be some out there – but there are most certainly many who are not. And over the next few months – when we go to sleep, when we sit around and talk, when we just sit there and listen to the sounds of this strange new world – we'll start to forget about what happened. But for today, we can grieve our friends and we can grieve our futures. And no matter what happens, I just want you to know – you're not alone down here."

"Thanks, Rai," Zain turned to her. Akiko took her hand.

"Call me Akiko," she smiled.

"Thanks...Akiko," she tried it out. "That does sound better."

"It's only meant for close friends," Akiko smiled and let go of her hand, standing up and stretching, "Get some sleep. You can worry about sorting out the pod provisions tomorrow."

"Ok," Zain agreed, standing up.

Akiko watched her walk back into the cave and unfold a sleeping bag before slipping into it. Nath appeared once she had settled in, still holding the scanner. He had a frustrated look on his face.

"What is it?" she asked.

"Can't nail down the noise. You get her figured out?" he asked, fiddling with the link in the alcove.

"She'll be alright. Just try not to push her buttons. She's new to this, even if you're not."

"I'll lay off her," he agreed, stopping to stare out at the landscape with her. The lake was almost green with the way the blue light hit its surface. Hardscrabble grass and sand that looked like glass gleamed on the other side. It was almost peaceful, if not for the eeriness of it all.

"At least one of us should try and get some sleep. You really should grab a couple hours – might help you think through the problem. I'll go with you once you get the scanner working."

"I'll think about it. I'll wake you up if I get it working before morning. Good night," he nodded, taking a seat on the rock. She left him there and retreated to her sleeping bag.

Fatigue overwhelmed her after a couple minutes and she slipped into a somewhat fitful sleep. When a hand shook her awake a few hours later, she briefly remembered dreaming about home, talking with Khiti after coming home from work – she never did that in real life. They weren't exactly the sisterly type.

"I found it," Nath told her. It was still night. Zain had woken up at the sound of his voice, pulling herself up off the ground. Akiko nodded to her to follow them out. She slowly pulled out of her sleeping bag and followed them to the cave entrance.

"One of us needs to stay," Akiko explained, "and it's best if I go, since we might uncover other survivors if we get it shut off."

"Where are you going?" Zain asked. Akiko could tell that she was apprehensive, thinking they might not come back.

"Over the ridge beyond the Rhineland wreckage. It looks like it's in the valleys we scouted out the other day. Can't believe I didn't catch it while we were there," Nath shook his head.

"How long do you think you'll be?" Zain asked, wrapping her arms around her shoulders. It was quite cool in the cave now.

"No telling," Nath paused, "but I'll see what we can get done today. If it's still nightfall and we're not back, then you can start worrying. I've got one of the bricks with me – if we get the source dampened, it should work. Listen for us."

"Alright," she agreed, looking back at the crates – the other brick was sitting on top of them.

"Hold the fort," Akiko nodded. Zain nodded back, watching the two of them leave the cave. Her face was still worried by the time they turned at the lake.

"Shouldn't we be bringing Ester with us?" she asked.

"No. I rigged another scanner from the other boxes we pulled from the other pods. She knows to start a search if we radio back. It's possible the pod radios will still be inoperable. What? You don't think I know what I'm doing?" he turned, grinning.

"You're enjoying this, aren't you?" she laughed, "in some sick twisted way, you like this."

"I don't think you'd be laughing if you didn't either. You never wanted to go exploring? Aren't you the least bit curious what it is?"

"Not as curious as you, apparently."

"Well, it's got to be something. I bet it's old war tech. Not *our* war, mind you – but the *old* war. The outreach ships. I think they used burst comms back then. That's exactly the kind of thing you couldn't trace with a simple scan. There could be some serious kit down here."

"You really think they got this far?"

"The old engines had quite a lot of reach. Their mission was to find anything they could land on...and this planet does have air. Imagine if that's it. That would be incredible."

"And we crashed almost right on top of them?" she pointed out the supposed flaw in his logic.

"You said yourself that Quint was on the mark. She was aiming for the lake. I bet they were, too."

"That's a lot of bets, Nath."

"That's what makes it exciting."

"Right," she mumbled coyly, following him over the ridges. He traded more theories on the way there – natural radiation formation and wartime provisions. He had so many conspiracy theories. The last was the most ludicrous of course, in that he seemed to seriously consider it. She had him repeat it just to be sure.

"Aliens?" she echoed as they crossed the ridge. The smoking radioactive ruin of the Rhineland lay beneath them. She tried not to think about the levels they had been subjected to after it crashed.

"Why not?" he looked back at her, swiveling the scanner across his shoulder, nearly losing his grip on it.

"Because it's insane," she shook her head at him.

"And what exactly, my dear, is so insane about it?" he huffed, catching his breath as he jumped between a few rocks.

"The Kolyov perimeter report, for starters."

"Oh, that old thing. You let a few scientists redefine life and we don't get to use the word 'alien' anymore. What's the matter with you people? You take the fun out of everything."

"If by 'a few scientists' you mean specialists from all classification missions that left Earth, then sure, we take the fun out of everything. There's no evidence of life or radiation made by it within the entire first wave perimeter. No aliens. No transmissions. No heat. No crop circles. Just space. Lots and lots of space."

"Well not *now*, no...but there could have been. It just requires a little belief *and* evidence. What if this is that evidence?"

"Now I *really* hope it's just that old war tech. I can't believe I'm talking to you about this," Akiko laughed.

"I've done my job. You're curious now," he cast a smirk back at her.

She rolled her eyes back at him, following him down into the valley, clambering down a couple slight rock slides. He guided them through an opening in the cave network in its center. She drew close to them as they strayed into darker areas. The radiation levels on the scanner started dropping steadily as they closed in. They glanced at each other quizzically.

"Why would they drop?" she wondered aloud.

The scanner then went dead altogether.

"Oh, that's not good," Nath spoke into the dark. "I just replaced those cards. Now why..." his mumbling grew too soft to hear. She heard him rustle around with it, pulling the plate and poking at things in the little light from the natural skylights above them – the sky had started to change from the blue-scale darkness to a white light day.

"Nath," she grabbed his shoulder. He stopped.

"What is that?" he squinted. They could make out pronounced lines of an object in the distance. The light on the scanner abruptly surged back on, showing the radiation had dropped to regular non-lethal levels. His echo program was wildly pinging the walls around them, overloading it again when he moved backward.

"Weird," he whispered.

"It's shielded," Akiko said, pulling a flashlight out of her pocket and clicking it on – they needed to conserve them since they had trouble charging off this sun's light – but she waved that concern for now.

"This thing is useless in here," Nath decided, pulling it off his shoulder and laying it back where it stayed powered down. He pulled out his own flashlight and clicked it on.

"Alright, Mr. Curious – what is it?" she asked. Their lights flickered wildly as they edged closer. As they neared the object, they realized the object itself was interfering with their lights, so they powered them back off, pulling back.

"A wireless sync? We probably shouldn't get too near it again if it can pump out enough EM spectrum to disrupt our electronics."

"Did you see any of it?"

"Just the lopsided outline. Looked like it was impaled into the ground – came in from up there," he pointed at the ceiling above them, where the light from outside was leaking down into a different part of the small cave.

"Does your old war tech do stuff like this?"

"No…but tech from *our* war might. Both sides were working on beacons for exactly this kind of situation – it would need to power itself through EM absorption of any kind. Radio, solar, you name it – but this is all a moot point. If this thing is a beacon, it's seriously malfunctioning. All it's doing right now is filling the local spectrum with noise. And in any case, it's bound to be packed with a ton of superconductor material…and you don't want to go poking at it for fun. With the energy it's gathering, the current inside is strong enough to evaporate carbon."

"And by carbon you mean—"

"Humans – us – yes," he said coldly.

"We have to turn it off," she said worriedly, "or we're never going to get a signal to the other pods, let alone into space."

"I'm going to need time to think," Nath drew back, picking up the scanner and tuning its electronics one more time. It whirred to life, the capacitors in its solid-state components singing eerily as he tried to hold onto a signal.

Akiko stood there, at a loss. She wasn't an engineer. She had treated her fair share of electrical burns, but never…evaporated limbs. Nath had better know what he was doing.

"Is there anything in the Rhineland that could help?" she asked.

"I was just thinking the same thing," Nath nodded in the half-light of the sun leaking into the cave.

"Zain would know where it is, right?"

"Depends on whether she ever fully synced the manifest. I think you're right. We're going to have to dig into the Rhineland to get the tools to tear this thing apart. But getting in there…" he trailed off.

She followed his gaze, looking at the ceiling. The light shifted from blue to green, then green to a deep indigo that reminded her of being bathed in decontamination lights.

"Look," Nath pointed at the object. It had become partially visible... along with something else.

"Oh my god," Akiko looked, then swore in Japanese.

A body lay next to it, still wearing a vacuum suit. The right arm and half of the right side were completely incinerated. The left arm was still holding a gun. The outline of a skull was visible beneath the broken visor, itself nearly shattered from a hole that had been shot clean through it.

Ryan could tell something was wrong when Akiko and Nath had come back from their excursion. They talked in hushed tones with Zain for quite a while before Zain and Nath took a pack of field kits and set off themselves. He decided he wanted to know what was going on, even if they didn't feel like telling him.

"Where are they going?" he asked Akiko. She motioned him over to the crates, picking up the brick radio on top.

"Into the Rhineland. Come on, I'll explain on the way," she told him. He looked back at Iris, who was playing a game with Nadia, Brit and Oliver. They found a few packs of cards in the provisions. She saw him leave, but he mouthed to her silently not to worry.

"What?!" he exclaimed, when she related the story of the beacon and the body. He couldn't believe it.

"We're not the first people down here. Nath is guessing that the wreckage of their ship must be near, but until we can disable that beacon, we won't be able to find anything."

"Any idea who they were?"

"We got as close as we dared and pulled the body away. The suit was crumbling, and their nameplate was disintegrated. The pockets were empty, and the gun was out of bullets. Decomposition had to be accelerated from radiation decay, so I couldn't give a guess on their age based on that, but best we could tell from the type of suit and its markings, they've been down here for at least fifty or sixty years."

"That's crazy," he remarked, following her over the ridge. "And the thing the sun did – what was that?"

"You saw the sky blink, too?" she guessed.

"Blink?"

"There's special nuclear material in the atmosphere that interacts with it – Nath was explaining it to me. They called it something else where he grew up, but he said as kids they just said it 'blinked'. Apparently, it was pretty common when they started nuking things from orbit."

"Is it from the Rhineland?"

"He wasn't sure. He didn't seem to think so – I'm inclined to agree with him, because the rad levels would be higher than they are now if that were the case. But we can't rule it out."

Akiko stopped at the edge of the ridge overlooking the crashed ship, typing a message into the brick. Nath sent something back a few minutes later. They were heading in from the remains of the frontside loop near the bridge, injecting extra anti-rad solutions. She told them to be careful.

"How are they doing?" she asked him, after a moment.

"They're all in shock. I am, too honestly...still hard to wrap my head around the crash. All those people...Kipp, Halim and Jin, the other miners, they've basically given up. Brit, with her son dead...I can't even imagine how that would feel."

"It will take time to come down from it. It's not easy – and for what it's worth, you seem like you're doing fine."

"We're stuck here...aren't we?"

"You heard us talking, didn't you?"

"Hard not to."

Akiko sighed. "It's going to be rough for a while...but we have to keep morale up. The easiest way to do that is build connections. Talk through things. Help each other."

Ryan nodded, then looked back at the entrance to the cave. He wasn't sure if he could do what she was suggesting. He wasn't exactly an extrovert. He wasn't sure any of them were.

"Where did you grow up, if you don't me asking?" Akiko asked, starting to type a message back to Nath. He said they had run into some trouble getting into the loop. It had caved in...they also had found a few bodies. Zain was getting uneasy, he said. Him too, to a lesser extent.

"Proxima. And you?"

"Earth. Though technically I was born in an orbital. Always thought that was why I liked the idea of being out in space. I grew up on the skyways between Osaka and Sydney."

"Don't know too many Earth-born natives, but if growing up on the skyways was anything like the continental lanes on Proxima, it was a hard life. Lot of moving around."

"A little like that. Mother hated living on Earth. My sister adored that blue planet. She still lives there with her...my mother's losing her mind these days. Khiti keeps her sane. Not something I could do," she paused, mumbling, "not after what I've been through."

Nath messaged that they had found the room with the tools they were going to need to crack the beacon open. Radiation levels were worse toward the end of the ship. Reactor seals must be leaking. She told them to hurry – the drugs could only flush so much out of their system before they became ineffective.

"Have you tried talking to the others apart from who you mentioned?" she asked, taking a seat on the ground. He did, too. It was oddly peaceful up on the ridge. The heat was sweltering, but this was the safest distance they could still message them.

"They're not really talking. Between bathroom breaks and sleep, you would barely notice they're there. Might help if we could get some other stuff out of the Rhineland – the theater projector is the first thing that comes to mind."

"And the popcorn," Akiko smiled. "After we shut this beacon off, we can give it a few days before journeying back in. I need to get the drug packs and some equipment out of the medical wing, too."

"About that...is Iris really going to be alright?" he turned to her. She averted his gaze, confirming his suspicions.

"I won't lie to you, Ryan," she said after a while, "any radiation poisoning that she's endured could progress into the baby and affect both of them. There's not an authorized panel for a fetus. There are blockers which I will inject once she gets near full term. Iris's own anti-rad panel is the only thing protecting the baby right now."

"Can we minimize it? Didn't you say the rad levels were low in that cave where you found the beacon?" he wondered. Her eyes seemed to light up at the idea, but quickly went down.

"The EM radiation would cause just as much, if not more damage in there. No...our best bet is to find a way to shield her during labor. That kind of equipment was on the Rhineland...but it needs power from a ship. When we make another trip back in, we'll see about finding some more static shielding."

"She can't die," Ryan said with a steely gaze, grabbing her arm and holding it in a tight grip.

"She won't," Akiko promised, placing her other hand on his. He looked into her eyes, trying to figure out if she meant it. Her eyes were tired...but he felt they were honest.

"I'm barely holding it together down here," he said finally, releasing her arm. She nodded in understanding.

"They found what they're looking for and are finishing up," she lifted the brick, typing another message back to them. "Nath estimates another ten minutes."

"What happens if we don't find any other pods?"

"Then who's left is who's left," she paused, eyes growing heavy, "simple as that." There was something there...but he didn't feel it was his place to push. She'd tell him if she wanted to.

"Dr. Rai, if you need to talk, I can," he offered. She didn't say anything for a long while, as they waited for Nath to respond. Once his message showed on the brick, Ryan decided to head back.

"It's Akiko, Ryan," she said, before he drifted too far away, "and I will, when I'm ready."

"I know it probably doesn't mean much to you, coming from me...but I've lost people, too. Not just my parents."

"It does mean something...but you're still young," she said ominously. He decided to leave her alone after that.

They had finished their card game back at the cave. Iris was doing her best to console Nadia – she was still under the impression her mom was out there. All of them knew the odds of that, now. How do you tell her that her mother was gone? You don't, he decided. Not until they knew for sure.

"Want to take a walk?" he asked. The pair looked up at him, the little girl getting excited.

"Not for too long," Iris said hopefully, "it's pretty hot, isn't it?"

"It's a little better today," he promised.

"Can we swim in the lake?" Nadia asked.

"I don't think that's a good idea," Ryan shook his head.

"Ahh, it looks like it would be fun."

"Maybe when we know it's safe," Iris told her, winking at him.

"Ok," she smiled, hopeful.

"Let's go, then," he said. They left the cave, heading down to the water. Nadia ran ahead, treading close to it but never going in. She seemed to heed their warning, at least a little.

"What is it?" Iris asked, seeing the look on his face.

"Nothing," he said, trying to erase the look, "just thinking."

"Can they get a beacon out? I heard the others talking...they said the mining corps wouldn't send a ship without an exact location. Is that what they're working on?"

Ryan hesitated. He knew the official rule now – he'd found it on the articles he'd pulled from Akiko and Nath's links when they offered him the files. He decided it was best to be honest.

"The mining corps won't send a ship unless they can gain value from it...the Rhineland is not salvageable down here. That's why most planetfall regulations tell you to get comfortable – we're not hauling our five years of heavy metals yet."

"But there are people down here," she stopped him, looking to make sure Nadia was sufficiently ahead. "How can they leave us here? What kind of people would do that?"

"I hate it too...but you have to see it from their point of view. The fuel cost – and the people cost – to send a rescue is just not worth it. We all signed waivers. Every tour has them. It's always a risk."

"I just...I can't imagine how they wouldn't send someone. All those people...they deserve better than that. *We* deserve better than that. I always thought they were better than that."

"Look," Ryan grabbed her before she dropped into further melancholy. "The others *are* working on a plan to get a signal into space. The mining corps may not send someone, but someone else might. The Consortium, the Coalition – possibly the transfer regime. A passing ship, even. No one's going to give up, ok."

"Ok," she took a deep breath, "ok."

"Everything is going to be ok," he promised.

"She's kicking," Iris said suddenly, breathing heavy as she found a nearby rock on the lake's edge to sit on. Ryan sat with her. Nadia was a bit of a ways away now, though still not in the water.

"Ryan says everything is going to be ok," she whispered into her chest. He put his hand to it, feeling another kick.

"Nadia!!" Brit shouted somewhere near them. They looked down to see that the little girl was dipping her shoes in the water.

"Oh, no," Ryan shook his head, leaping into action. He and Brit rushed down to get her before she took another step.

"What were you thinking?!" Brit shouted at her. "We don't know if that's safe," she said more softly. Nadia had started to cry, asking once again for her mom. Brit looked at Ryan before looking back at the girl.

"It's alright. I'm sorry I yelled at you. We're still looking for your mom, ok? We'll find her."

"What about the other kids? Maybe she's with them," she said, wiping her eyes with her hands.

"Maybe," Brit lied. "But we have to just wait for her, ok?"

"Ok," she said sullenly.

"You didn't put your hand in the water, did you?" Brit asked. Ryan looked at her hands – they were dry. Her shoes were wet.

"No...I just wanted to make the squishing sounds with my feet, like we did when we went to the beach once. I'm sorry. I won't do it again," she promised.

"Let's head on back and get your shoes dried off, ok?" she said, hurriedly pulling her back to the camp.

Nath and Zain were walking into the cave with Akiko by the time he and Iris got back. They were carrying a couple crates, placing them near their cooler they had set up in the other corner, where they had been meeting the last couple nights.

"I'd like to help," Ryan offered, when they had offloaded the tools onto the ground.

Nath looked up at him, a bit of a tired look in his eyes. "Do you have any experience with sinking heavy currents?"

"I have on one of the ice miners."

"Hmm," Nath paused, "ice mining. That could work."

"What exactly do we have to do with the beacon?" Zain asked.

"Well we've got two options. Sink it to another controlled source...or let it sink to its own source."

"One big arc flash," Ryan guessed.

"Right," Nath pointed at him, making a clicking sound.

"We need another coil or a some kind of giant rod to short it with," Zain summarized, "and since I don't remember lugging another battery over here, I'm guessing we're going to short it."

"A bit of both, actually," Nath explained, "from what I remember about electronics before I specialized in comms networks, superconductor coils are notoriously difficult to discharge. If we try to short it, it'll just burn up the wire. We need a legitimate load resistance to put between the leads before it burns up so we can actually discharge it enough to disconnect it."

"What about the computing network in the Rhineland?" Ester suggested, startling Ryan. He hadn't seen her come in. He had only talked to her a few times while she had been busy working on dissecting the pod radios. Nath seemed to consider it, but shook his head.

"I think we have to rule it out – the terminals were fried when Zain and I went in. The network wouldn't even light up with a simple connection."

"Why not the simplest solution – the electric heaters?" Zain pointed out. "Just burn off the resistance as heat."

"Let's call that option B," Nath agreed. "Because we might actually have use of those if the climate changes. I'd rather not break them if we can avoid it."

"So, what's option A?" Akiko asked.

"The lasers," Ryan lifted his head. Nath nodded.

"Originally, I was thinking of pulling one of the engine frames...but then you mentioned laser sinks. They are very dense, for what duty they perform. We just need to get one of the smaller ones out of the mining platform. That should be enough to sink the current without killing us."

"That sure would cut the time down. How long before we can go back in, Akiko?" Zain asked.

"You two – at least another day."

"Tell me how to disassemble it. I'll go get it," Ryan offered.

"Me, too," Kipp said, walking up behind them. It was the first words he had spoken in the last couple days.

"Alright," Nath agreed, after a little hesitation. They spent the next few hours going over how to approach the mining section. Zain told them where to find the other tools they would need that they hadn't pulled during their first run. Akiko warned them about the dangers of increased rad sickness, and when to inject the denser blocker if they couldn't make it out in a preferred amount of time.

"Don't go, Ryan," Iris pulled him away, once they had finished prepping. The others had gone out of the cave.

"It'll be ok," he promised.

"Do they really need to do this?"

"We have to get that beacon off. If there are other people out there...the conditions in the pods won't last long in this heat."

"Can't someone else go?" she said worriedly. He looked around at the scattered people. They had all heard. None moved.

"I can get us in and out of the mining section faster than anyone else. I'll be fine," he nodded, wrapping his arms around her. He turned her slightly so he could kiss her without the others seeing.

"Come back, ok?" she urged.

"I will," he nodded, leaving the cave. Oliver came up to her just as he was leaving – he was their reserve should things go south – laying his hand on her shoulder, whispering something to her before heading out after him. He came up to Ryan.

"I told her I'd make sure you got back," he said.

"If she understood what kind of radiation levels are in there, I'm not sure she'd let me go," he lamented.

"She understands. I get the feeling she's not a selfish person," Oliver gave him a weak smile.

"We'll find Junie," Ryan consoled him, "with the beacon down, we'll find the other pods. She's bound to be out there."

"At this point...for Nadia's sake, I really hope you're right," Oliver nodded, lowering his head in resignation. "I don't think I have it in me to tell her that her mom isn't coming back."

"We'll find her," Ryan put his hand on his shoulder.

It took them a half hour to get back to the wreckage. Kipp was talking with Akiko and Nath while he and Oliver trailed behind. The doctor had injected them all with booster blockers before they left the camp in the cave. Ryan could feel an uneasiness in his stomach as the wreckage loomed in the distance.

"Euler, you ready?" he asked. It was pronounced like Oiler.

"Yeah," he nodded. His face was still as blank as it had been the past few days, but something new was hiding behind his eyes.

"You have an hour before the boosters can't keep up with the levels in the mining section. Get in, get out, and get the laser sink over to the beacon," Nath told them.

"Depending on the state of the energy network when she crashed...the lasers in the mining platform are probably still live," Zain warned. "You need to be careful not to discharge the sink inside the ship. It's one of the parts we don't store because of how dangerous it is."

"We're going to start imaging the beacon to figure out where to plug the sink in to turn it off," Nath continued, "but Rai and Tam will be waiting here in case you need them."

"The radiation leaking off the sink will be just as much of a problem as the ambience in the ship. You don't need to stretch the time any more than you have to, ok?" Akiko warned.

"Got it," Ryan nodded. Kipp did the same. Without further delay, they went inside the opening in the inner loop. It was a relatively short trip to the platform entrance, but the climb through the substructure wasn't fun. The clock was ticking. The weight from the pack around his shoulders dug into his skin. It was filled with part of the tools they would need to extract the sink and some extra radiation packs. Zain had told him it was essentially an open coil. He hoped it was enough.

"There," Kipp pointed. It was the base of the laser assembly that trailed into the vacuum quarry. They were deliberately avoiding the bodies...a lot of their friends and fellow miners were in there. A quick stop at the supply base gave them the rest of the tools they would need.

"Let's work quick," Ryan insisted, climbing onto the nearest laser, pulling the bolts with the large omnitool. The exposed sink was smoking. Kipp pulled the bolts on the next one. Same. At the fourth of five lasers, they found a sink that was still intact. He messaged Akiko and Oliver.

They had a little under thirty minutes to get out of the ship before they risked radiation poisoning.

"Don't touch the leads," he warned. They pulled it out with the clamps from the supply closet. It was extremely heavy for something so small, weighing in a little over a hundred kilos of solid coil, encased in composite insulating layers to prevent direct contact. They heaved it out of its socket, both bowing under the strain.

They pulled it down off the laser assembly, stopping every so many meters to catch their breath. It was a lot to haul.

Kipp stood up and suddenly broke off for the entrance to the barracks, twisted in the way the ship had landed.

"Where are you going? Kipp, we don't have time, man." Frustrated, Ryan rushed off after him, pulling his aching muscles over the door laying on its side.

"What are you doing?" he called out. No answer. "Euler?"

"He's dead," Kipp's voice answered weakly as he crossed into the last room. He was holding the small body of an animal. A chinchilla by the look of it. It was dead, either from radiation, the impact, or both.

"Euler, man...I'm sorry, but we need to go."

"You've got Iris. All I had was this little guy...I hoped...I thought that maybe he was still alive. I pumped him full of anti-rads for the trip."

"Kipp..." he trailed off, not sure what to do. He was sobbing.

Kipp yelled, slamming his fist hard into the lockers. It dislodged something in the fragile floor hanging above them, sending it crashing down on his leg. He howled in pain. Ryan pushed the debris out of the way, but it kept coming down. A last piece came down on top of Kipp's head and he went silent. Ryan could see blood as he tried to get around to him, but the barracks were starting to collapse.

He left, running back to the sink. His hands clambered for the brick, typing in a quick message. Akiko soon typed that Oliver was on his way in. He heard him after a couple minutes.

"Mainer?" he yelled.

"Over here," he shouted.

"What happened?" Oliver asked, watching the barracks collapse in all the way as Ryan pulled himself out of the small corridor. He grabbed his hands, helping him through the last part.

"Euler...he went in after his chinchilla. It was dead...he got mad and started punching the wall. He must have hit something structural. I...I couldn't save him."

"Nothing we can do for him now," Oliver consoled him, grasping the holds on the sink. They both continued carrying it out, with Ryan trying to hold back tears of anger and regret. With ten minutes to spare, they exited the ship, where Akiko was waiting.

"What happened to Euler?" she asked.

"Dead," Oliver said quickly, cutting off any further discussion, "we need to get over there. This thing's heavy." Akiko added what strength she could, and the three of them started for the edge of the valley, heading into a cave entrance that Nath had marked by scraping a rock across the front in the shape of an X.

"In here!" Nath shouted further in, hearing them groaning.

"Put it down here," Ester pointed. They had setup some lamps around the object. The body that had lain against it was in the opposite side of the small cave.

"Where's Euler?" Nath asked.

"He went after his pet...barracks collapsed on top of him," Oliver summarized, seeing Ryan was still suffering from shock.

"Another one...gone," Zain shook her head, staring at nothing.

"Rhali – focus," Nath snapped his fingers. She did, grabbing the cables and testing the sink with a scanner outside the cave where it wouldn't have as much interference.

"Get them out of here," Nath ordered. Akiko did as he said, pulling Ryan and Oliver back out of the cave and a good distance away. "Just wait here," she said. They did, knowing it was for their own safety.

Ryan's heart was beating fast and his arms were aching. He slumped against the wall, waiting for the word from inside. He wasn't sure what he was expecting: a loud explosion; lightning raining out down from the sky; some climactic end to their crusade that had just cost a man his life. All he wanted was his pet. Poor guy.

"It's discharged," Zain told them, a few minutes later. Her face was very pale. Something had unsettled her.

"What's wrong? Zain?" Oliver asked, waving at her. She turned to him, not sure how to form the words.

"What is it?" he asked. "What did they find?"

"Nothing," she shook her head.

"Nothing?" Ryan muttered, half to himself as much to her.

"The pods. Other radios. You're saying they found nothing?" Oliver asked, standing up to her, grabbing her by the shoulders.

"No pods. No signals. Just desert. Goes on forever," she shook her head. "We're all that's left."

Akiko took a large drink out of the metal tumbler, waiting for the mild mix of cold-brewed herbs to calm her nerves. It had been a rough couple of months. They had made several trips back into the Rhineland for anti-rad drugs and the equipment to make more, then they began the laborious task of removing what few of the bodies they could find. One vigil was all they could stand to hold. Candles on the lake. It was beautiful, despite the circumstances.

They had made sure the water was safe, and Oliver carried Nadia into the water so she could place a candle for her mother. The girl was only ten. It broke her heart to watch that. Nath had been in bed for much of the time – he had caught the discharge on his legs, cracking his bones with the tremendous force of electric current.

Nik was dead, she had told herself, night after night. His body wasn't one of the ones they found, which she was mildly thankful for – the sight of him might drive the last shred of sanity left to her. He was the only reason she was out here...and now he was gone. Her life, whatever was left of it...would be spent here on this nameless planet.

Nath was on his feet today, though, giving up the bed for Iris. She had entered labor a little while ago, and the whole camp was abuzz with waiting. Camden and Brit were taking bets on the color of her eyes and her hair, though Akiko warned them that they could change over the next year – which they found amusing, as it only made the bet more interesting.

Ryan was sitting with her, dozing off. He hadn't been sleeping well, and she could only guess why – he was worried about the first radiation therapy. They had setup the shielding around the bed in the corner, forming a small room. The scanner was sitting next to the bed where Akiko could keep her eye on it. The levels on the display were much lower inside, but it was very hot in the room. On top of the scanner, a makeshift fan was pouring a small bit of relief for Iris. Along with a half roll of isocaine tabs she'd already chewed.

"Drink some of this," Akiko said, handing her another tumbler with cool purified water. She took a long drink and handed it back.

"Ryan! It hurts!" she yelled. It was getting close. His eyes shot open and he squeezed her hand.

"I'll be right back," Akiko told them, pulling out of the box and into the open air, shutting the shield.

"My trunk – did you get my trunk?" she looked around.

"Yes, right here!" Zain echoed from the front of the cave. She and Oliver were carrying a heavy trunk with them.

"Put it down, put it down," she waved them, "quickly now."

They dropped it on the rock. She rubbed the sweat out of her eyes so she could see the lock. It was an older pattern entry with 8x8 squares. She traced what she could remember, missing it a few times before it finally clicked open.

Her books had shifted to one side, but the box she was looking for was still stuffed into the side, wrapped in some of her old favorite clothes. She extracted it, clicking the locks and flipping it open. It was her old kit, but it still had the combos she needed. Iris's screams from the other side of the cave renewed her speed. After finding the one she needed, she pulled the injector from her jacket pocket and slowly trickled the vial into the filter.

"Alright, be ready and listen in case I need something else," she told them. They nodded, still breathing hard from the trek back.

Akiko pulled the shield open and closed it back in once she was inside, pushing the injector against Iris's arm. She relaxed, but her cries of pain were still resonant.

"Push," she told her. "You can do this."

Iris grabbed her arm, looking her in the eyes with a violent worry, "Don't let her die...please." She held the young woman's hand, telling her to breathe. After an intense few moments, it was finally time. Iris closed her eyes and her screams filled the cave.

Akiko cut the umbilical cord and wrapped the baby in a hazard blanket before carefully pressing a patch to her tiny shoulder. She wasn't crying, just looking up at her. Her eyes were the strangest sight she had seen in a long time – two eye colors. It happened...but the radiation made things questionable. She nodded to Ryan, motioning that the baby was fine.

"Ryan...is Emma alright?" Iris asked, collapsing back onto the bed.

"She's alright," he told her. "How are you feeling?"

When she didn't answer, Akiko knocked on the shield. Ester came inside, taking the baby from her as she hurried over to Iris.

"Iris?" Ryan nudged her, "Iris, wake up...what did you give her?!" he yelled at Akiko.

"Nothing that would do this to her," she said as calmly as she could manage, pulling Ryan's arm away so she could get at her pulse. It was far too low, and it was nearly gone. She injected the reversal, but it was useless. She shouldn't be dying...but nothing had gone as it should down here. In that moment...she felt the most powerless she had been in decades. Powerless to save a life.

"Iris, wake up..." Ryan started to cry, "please...just wake up." He yelled into the blanket when he felt her arm go limp.

"Ryan," Akiko said after a few minutes, taking his arm, "Ryan, come on." She nodded at Ester, who knocked on the shield. Oliver came in, his eyes dropping when he realized what had happened. He held the door while she slowly carried him out, taking him out of the cave, past the others who stood waiting.

She pulled the brick out of her pocket, telling Ester to check on the baby like they planned. She messaged back that her exposure check had come back at permissive levels, as Akiko had guessed. She pocketed the brick and helped Ryan to a rock on the edge of the lake, far from the camp. He was inconsolable.

The sun was coming up, going through its slow phase where it interchanged the light, green and blue shifting into black. Her hands were covered in blood and fluids. She went to the lake's edge, dipped her hands in, then pulled off her jacket and used it to wipe them off before she sat down next to him. She put her arm around his shoulder, holding him as her mother once had held her.

"I am so sorry," she whispered, "I'm sorry I couldn't save her. Sorry that I broke my promise." He cried into her shoulder, trying to hold back his sobs but failing.

"You did what you could," his voice cracked, looking up at her. His eyes were bloodshot. He was tired, he was depressed, and he wouldn't be ok for a long while. She just held him there, and after a few minutes, she started to hum softly as the dark lake gleamed in the strange black light.

"Where you go / I cannot follow," she sang, "Wading in / the fathoms deep. Treading stars / awaiting sleep. I dream awake / on nights like this. Wishing for / one moment more. But I can hear / if I listen close. The drum / of our heart's twin beat."

The sky stayed dark for several more minutes, and when it lifted, Ester and Oliver were standing near them, carrying the small baby. Akiko had told her it was safe to expose her after the patch had taken its course. She came over to them. Akiko let go of Ryan and took the baby from Ester. Oliver put his hand on Ryan's shoulder.

"What's her name?" Ester asked Ryan. He took the baby in his arms, flexing them to hold her steady.

"Emma," he said, trembling. Akiko put her hand on his shoulder. His shaking slowly calmed down.

"Emma has beautiful eyes," Ester whispered.

"Is something wrong with her? Is she...ok?" he looked at Akiko.

"Her eyes? No. It's a genetic condition. She wasn't exposed – it's not radiation. She's going to be just fine," it took all the strength she could muster to smile at him. It wasn't a lie. She *would* be fine. Nothing would happen to this little girl, Akiko decided. Nothing. She wouldn't let it. Not while she could still draw breath.

"Hey Emma..." Akiko grinned at the baby, trying her best to hold back tears, but she could no longer. "This is Ryan. He's going to take care of you."

The sky's blink started to recede, shining a long blade of blue light across the green lake. Ryan stood up, walking out to the water. Akiko followed behind, trying to hear what he was whispering to her. He was too far away. By the time she made it to him, Emma was closing her eyes as the blink finally ended, shining cool blue light down on the five of them.

Akiko looked across the lake. Nath, Zain and the others had gone back inside the camp, dealing with the fallout of the tragedy. Her heart beat wildly in her chest. It had been so many years since she lost a patient. It always hurt. Nik would know what to say...he always used to know what to say. She wanted so desperately to talk to him. Just one last time.

Nik breathed in harshly, coughing as the pain ballooned in his chest, searing his throat. He was in a pod crash seat. It was still in space – he was floating in zero gravity. He reached up to his helmet, looking for the crack he had felt when the outer ring smacked him. It wasn't there. He couldn't find it. Twisting in the vacuum was difficult, shooting hot pins and needles up his spine and down his legs, where the limb under his brace throbbed in terrible pain.

A body floated at the bottom of the pod; its face flash frozen. He could barely make out the features of Mikhail Torv. He held Nik's cracked helmet in one hand. Nik had little time to mourn for him before the radio burst with static. He swung over to it, screaming in pain as he clicked it off. It had patched into a source somewhere…the Rhineland maybe.

Gravity had started to build in the cabin, pulling him down into his crash seat while lowering Torv's body to the floor. The small craft shook violently as he grasped the straps, securing his body in shortly before it rocketed into the ground. He blacked out.

When he came to, an enormous surge of pain and nausea overtook him as pulled off the straps. He collapsed to the ground next to Torv, unable to stay conscious. His stomach had returned to normal by next he woke, now filled with a gnawing hunger. He pulled the tab on the provision drawer nearest his face, grabbing the box and pulling out the first ration stack. He smacked the helmet with the wrapper.

Annoyed, he jerked the helmet off his head, pulling the wrapper away and swallowing a good few pieces, chewing enough to get it down. It was possibly one of the best meals he had ever tasted. It made him forget about the body next to him for a couple minutes, while his head processed everything that had just happened. Not a single logical thing led to a crash in his mind. They were not in an asteroid field. Surely, he thought, Vauss could have seen something big enough to tear the outer ring off and course correct in time.

What else could it be? If someone was shooting them down, they would have kept firing. Maybe it couldn't be picked up by the ship's lidar...but what could absorb the light and hit them that fast? He had no idea...and the only way he was going to get one was if he could get to the Rhineland and figure it out. If anything was left of it.

His next thought was the crushing reality of the people that had just died on his watch. There was not nearly enough time for them to get off in an orderly fashion – it had been night on the ship. Most of the crew was asleep. Not to mention the descent itself was too fast and too close to the planet. Some pods would have just burned up...others would have floated out into space without oxygen. He stopped thinking about the numbers.

He picked himself up, staggering under the pain but managing it so he could look at Torv. His side was impaled with shrapnel, but he had plastered thermal paste on it...he would have lived, if he hadn't given him the helmet. But why?

"Why didn't you save yourself? Why couldn't you just..." he trailed off, coughing to regain his voice. Why couldn't he just let him die? The naked thought hung there, echoing in his mind.

The pod door was cold to the touch. He picked up the helmet, brushing off the fingerprints inside before reseating it. The vacuum seal tightened, the small display in the corner of the helmet showing him how much air he had used. Almost all of it. He did the math. Three days in space. The suit's IV solution had kicked in to keep him from getting dehydrated. At least another two days down here. No wonder he was ravenous. He pulled the helmet off one more time, eating the rest of the ration bar before replacing it on his head.

He tapped the sequence into the door lock. It opened a few centimeters, enough for him to get his fingers inside. He dug in, pulling one side open, then the other. A dark sky showed above him, along with a shrill wind in the suit's mic. The temperature was below freezing, rising slightly. He keyed the door sequence again, making it shut now that he broke the flash frozen seal.

He sat back in the ship, picking up the provision box and hunting around for the isocaine rolls. Once he found them, he pulled his helmet off a third time and swallowed half the roll. It eased the pain in his leg, but it wouldn't work for too long. He had to conserve them – there were twenty more rolls in the bins. He shoved the remaining half and two more in his pocket.

Swallowing hard, he pulled the helmet back on and stood up on his leg. It hurt far worse than it had earlier, almost sending him back to the floor. Real gravity, his nemesis, had arrived. He keyed the door and it popped open. The wind returned; he dialed the external mic down to a whisper.

There was no moon in the sky, and barely any stars. He couldn't piece together the constellations, even if he knew them. Outside the pod, the landscape was mostly tundra. Tough grass grew in tufts on top, but no other plant life. No trees. The pod had crashed into the dirt and its thrusters burned up, covered in black marks from the afterburn.

First things first, he decided. He went back into the ship and dragged Torv's body to the side, pulling the helmet out of his hand. There was a bag in the provisions. He pulled it over him and started zipping it up to seal him against the elements. As he got to other hand, he realized it was clutching something else. It took a lot of effort to pry his fingers apart. His link was half crushed in his palm.

He gingerly took it, trying not to bend it further as he laid it on the pod's forward console, next to the radio boxes. The radio display was reporting madly, but even through the noise he could tell it couldn't mesh against anything. If there were other pods down here, he would have to find them on his own.

After he finished zipping up Torv, he pulled his body to one side of the small pod, away from the provision bins. Until he could find something to bury him with, he would just have to leave him here. He shook his head, the thought of the younger man's sacrifice still tumbling around his brain. It was a noble thing...and he was sure he didn't deserve it.

There were a few batteries in the bins that fit his suit. He ejected the slim tube out of the shoulder pack and pushed another inside. The display gained a little light in his helmet. Then he replaced his air mix tank with one of the tubes in the next bin over, shooting the oxygen sensor back from red to green.

Next he needed to figure out the source of interference that was jamming the radio. Thanks mostly to the loss of Torv, the pod provisions would last him for a solid few months. Whoever else had made it down might not have that kind of time. Amplifying the radio to reach them was going to be tricky. The last time he troubleshot comms, he still had a knee.

He connected his link to the radio box, pulling its program and mirroring the protocols. It took a few tries before he got it right. Brain fog from the crash kept him stymied, but eventually his link connected to the radio. He exited the pod, going a good hundred meters without it giving out. That was good, in that it meant he could stay in contact with the stronger tech in the pod – and bad, in that it meant the radio likely couldn't find a sister radio to mesh with in the surrounding fifty kilometers radius.

After another hour of analyzing the signal ratio, he decided the direction of the interference and followed it – there was no magnetic north on this planet, and no reference for its axis. His boots made a crunching noise as he tread across the tundra, dragging his maimed leg before the dull pain was too unbearable to continue.

Stopping was painful, too. He breathed hard against his helmet, thankful for the small heat the suit could provide. All his adrenaline had worn off and he was starting to feel his bones creak in the native gravity. Before it could get to him, he set off again, slowly coming up to a break in the tundra. He swung his head down, letting the lights from the helmet flood the small ravine.

Except it wasn't a natural one. Something had carved it into the surface – something large. His heart skipped a beat as he swung his helmet upward, expecting to see the Rhineland's body exposed in the cold, unforgiving wind. The lights flooded a rusted gunmetal hull, cracked in several seams and falling to pieces.

It was not the Rhineland.

In fact, it was not a design he had ever seen up close – and his time in the war had given him a lot of experience with ships. The telltale outline of the hexagonal engines were late stage blueshift models, placing their date of manufacture over the better half of a century ago. The last blueshift cores were retired a few years before he was even born. His mind spun as he climbed down, hoping to get a better look. The suit's Liev counter was reporting a significant pickup of autonuclear radiation – but thankfully nothing that would kill him any time soon. He was still at least five or six kilometers from the pod.

The vacuum paint had faded, preventing him from making out the name of the ship. Maybe he could see it in the daylight, provided the day cycle on this planet wasn't terribly long. His link told him that the pod radio was still solidly convinced the source of interference was within the wreckage. He sighed.

He paused, took a deep breath, then popped his helmet slightly to feed a tab of isocaine into his mouth. He chewed the chalky blue substance and let it dissolve as the wind blew into his face. It was still quite chilly. Once the small relief hit him, he started into the wreckage. Of the few hangar doors that might allow ingress, only one was rusted in a place he could squeeze inside. He strained, trying not to imagine how he would feel later.

Inside, he couldn't help but feel like he had stepped into the past. Once, when he was very young, he had visited an old war museum with his dad. They had ocean submarines, water navy ships, and the first explorer ships. He still had a strong memory of stepping into the cramped cabins, overwhelmed by the controls and switches – here was no different. For a moment, he felt like that kid again.

On every bulkhead, a small panel was inlaid in the corner, fed by a box of thick wires running behind the rusted metal. Each fed the next one in line, all the way down the small corridor. Every piece of the ship had to be constructed in such a way that it could be folded and molded back into the next module, in case of rupture. Modern ships were built with little more than a crash contingency...the art of "exploring" was lost. He shook his head at the thought of his own ship and its crew, their futures evaporated by a single hit.

He followed the wires to the center of the old ship, looking for any sign of general amplifiers. Even the old ones could pack a punch, given a strong enough power source. While he searched the ship, he kept a careful eye on the rad counter, watching it tick slightly upward as he rustled up some dust. It stayed just on the edge of lethal. The engines on this ship had expended enough half-lives. Small miracles.

In the center was the bridge. Its door had been cut out, as if someone had taken a torch to it...from the outside. What he found inside didn't shock him, but it did change his suspicions. There were three bodies, each mummified. They hadn't decayed down to the bone. Two were on the floor, bullet wounds in their necks. The third was in the navigation chair, head erect, and arms relaxed...they had died just sitting there. Had they killed the other two?

This deep inside the metal ship, he had lost contact with the pod. The source was here though...somewhere. He looked around the small bridge, barely ten meters square. All the terminals were bulky and used the archaic plug and play ports for the old links. If he recalled correctly, they needed common-connect-cables, or what the old comms books called a "C3" as shorthand.

No maps or overviews were tacked to the bare walls. He would need to look in its computer to find a layout of the ship...if it even still functioned after all this time. Older ships like these used hardened solid-state electronics. The real threat was the prolonged exposure to autonuclear radiation – late 21st century physicists' gift to humanity. Self-sustaining micro-fusion. Its lasting effects sat between background cosmic radiation and traditional nuclear byproducts. The first space pioneers lumped it all into "storm colds" – temporary sickness that often happened on long routes without any viral or bacterial origin, peaking during ion storms.

"Great," he kicked the console, sending up a plume of dust. "If Nath were here, he'd be having a field day." He wondered if his other friends had managed to get off in time. Then the next thought hit him so hard he wasn't prepared – Akiko. He had nearly forgotten. His feet gave way and he collapsed into an empty seat.

Akiko had gone on this trip at his request – Getty had told him he was finally done...two weeks before they left for open space. The mining corps had assigned a fresh-out but he said no, leaving him without a doctor. He had scrambled, knowing there were few qualified people in the medical corps who would even consider it. He had come up short. She was his only hope. He closed his eyes, picturing the moment he hit send on the mail. He had left it in his drafts for a week, hoping it wouldn't come to it. Someone would come up. No one did.

But she did. He knew she would. What had she said? He had mentioned his dad. He barely even remembered that...what had he actually said? He was not a good man – he had hurt him and his mom, splitting them off from the other side of the family. She died and he was left in his custody. He shook his head – it was so long ago. Why was he thinking about it now?

Her eyes. He missed her eyes. It was the first thing he had seen, when they met – her face had been covered with a scarf to keep the dust out, her helmet hiding her hair. Only her eyes were visible. She wore contacts that gave them a violet hue, even though they were blue. His friend had been shot, and she was the only medic left to patch him up. She had fixed him... and he had gone back out to get shot again, dying a few days later.

They had gone to the only bar left in the Juno – the orbital space habitats they fought on – and they helped each other drink their woes away. She had never lost a patient before, not like that. He had never lost a friend. It was a horrible night, but they were there for each other after that. Until the end. And she was there for him when he needed her...and now...now the odds were not in his favor that he would ever be there for her again. The air grew close in the small cabin. He had to go on. If she was out there or not – others could be...and they would need his help.

Done reminiscing, he refocused his mind on locating the ship's computer. Older ships usually liked to centralize them to the engine frame, since the loss of either one would be the loss of the whole ship. Distributed networks came later, when hardened net cards and fiber shielded against cosmic radiation were cheaper to produce. That said, it wasn't on the bridge – it was in engineering.

"Stay put," he whispered to the corpses, heading back out of the bridge and past the entrance corridor he had followed from the hangar. It was about a third the size of the Rhineland, based on what he had glimpsed outside. Engineering had to be in the center of the front or rear. A cursory examination of the cables in the front told him it was likely to be in the rear – they all trailed that way.

Rad levels ticked steadily upward as he pushed into the rear. They would be lethal if he stuck around for too long – a booster shot would be necessary after more than an hour. He started a timer on his link. Back in the pod, he had strapped one of the small field kits to his suit's shoulder pack.

The door was cut open here, too, the discarded plate laying in front of the entrance. Another body, sitting down normally at the reactor management console like the one on the bridge, as if they had just...died there. The radiation shield had cracked in several places, causing it to lose a significant amount of coolant. What was left shimmered behind it, glowing blue with radiation leakage.

There was a ladder down. He took it, trying not to break the rungs that had grown weaker from time. On the lower level, the shield was still intact, and no coolant had spilled out down here. Behind him was the telltale bundle of wires terminating from the front of the ship. A mass of cables fed stacks of server blades behind the heavy glass, acting as an electromagnetic shield.

Several of them were still blinking their ancient LEDs with regular pulses, trying to talk to the rest of the ship. A handful had gone totally dark. Permanent resilience was the old mantra – never stop communicating. Unlike the Mining Corps, which dictated that only network techs be required to train in comms, the Consortium required minimum courses in networks for any officer or enlisted rank that would be exposed to vacuum.

Granted, he had forgotten a lot of it...but the basic knowledge was still there. They had trained on basics and old connections – it was how he knew about the C3 ports. Speaking of which – he pulled open the locker in the server room corner. Several large pads were seated in the alcoves along with a bundle of C3s. He took out a stack of pads and all the C3s, stuffing a few of the cables into his pocket.

At the center of the server stacks was a pillar that contained net connections to each server, a single port for each of them. He thumbed down the dusty numbers and found one that corresponded to a working tower. He set the stack of pads down on the open bay of the pillar, picking up one in his hand, plugging the cable into the working tower's port and the pad's jack.

It lit up, missing a few chunks of pixels here and there, but otherwise remaining readable. The ship's real-time OS was still quick, so the electronics were still serviceable, at least. It gave the lag times in input on one corner, under 100 milliseconds. A tree of the ship's functions flashed up on the left, requiring elevated access for anything more than the most basic readouts.

Kilimanjaro. That was the ship's name. There was no colonial, coalition or consortium designation. Either it was an independent rig, or it was flying unlisted. The size of the ship *and* its name were evidence that pointed to the latter, rather than the former. The Mining Corps had always named their in-service ships after Earth rivers, which was built on the tradition of using landmarks, borrowed from earlier explorers. Mountain names were reusable designations when transferring between companies...or extra-planetary states.

It was a longshot, but if this ship was a state build, it would have the buoy and dark protocols – scuttle was added during the war. They had remained largely unchanged since then, he remembered, because they were meant to be the least common denominator when ships were endangered. Buoy enabled comm buoys with maximum amplification. Dark disabled comm buoys in hardware to prevent noise transmission due to viral data. Scuttle was a different story.

The trouble was that the opcodes were on his link. Due to the nature of the protocol, they were rolling bytecode, preventing anything but personal use of his link to activate them. He would need to connect it to one of these pads...but how? Nath would know how to do it. He always knew what to do with these old things.

Nik sighed. There was nothing else to be done for now, and he was exhausted. He laughed at the audacity of thinking about where he was going to sleep – there seemed to be no shortage of the dead, here or in his own pod. He'd find time to bury them all when his mind stopped racing and he didn't feel like he would collapse. For now...the server floor looked great to him.

His rad counter warned him otherwise. Leaving the wreckage was for the best, at least until he could figure out how to reduce or balance his exposure. The provisions included several field kits with anti-rad boosters; the assumption of any crash was reactor leakage. They would have to last until he was done with the wreckage...and he would need to keep some in reserve when he went looking for the Rhineland. She was out there, somewhere. He could feel it.

Another half roll of isocaine tabs and an hour later, he collapsed inside his pod, looking at the bag which contained Torv. Leaving him outside was not a respectful option...but he couldn't sleep here with him. The provisions contained some environment tents, and it took him another hour of excruciating work to set it up away from the pod. He took the body and placed it under the tent, hammering the clamps into the tundra to keep it steady.

The pod felt empty without him, but in a way he could handle. He'd slept in worse conditions, just preferably not in a morgue. He leaned back, feeling his knee tighten as the world slipped away. His dreams were vivid, mixing between the Rhineland and his old cast of nightmares. He felt much the same when he woke up. Leg was still throbbing. He swallowed more tabs.

Outside, the sky had turned a strange hue of green. It reminded him of the northern lights back home...when he had a home. He couldn't shake the thought of it. He hadn't been what he would call "homesick" for a long time. Fighting on the hinterland Junos, when it got bad...he thought of going home. Then he remembered his dad and the trenches didn't seem so bad.

He made a trip to the Kilimanjaro, scavenging the ship for any usable supplies while his link recorded the old ship's RTOS from the old link. What little he found had mostly been picked clean, but eventually he found the jackpot – there were still food stores. Irradiated, of course, but edible in small doses with his own anti-rad panel working full blast away from the wreckage.

Days passed while he wracked his brain for a way to connect the modern tech to the old cables. He simply didn't have the technical knowledge to do it. His leg slowly began throbbing less, as the brace adjusted to the natural gravity and his natural tolerance for the dull pain returned. He knew he was getting better when he only needed a tab or two during the whole day.

Nearly three weeks after he landed, he found a box of tools in one of the old ship's hangar that had some picks and a retractable tool that could act as a passable shovel. He'd dreaded the moment, but knew it was time. He had put the other bodies in bags and removed them from the wreckage, stripping any useful items they still had on them. The body on the bridge that hadn't been shot was carrying a link which was marginally more up to date – a few millimeters thinner and a handful of centimeters smaller.

He buried the bodies, all five of them, out on the tundra.

All their suit tags sat atop their graves, but only Torv's was still legible. He was no closer to knowing who the others were or what they were doing down here. His efforts to crack the Kilimanjaro's old encryption were fruitless. He plugged the smaller link in, hoping for a miracle, but it showed the same minimal information.

It became warmer during the time of day when the dark green sky replaced the inky black starscape, enough for him to leave his helmet off. The sun still had not shown itself. There was enough light for the pod's minimal solar circuit to charge. He kept batteries in reserve for when the season would shift back. At the very least, he could breathe in the open without furthering his exposure.

At night, he alternated between reading some of the stored novels on his link and watching the small blocks of footage it took when he let it record the old link. There were blips in the response time – sometimes rising over a second, which was odd in any real time network. 250 millisecond response time was standard. With a few months of data, he could now see the blips were happening at regular intervals.

Then he had an idea.

Ryan watched Emma try to walk, but no matter how hard she tried, her legs wouldn't work like she wanted. He couldn't believe it had been almost eight months since she was born. Her eyes were still different – Akiko said they could still change, but this condition usually persisted. The little girl looked up at him, her blue and green irises shining in the sunlight.

They hadn't come up with a name for the planet. It was one of the topics at their weekly meeting. The first few months were very hard. Every time he looked at Emma...all he could see was her mother. Akiko made sure to check on her constantly. Almost to the point of being annoying...but he still appreciated the gesture.

There were thirteen of them now, counting Emma. Jin Greer and Halim Kalash were the only other miners aside from him that had made it off, except for Kipp. He still had nightmares of seeing him holding his chinchilla. Oliver Tam, Elyna Quint and Brit Jameson were the only deck officers left. Ester Kim and Camden Senia had been department techs.

Nadia Lowe had taken to sneaking out of camp when she wasn't volunteering to help babysit Emma. Oliver and Brit had become her de facto guardians. No doubt trying to fill the holes left in their lives after the tragedy. She had mentioned her mother less and less as the months drug on, but he knew how much it hurt her to know that she would never see her again. It was different for Emma. She had never known Iris.

Aside from himself, that left Akiko, Nath, and Zain. The four of them had taken up leadership of the group. Akiko took care of everyone, checking exposure and nutrition along with healing the daily scrapes and bruises. Zain had similarly taken up her old role, plotting out ration limits and keeping track of equipment.

Nath seemed aimless for a few months, but eventually started collecting the old components off the Rhineland wreckage, creating a solar network – Ryan and Zain were delegated to setup and maintenance. His latest achievement was getting the theater projector working last month. A whole stack of shows and movies had been archived in its static storage. Morale had lifted significantly. After that, he had gone back to his own personal projects, trying to resuscitate the old network so he could make sense of what happened.

Ryan was everyone's handy man. They had moved a bit further away from the wreckage to avoid radiation levels, finding a nice cave network that got them out of the occasional torrential rains – they quickly found out why the lake existed. The desert's hardscrabble mud was a byproduct of the quick rains and long dry spells. They made rooms and installed some limited soundproofing for privacy.

Most were partitioned, with everyone having a choice of singles or doubles. Nath, Zain and Elyna opted for the singles. He figured Jin and Halim would too, but they seemed ok to room together, as they had back on the Rhineland. He didn't share the need, but he understood it. Oliver, Brit, and Nadia were in a slightly larger double. Ester and Camden decided to take a regular double together. He and Akiko were in singles that connected, so she could keep an eye on Emma when she wanted. It was the only compromise he made. He wanted to be alone.

They had rigged lights and some makeshift hydroponics in each room, to give some fresher oxygen and keep things from getting too grey and dull. The center of the cave network had been open to the sky, but they had mounted transparent metal scraps over the holes so the rain wouldn't rush in – it still dripped, but not enough to cause any damage.

Ryan was sitting on the edge of their commons table, watching Emma crawl across the ground, smiling at her attempts to stand up. He often thought about his mom, wondering when he had learned to walk. Akiko was more than happy to tell him all about the stages of development. She reminded him of his mom in certain respects...but not when she was angry. His mom had been loud when angry. Akiko stayed silent. He had quickly learned to avoid her when she was silent.

Someone had been stealing medical supplies and she left them all a scathing notice on the message boards. That was how most of them kept track of things. It made it easier. Elyna and Halim never really talked, but they would answer messages. Nath had shrunk the bricks down to something more like the link size, which could work over a 25-kilometer radius. He was a wizard with communications, but no matter how hard he tried, penetrating the atmosphere was next to impossible without a higher power output.

That was the sad truth. This was their home, whether they had intended it or not. Everyone was coping in their own way, looking for something to focus their efforts. Nath had helped Jin get into voxel programming when he started pulling out the nav suite components from the Rhineland. His creativity would have remained hidden had they never crashed.

Most people read – book clubs weren't his favorite thing in the world but listening to the others not despairing over their situation was better than nothing. Akiko urged him to read *something,* but he usually found a way out of it. Taking Emma on walks and exploring the strange forests on the ridges was his favorite pastime. Swimming in the lake was a close second, when the weather permitted.

"Ryan, there you are," Nath exclaimed, carrying his usual box of electronics he lugged around in his spare time. He laid it on the table, smiling at Emma when she looked over at him. "I wanted to talk to you about something – if I can expand the radio field, we can explore a little further. Finding pure water would be a big help."

"You really think there's a cleaner river somewhere out there?" Ryan asked, turning so he could face both Nath and Emma. She was amusing herself with a rock. They had laid down plates, so it wasn't too dirty. She hit the metal with the rock, making *chinking* noises.

"Groundswell, more likely. Something must be feeding these forests. They're growing too tall with this planet's weird cycle of photosynthesis," Nath explained. He had been reading his own share of science texts in the old manuals he still had in his link.

"How can you expand the field? What do you need from me?"

"Manual labor, mostly," he laughed, "but ingenuity, too. You think you can make these numbers work?" he pushed his static pad over to him. It was a small schematic of a comms array.

"Zain said our store of aluminum molds is low. Unless you can find some ore on the way, that's going to be difficult to source."

"Which is why I asked a miner – you think you can find ore?"

"Normally they bring it to us," Ryan chuckled, picking up the pad. The right half had the array – they needed material for seven. "You'll need to trace bauxite. How good's your scanner now?"

"Better than the first month we were here," he pulled it out of the box. It was marked up in several spots and the screen scratched up, having been dropped. It was a resilient device.

"If you can find it, I'm sure I can mine it."

"Good man," Nath grinned. "I'll get started on the scanning algorithm – bauxite, you said?"

"Yeah. Or any other deposits with high aluminum mineral content."

Nath nodded, putting the scanner back in his box and heading back to his room. Ester and Camden walked into the room sometime later, taking a seat near him.

"How is she doing?" Ester asked, nodding at Emma.

"Fine," he smiled, "though I don't think she likes the storms. Or night. Can't tell. She starts crying."

"You try rocking her?" Camden asked, picking her up.

"Didn't make a difference."

"She'll grow out of it," she assured him.

"Nath wants me to mine for aluminum."

"What does he want to do now?" Ester rolled her eyes.

"Expand his radio field so we can explore further out. Needs to build seven more pylons."

"That doesn't sound so bad," Camden said as Emma grasped her hand.

"I guess it could help find water," Ester sighed.

"Yeah," Ryan confirmed.

"What are we watching tonight?" Oliver asked, approaching the table and setting his mug of coffee down carefully. Nadia was now in the floor with Emma, giving her different sized rocks and a toy she had made herself, which lit up when she hit it on the ground.

"Swordfell and Retroactivity," Camden read off the message board from her mini-brick. "Swordfell – a medieval knight comes face to face with his old king, who's bent on terrorizing the region. Then there's Retroactivity – a time traveler who goes into the future to find humans have been enslaved by an alien race. Another reimagining of H.G. Wells' *The Time Machine*."

"Never seen The Time Machine?" Oliver asked.

"It's a book. Well, a short novel really," Ester nodded.

"Any good?" Ryan wondered.

"It's a classic."

"That doesn't answer the question."

"No, it doesn't," she smiled impishly.

Not everyone came in for the movies. Only Zain and Elyna joined them later. Halim and Jin were playing voxel games. Ryan and Ester sometimes joined them to play teams. Akiko would only watch a movie on occasion – had to be one she "really liked". He told her that's how he felt about books, and she just shook her head at him. She did come and take Emma shortly after the movie started so he could watch it without waking her.

Swordfell was better than Retroactivity. He wouldn't have called that, since sci-fi was more his genre – but they were indie films. You could only get so much out of the money. Everyone went to bed after. Akiko had fallen asleep in her chair with Emma, her door to his room slightly ajar so he could see within. He left her there.

A few days later, Nath had his program ready. The two of them went out together early in the morning, before the blink. His scanner was picking up dead ends for most of the day. Before nightfall, they finally found a cave network with open bauxite, about ten kilometers away. They marked the spot on their running map he had stored in static data on the radio network.

"I read it's not a good idea to mine alone – I'm happy to help but I really don't know how much good I'll be," Nath shrugged.

"I'll get Camden or Zain to come along. You can focus on the layout. Looks like you still need to map it out anyway."

"Works for me. Let me know if you run into any problems, alright?"

"Will do," Ryan agreed, waving him good night.

They soon arrived back at their home cave system, splitting at the fork to their rooms. Akiko was waiting for him.

"I know it's late, but can you help me with something?" she asked. Emma was asleep in the crib they had made for her.

"Sure."

He followed her out to the part of the caves where Zain kept the stores. A fresh set of pallets and crates were in the sorting area.

"That's Nik's old trunk. Zain messaged me to say she found it. Can you help me get it into my room?"

Ryan nodded. Normally they would use the loader, but it was still charging, and the walk wasn't that far back to her room. She seemed stronger than she had when they first landed. It was the same for everyone, it seemed. Early on, at her advice, they adopted an exercise routine to adapt to the new gravity.

"Right here," she grunted, heaving her end into the corner of her room. Her own trunk was next to it. Both had identical 8x8 grid locks on the front, tiny black square keys.

"You know his lock?"

"No...and I've read about the dangers of trying to slice into these old types. I don't want to damage anything. Figured I would try some of the old standbys, when we were caching supplies. He wasn't one for unique passwords...at least not back then."

"That will take you forever," Ryan smirked.

"I suppose you'd just laser it open?" she quipped.

"Well, I don't have stuff I store in a trunk...so I guess I shouldn't have an opinion here."

"Right," she smirked back.

"Well, you let me know if you change your mind."

"It's a puzzle. I like puzzles," she smiled. "Good night."

"You, too." He shut their interchange door, then soon went to sleep.

Mining the old way was rough. Getting the laser field setup over a large area was difficult, since his only experience doing it manually was on the first small pass he did on a "starter" ship, where the corps trained miners. He appreciated the auto fields far more than he ever did after he finished, sweating from every pore.

Halim and Jin were not interested in reprising their old careers, and as he predicted, Camden helped him. She was as strong as he was, if not stronger, despite being just a bit shorter and good bit smaller than he was – curse of his particular mining diet, he guessed – he didn't want to be wiry, so his build was just a little bigger. They worked for the next few weeks, finally getting enough ore to process. Nath had finished his layout and identified future mining sites.

It took another week or two to setup the ore processing, most of which was automatic, except for the output. He had taken to watching Emma in the morning while it soaked up the excess energy from the solar network. She was almost nine months old. He nearly dropped the aluminum briquettes when she stood up and started walking on her own. He showed everyone later, and they all had a good laugh while taking some photos and videos. It was a welcome milestone.

Zain helped him heat the briquettes for the mold when they started on his array design. Once it was finished, the two of them spent the next few weeks putting it up. Ester decided to help on the last day, when the array would be activated. Camden joined too to see what their work had been worth.

"Alright, dialing up the field strength – we should be able to get scan depth and radio waves back through these," Nath nodded. Ester ran her own programs, often to check his math.

"Still no other pods," Zain whispered, seeing the scans.

"That's probably a good thing," Ryan put his hand on her shoulder. No one else had heard them. She nodded, shaking her head as if to wipe away the expression on her face.

"Ok, looks like we have some promising areas on the 80 degree and some on the 170 angle. Totally opposite...but hey, no one said it was going to be easy. Ryan – you want to help me scout the 80? Camden, you and Zain can try the 170? Ester, you good to run radio pings from home?"

"I'll handle it," she agreed.

"Alright, turn back when the signal stops pinging – still could be dangerous to get out of range. Let Akiko know what we're doing, too, so she doesn't get too worried."

"Will do," Ester nodded, heading back home.

Zain nodded, taking off with Camden.

Ryan could tell it was going to be a long day, which made it a bit exciting. He and Nath crossed the outer radius, still getting an ok from Ester – the array was working. Nath clapped him on the shoulder. He seemed overly excited, though he was always giddy when he finished a project.

"She'll be one here in a couple months, right?" Nath asked, as they crossed a new ridge. A whole forest of strange new trees stretched out beneath them as they towered above it. There was not a single sound of life. It took a moment to rewind his mind to hear what he had asked.

"Yeah, she will," Ryan smiled, thinking of Emma...then of Iris. It was also the anniversary of her death.

"Hey, I didn't mean to..." Nath stopped, seeing him frown.

"No, it's alright," Ryan shook his head, as Zain had, erasing the frown from his face.

"Anyway...I figured we could have a party for the little tyke. Not that she'll remember it...but I have some ideas."

"Sure. I guess. Didn't think that was your thing."

"It's not, normally...but Akiko asked about it the other day. I figured I would placate her."

"You still like her," Ryan smiled mischievously.

Nath only gave him a thin wry smile in return.

"Yeah, I'm down with that," Ryan agreed.

"Alright. I'll let it be a surprise then. Just wanted to make sure you were ok with it."

"Yeah," Ryan agreed.

"Hold up," Nath stopped them. The pings on his brick had stopped a few seconds ago. He handed him his modified link and told him to walk back. Ryan did as he said, and the pings started to make it through again.

"Looks like this is it!" Nath yelled up the ridge, retreating. "It'll have to do," Nath sighed, reappearing next to him.

"What's that over there?" Ryan pointed. A break in the forest that didn't match up with a natural formation had caught his eye.

"I don't know," Nath said, pulling a small pair of binoculars out of his pants pocket. After looking, he handed them to Ryan.

"Don't drop them," he warned.

Ryan gave him his link back and took the binoculars, looking through them at the clearing. It was slightly outside of their new radius. Something had split the trees.

"I want to check that out," he said, lowering the binoculars.

"Agreed," Nath said, taking them back, "but not today. It's already late and it's not wise to go outside the perimeter, even this close."

"Alright – tomorrow then?"

"Tomorrow," Nath agreed. They made the long trek back, arriving home after nightfall. Zain and Camden had found roughly the same perimeter. They exchanged their findings and agreed to regroup the following day.

Ryan was exhausted when his head hit the pillow, and he was grateful that Akiko had taken Emma for the night. He had a dream that he was on the Rhineland...or maybe one of his older ships. They all seemed to run together. One of his older girlfriends was in his arms as Iris had been, looking up at the outer ring. She fell asleep in his arms, but she wouldn't wake up. He tried to shake her awake – and that's when he woke up himself in a cold sweat.

He took a shower to shake off the haunting thoughts, using as little water as he could. Nath, Zain, Ester and Camden were waiting in the center room. They laid out a plan to search that side of the perimeter – Nath had cobbled a mobile array together from the last of the parts left from the original array's construction. They would plant that on the ridge and link it up.

They all set off together, arriving at midday. Ester stayed at the ridge, monitoring the mobile array. Nath continually tested the ping as they made their way to the break in the forest. It seemed to hold the signal. The four of them could see Ester on the ridge in the distance. If need be, she would camp there for the night – they had watched the weather patterns to make sure nothing would surprise them.

"They're splintered, but not from lightning," Zain commented, tracing her hand across the broken trunks. There were no burn marks usually indicative of the such a strike.

"What's that?" Camden pointed past them, starting that way. The trees had hidden what lay beyond the break. They all followed her.

"Another one," Nath whispered in wonder. Inside the clearing past the break, covered in dust shaken up from the storms, was the wreckage of a small indie explorer ship – and it was very old. Nath was trying to make out any markings. It was marred by weathering and time. If they were going to learn anything, they would need to open her up.

"You think this belonged to your friend with the beacon?" Zain directed at him. He shook his head.

"No...this is older than them and the beacon. Early 2100s. How did she even get out here?" he muttered to himself, looking for an entrance to the cockpit. It was barely twenty meters long. He finally found what he was looking for – it had been sealed.

"Royce – you don't know what's in there," Zain warned. "These old ships were known for hyper pressurization."

"You're right," he stopped himself. "Give me the bag." He spent the next twenty minutes rigging an actuator to an omnitool, shoving it inside the lock. He waved them all away. They all took up behind the broken tree lines. Camden messaged Ester what they were about to do. Ryan could see her stand up on the ridge.

"Now," Nath triggered it from his link. Nothing seemed to happen at first, but a small quake told them otherwise. He took out his binoculars and saw the smoke rising out of the slightly open seal. They waited a good fifteen minutes before approaching.

"Masks," he suggested. They all put them on.

Nath opened the door, spilling the last billows of smoke out of the ship. Inside there was nothing. They were all expecting to find another body. An almost anticlimactic end to their discovery.

"Look," Nath pointed at the door, "it slammed shut and sealed midair. You can tell by the latch – it's broken. Whoever was in here jumped out before it crashed."

"What kind of ship is it?" Camden asked. She approached the front controls, looking at the older bulky arrays of dials and switches that covered the front cockpit. There were three seats. It was all one room inside. A small cargo section was separated by lines in the back. Other than the remaining fog, the inside had been preserved.

"Definitely indie series – I'm guessing blueshift engines by the control configuration. I was right – that puts its manufacture date at 22nd century. Maybe even late 21st, if the fuel mix is older. But why – not to mention how – is it out here?" He asked, flipping a couple of the dead switches on the front. It was totally dead.

"Tell Ester to radio Akiko. Tell her we're going to need loaders. Probably not safe to open these old containers here – we'll want a controlled environment," Zain motioned at the old crates.

"I'll pull the net cards and the black box – they were all in the same spot in these old ships," Nath said, ducking down under the front console and whipping out his omnitool.

Ryan looked at the old radio on the console. Its digital readout was blank, and the analog controls were old and worn – it had been used quite a bit by the ship's owner. Something caught his eye. Nath hadn't even touched the console yet...and granted, the smoke was still in his eyes, but... he could swear the readout had flickered. The numbers had gone by too fast for him to notice. He had a flashback to the crashed pod in the forest. It had happened then, too.

It had to be a coincidence.

12
OLD CREW

Nik woke up, and for a few brief moments, he forgot about his knee. It almost seemed like it didn't hurt at all. Then he put pressure on it and his hopes evaporated. The crunching pain came back and he popped a quarter tab – he found that spacing them out was enough to keep him from getting too overwhelmed, and his stash of tabs wouldn't dwindle as easily as it had at the start.

It had been over a year since he crashed. He tried not to think about it – maybe the pod clock was wrong. But it wasn't. It was hard to tell without real sunlight. He had rigged the pod to have some artificial sunlight during the hours the pod clock held, since it was still synced to the cycle on the ship.

Today was going to be his first real try at getting into the old ship's computer. It had taken months to find the parts and manuals needed to resuscitate a frequency generator he found in the bowels of the storage hangar. If he could catch the inputs on the blips, he could inject a full reset opcode. It would revert to the shipyard RTOS defaults and he should have free reign inside the system.

A few months after he crashed, he came to the conclusion that the ship was forwarding the source of noise, as opposed to *being* the source. The blips were the result of electromagnetic overload on the ship's computer network. It was exactly the situation that the dark protocol was designed to stop, but his link was just too new, and the ship had no wireless entry points.

He was in the server room. The leads from the resurrected equipment were plugged into the serial ports on the bottom of the pillar, labeled with the color-coded dock connections. A few of the manuals stuffed into the old machines had notes about how to use the connections, presumably written by the original engineers who were reprogramming the ship in dry dock.

If he did this wrong, the ship may not power back up. Either way, he was sick of waiting. He watched the analyzer, seeing the blip in the input pings – and he twisted the knob, sending a surge into the mechanism. The servers went dark, followed shortly by the ship. The only light came from the blue bleeding off the reactor through the glass shield.

Nothing came back on. He yelled and slammed his fist against the pillar in anger. The air was still filled with noise from this imaginary source, according to the pod sensors. Either the comms were still online, or he had been wasting his time for a whole year. Both conclusions made him angrier.

He went back to the bridge. No running lights, just as before. He took a seat and plugged the links in, hoping for a new outcome. They all remained blank. He yelled again, swearing to the empty air. This was what the manuals had said to do – could they be wrong? He collapsed back in the bridge crash seat, laughing at his luck and the fact that he was angry with some engineer who'd probably been dead for sixty years.

Then it happened.

"...protocol extant. Binning request. Protocol extant. Binning request. Protocol extant. Binning request..." the noise continued, coming out of the 8-bit speakers. He couldn't find where it was coming from, spilling out of every speaker on the ship. He walked back to engineering, checking the links. Nothing. He investigated the few rooms that were closed off, but they were silent.

"Where are you?" he called out, hoping it might respond to voice – the old ships sometimes were coded for that, before they decided to restrict all input to physical touch. He wasn't lucky. It kept on spitting out the same four words: protocol extant. Binning request. That was a debugging message.

He turned the mic down on his helmet so he could think. It was still there, a dull lull. He thought about the words. Protocol extant – that meant it was still processing some previous protocol. It was ignoring (or "binning") any further requests. But what protocol was it possibly acting under? It wasn't any of the three he knew – comms weren't amplified, they weren't off, and the ship wasn't blown up. What was going on?

"Tell me what it is!" he yelled into his helmet.

The manual was open on the pillar's open bay. Nothing in the pages or the handwritten notes mentioned any kind of extra codes for protocols. Sometimes docks had empty protocols installed when they were decommissioning ships...but they were wiped as a result of the new OS. For another hour, he just sat there, trying hard to think of an answer.

Eventually he gave up, heading back to the pod so he could get away from the noise and take off the helmet. It was still echoing when he left. The season had grown cold again, but he hadn't paid much attention since the weather seemed to have a mind of its own. Since he never saw the sun, he wasn't sure what to make of it. He went to sleep, dreaming of the words hammering in his ears.

When he woke up, he noticed the radio in the pod had synced. He nearly gave himself a concussion hitting the ceiling on his way over to it.

"Hello, hello," he spoke into the shortwave. He hit record and set the message on auto-replay. It would drain the power, but hopefully whoever had synced could hear it. The signal came in, but it was weak. He adjusted the dials.

"...extant. Binning request." He slammed the switch off on the auto-play, lowering his head and breathing hard. His heart was beating wildly, the well of disappointment from yesterday resurging.

"Wait," he whispered aloud, looking at the radio. He pulled the rolled-up manual out of his pocket. The yellowing paper was warped, and the old metal spine was bent. Some of the notes in the margins mentioned radio problems. They were fixing some signal ghosts in the equipment. At the time, he hadn't paid attention to it. Modern sync protocols wouldn't mesh to anything that couldn't mesh back – something was active on the Kilimanjaro, despite all appearances to the contrary.

"It can't be that easy," he whispered.

He pulled the link off his wrist, shoving it into the alcove on the radio, and pulsing the 'dark' opcode. The noise on the radio stopped altogether, including the strange source being forwarded from the other ship. The relief of what he had just figured out was quickly overshadowed by the sudden realization that the ship was resetting – he still needed to trigger the switch into the dry dock defaults.

He swallowed a whole tab and took off, ignoring the mounting pain in his leg as he neared the old ship. The server room was just starting to blink when he made it to one of the old links. He jammed his thumb on the link and turned the signal generator to the reset code the manual expected.

"Yes!" he shouted, voice echoing. The ship's RTOS root screen flowed over the old link's screen. He was in.

A large directory of files filled the base tree. Many of them were corrupted. Before it got second thoughts, he needed to dump those files onto something else...maybe to his link in the pod. He followed the external device management and found his link in the mesh network – nothing else was meshing, of course. His first guess about there being no other pods was correct.

At least it recognized his link as static storage. He dumped the entire ship's file directory onto it, hoping none were too dangerous – if they were, modern file scrubbing would have to be his saving grace. He couldn't risk the ship's power going off again. The copy took a few minutes to compress and transfer, his palms sweating as it did. The ship slowly lost power as the old systems turned on then sputtered, blaring warnings from the engineering section.

When it finished, the Kilimanjaro was dark again, save for the glowing screen on the old link. He decided that nothing else would be gained here today, toggling its low-power state. From the basic diagnostics in the link's right-hand side, the electric batteries were fused to the core, having lost most of their original capacity.

He left the ship and headed back to the pod. It had risen above freezing in the green half-light, prompting him to remove his suit helmet and take a deep breath. Without a significant source of water, he hadn't showered in far too long...and it sometimes got to him. He had let his beard grow long, not bothering with it. Without scissors or a reflective surface, his hair was the same kind of mess.

Back at the pod, he laid his helmet down on one of the seats, peeling off the outer layer of the suit with it. Free of the bulk, he re-emerged in the brisk air, feeling the small breeze blow his under shirt against his thinning stomach. Rations were hard to live on, but he had made do, shedding weight he had gained over three tours.

Sparse tundra grass had grown over the five graves, making it where he could barely make out the glint of their suit tags. He still thought about

Torv sometimes, wishing he had known the man a little more. When he first met him, shortly before the tour started, he was uncertain about him – no one could replace him easily among his veteran crew. Cole and Nath both had their reservations, though Cole was more apt to voice them.

The engineer had not liked a particular line on his resume – the one that stated he was a declared transfer regime member. That meant he had migrated from one side or the other, choosing not to hail from either. It was a touchy subject for those who spent their lives in space, staying away from politics like that for years at a time.

But Torv had managed to impress even him. That was the last words he had heard from his engineer – praise for "Alexei." Nath had read more into that name drop than he had. He hadn't made up his own mind about him yet...Torv had wanted to separate that poor girl Iris from her child. He thought about her, too. Prayed that she somehow survived this nightmare...or if not, that she had gone quickly. Doubtless others had suffered when their pods ran low on oxygen, lost floating in space like flotsam and jetsam in a stellar ocean.

But...Torv had been with him on the outer ring. Where the captain should be, trying to save their ship. Together they had separated it from the ship, what good it had done. In the turmoil, Torv had carried Nik to the pod and saved him from dying in space. Now the younger man lay in the ground of a world where no friends or family would see him again.

He pulled Torv's link out of his pocket. Over the long weeks, he had carefully removed the broken pieces and picked out the tiny embedded storage card where the files were stored. None of the old equipment could read it, and he was worried about damaging his own link by doing a transplant. One of the pod boxes might have an adapter, but he couldn't bring himself to pull them out.

What was he likely to see? Photos and videos, better meant for his family or forgotten loves? It made him think on what he would leave behind if he had died. What would be on his link? He hadn't taken a picture in years. The official crew shots were handled by all the bureaucrats now. Nath was the one who liked to take videos and only when they went on their end-of-tour stops. His heart ached at the thought.

The three of them – he, Nath, and Sebastian – they always went for a round of drinks on the last roundabout to the mining yard. It had always made him reminisce over the quiet times of the war, when they hunkered down in the local pubs on all the Junos, where many of his friends would disappear with strangers in their arms and reappear days later when it was time to leave. They were the only family they really knew.

And now...now he would never do that again. Eyes closed, he imagined what it would have been like to have a drink with Torv at the close of this tour. They would all have been friends. He would have annoyed half the crew to death, but they would have embraced him by then, ready to let old Nik go with his ship in good hands. The thought both warmed and froze his heart.

It was a dream now. Like the dream of seeing Akiko again. He could stomach losing friends...he had lost many in times past...but losing her? He had asked her aboard. She was out here because of him. She had *died* because of him. It made him sick.

He swallowed a quarter tab and headed back inside the pod. The link was waiting in the alcove, ready for him to dive into its secrets. He took it out, leaning back onto the handful of sleeping bags he had bunched up as a bed, pulling up the file structure. Most of the usual boring bits and pieces of ship firmware filled the folders, but a few caught his eye. Logs. He keyed into them.

SOURCE: personnel-log-17
RAW: 302483
DIGEST: d1c6a1cca651e86329d80c6e8942040a89af9022
CREATED: 2178-08-05 01:24:04 EC
AUTHOR: Eru Fowler [kil-26]

We finished the decommissioning procedures, but the last crew left
several personal items aboard. Requested a return requisition but
Ancillary won't ship it out without someone's authorization. I went
ahead and signed for it. Suki can be angry at me once we get out in
the deep. We can't wait forever.

I'm going through the old manifest – there's some cargo they forgot
to flush out. Looks like Northcomm tech. After we run the test
flight on these old engines, we'll drop them off. Figure they can
stand a few months without them if they've left them in here this
long. Not to mention they weigh literal tons.

[FILE END]

All the remaining logs were made by Eru Fowler. They were a skeleton
transfer crew out of the old colonial yards. Five people. This Suki was the
interim captain, while Fowler was its commander and requisitions officer.
The others were an unnamed engineer and two techs named Weston and
Barret. He could only assume that the four bodies on the ship were what
remained of them.

One was unaccounted for; based on his assumptions of their gender and
the log's narrative, he guessed it was the captain, as she was the only
woman. The four bodies he buried were male. He spent the rest of the

night combing through the logs, finding only one entry by a different author. At first, he thought it was a corrupt file, but the contents did pull up on his link. It occurred to him that it might have been erased by the transfer crew, but his link had recovered it from the data blocks he pushed over. He opened it.

SOURCE: 250-395022-3304-recovered
RAW: 258304
DIGEST: unknown
CREATED: 0000-00-00 00:00:00 EC
AUTHOR: unknown

under the deck. punchcode 8-series, a82m3foi.
resonant frequency: 200 hz
do not deploy.
repeat.
do not deploy.

[FILE END]

Under the deck? Punchcode? He was tired, but his mind was now fixated on the new mystery. What was the old crew hiding? The file had default values and a raw source id that put it way before the other files in the ship's static storage block. He had assumed it was *this* crew that had created its own bad luck, not the previous.

One of the other ship directories held the crew manifest. The old pictures confirmed his assumptions. Their names were captioned beneath them. Suki Nugyen, Decom Captain. Eru Fowler, Decom Commander. Weston Christchurch, Decom Network Technician. Mendel Barret,

Decom Navigation Technician. Hunter Roberts, Decom Engineer. But... how had they died? Did Nugyen kill them? Or were there others aboard?

He didn't know when he fell asleep. The sky was dark when he woke up, and his leg was aching from the day before. After a quick set of stretches to get his blood flowing, he returned to the old ship with his link. Finding this supposed hidden compartment under the deck was his new priority. It proved difficult – he had pulled up many deck plates during his isolation and there was nothing under any of them.

Except for one. There were plates under the reactor housing. It was the one part of the ship he had been afraid to breach – staying near the leaking reactor was not good for his health. Mapping it out was a low priority up until this point. However, with the ship's old layout on his link, he wouldn't have to guess at it.

According to that layout, there was an auxiliary coolant reservoir in the surrounding layer – the main reservoir may have ruptured sometime *after* the crash. If he could drain the remaining fluid into the auxiliary space, he could power down the reactor and run the ship's last systems off the electric batteries.

Coding the program took him a while since he had to write it from the limited manuals he had on hand. The firmware commands were listed in the Kilimanjaro's files. After a few days of troubleshooting, he finally got the flush commands to work right, beginning the slow shutdown sequence on the reactor.

Another few weeks went by before he felt safe enough to start looking under the plates. The electric batteries were spent, barely getting charged from the dusty solar arrays plastered to the outside of the ship. The Kilimanjaro's RTOS was rebooting daily. The rad counter wasn't happy about him being in the reactor section, but its screeching warnings weren't screaming "imminent danger" either.

Pulling up the plates took time since they were bolted down and escaped rusting while submerged in coolant. Once the last plate was free, he lowered himself down into the subfloor. A large industrial crate was shoved into the space. The old black punchcode square was waiting for the code, its 64 obsidian keys beckoning to him.

This part was easy. He had already mapped it out. Eight characters encoded in old ASCII to hex, then finally 64 binary digits, eight per row. It didn't seem to form any quaint picture, but it did pop the steel plate trigger. It was empty. He wasn't sure what he was expecting...but it wasn't this. No – not empty. He fished out a small trinket from the bottom of the box. Another link. It was even newer than the other links – it had a wireless control chip embedded in the corner – and it was *on*. There was a message left on it, dated decades ago.

Follow the noise.

Akiko raised her arms, and Emma raised hers in kind, giggling madly. The little brown-haired girl would be two in another month. Her heterochromia had settled into two definite eye colors: a bright blue and deep green. She picked up the young girl after she ran toward her, giving her a quick hug before placing her in bed. Ryan was out on another project for Nath. When he wasn't spending his moments with Emma, he was working with Camden or Zain on whatever fancy Nath developed this week – he had an infinite imagination for expansion of their tiny domicile.

It was for the best, she supposed. If Nath grew too idle, he would wax on about the lives lost aboard the Rhineland...lives they both could have saved. Zain had lived a bit before joining as quartermaster, but she didn't have the world-weary eyes she and Nath shared. The less he talked and the more time she watched him, she admittedly found him interesting.

They had spent a few nights exploring together, learning a little more about each other. She had told him about Sydney, about Khiti and her mother. He had in turn told her about his sisters still living on the frontier. Fine English colonists, he said. Had not talked to them in years.

After reading Emma a bedtime story, she closed the door between her and Ryan's room, then took a shower. The steam fogged the small mirror on the side of her locker. Once she dried off, the lines of her face seemed to temporarily melt away and her feet grew a little unsteady. This planet was doing something to them. The manual chapter on "atmospheric adjustment" said it was a process that took years. The colonial almanacs called it ground sickness. She thought that term fit better, somehow.

Radiation levels had dropped, but the exposure traces were still reporting in decent amounts. Convincing Ryan to stop swimming in the irradiated lake was a difficult task – then Nath had suggested making a pool with scrubbed water. For Emma's birthday, of course, he had quickly said. In truth, she thought it wasn't that bad of an idea and gave it her blessing, so long as the levels weren't going to melt their skin off.

As for the others, Jin and Halim were inseparable. They reveled in designing their voxel games and getting the others to test them out – they even made a couple small demos for Emma. She loved every second of it, often joined by Ryan. He had taken Iris's death very hard. When he disappeared sometimes, she knew he was visiting her grave, situated with the others on a tall ridge.

The mysterious crashed ship still baffled and fascinated Nath, as his efforts to re-power its ancient electronics had been fruitless. It was a strange curiosity, even to her. They had trucked back its cargo and pulled apart its old systems. He had nearly rebuilt the cockpit in one of the dedicated workshops. It was his belief that if he could learn what grounded it, he might be able to find a way to reverse the effects that kept them from radioing out.

Oliver and Brit were trying to have a baby, as if Nadia was not enough for them. The twelve-year-old could be helpful and helpless all at once, depending on her mood. She and Brit had a somewhat unpleasant, but necessary talk with her about changes in her body. Overall, she was handling it well enough.

She had to tell Oliver and Brit they couldn't clinically have one. The state-mandated birth control for deep space crew was very potent and extremely resistant to reversal. None of them would be having children, not for years. Iris had been a special case, and they didn't have those same odds. They were disappointed, but able to cope. Akiko knew she missed her son Ty. How could she not?

Camden and Ester found Emma most entertaining, playing with her during the day between the little jobs and semi-constant stream of Nath's requests. They often watched Nadia and Emma both while she and Ryan were occupied. Overqualified babysitters. The thought made her laugh. But the little girl was safe...and that made her feel better.

She pulled on her jacket, looking at the stitching where she had pulled it in to match her subtly shrinking curves, due to the new gravity and diet. Her eyes rested on the old picture of her and Nik she had rescued from the Rhineland, tacked to the locker with the rest of the hard-prints they'd managed to generate with an old machine Zain recovered. Emma and Ryan smiled back at her from the picture beneath it. He had lifted her up to see the floating candle lights on the pool Nath had made to celebrate her first birthday...and the anniversary of her mother's death.

It was the things like that she found surprising. Nath was playfully insulting and sarcastic whenever he pleased, but he could be thoughtful, too. He had invited her out again. She had initially wanted to decline, but Ryan had vouched for him, telling her the offhand comments he made when they were together. Good old gossip. She finally relented. He was there now, waiting for her up on the ridge.

The walk was brisk, now that the sixth seasonal shift had set in. It was a strange orbit on this planet – it was totally tilted where their half stayed perpetually pointed to the sun, occasionally drifting out and causing the atmospheric mist to light up in that strange blinking pattern. The rapid rain brought a chill front that sometimes took a week or two to evaporate before the scorching sun returned.

She left the camp and started for the ridge. It had rained a few days before, leaving it balmy and humid. The sky was a mix of green and blue with the subtlest hint of red as the sun disappeared in the planetary turn. He was seated on a rock, staring up at the darkening sky.

"Romantic," she smiled, taking a seat on the rock next to him. He stayed silent. "Hey, you there?" she asked, waving her arm in front of him. He broke from his reverie, turning and smiling mischievously at her. His face had relaxed too, blurring some of his age lines. She could never place his age. He was younger than Nik, but still older than her.

"Sorry, just thinking," he whispered, planting his hands on the rock and leaning back to look up at the stars.

"About what?" she wondered, leaning back with him.

"If we never leave this place. The smart meds will stop, and the others will eventually get their chance at kids again."

"I wonder if that wouldn't be so bad," she admitted.

"The manuals don't have a chapter on hope."

"Back then, they didn't have much. Out here on their own, flying past a desert of stars, looking for any scrap of air and metal that could serve as safe harbor. Their hope...it was in each other."

"And here we are, in a tiny little oasis...as long as it can last."

"I want you to know...whatever you feel about the crash, most of them would have given up if not for you. Because of the work you've put in...they believe they can have a life here."

"Not everyone," he paused, "I miss him."

"Me too," she whispered.

"I haven't really told you why I joined up with him, have I?"

"No," she nodded, moving closer to him.

"Well, like I was explaining once…I was done with comms rigging. I had a dream and it wasn't being stuck doing field tests. The mining corps was drafting heavily when they found those big asteroid fields a couple decades back. Easy sell to get their aging fleets up to spec. I told Nik I could patch up the Rhineland's networks at half the cost the corps reps promised. He asked what I wanted. Probably figured I wanted a triple bonus clause."

"Sounds like you," she chuckled.

"Well, you're right. I did want a triple bonus clause. He said no. So, I said just put me in charge, then. He didn't agree to that either. He knew people and he knew when they were trying to pull one over on him. At the final pre-tour stop, I was still on the ship. He made me a tech when I told him I wouldn't leave. Good thing, too."

"Why's that?"

"Because when the last stop got there, the corps took away the network admin position. Said they didn't need it."

"Of course," she chuckled, "he was watching out for you."

"After we left dry dock, he said 'Do what you promised and I'll give you that triple bonus'…at a tech's tour salary, of course."

"So, could you do what you said? Did you patch the Rhineland?"

"Are you kidding? No. You can't fix that thing – it's probably in better shape *now* than it was when I first started. I had no idea what I was doing. I just wanted to be out in space. And he knew that."

"How did you stay on?" she laughed. He smirked.

"Between the corps regulations and the impossible budget constraints, all you can hope for is to keep the terminals online, let alone get them fixed up. The new ships have had voxel terminals for a couple decades now. Not two-dimensional relics…*but* the corps does love to recycle. Thanks to me, there's terminals on the Rhineland from a dozen different shipyards."

"You'd think you and Zain would get along more," she chuckled.

"I am a *networking specialist*. I do most of my talking with machines. And trust me, if you want to get a hold of good screens and entertainment out here, you better be *good* at talking to machines. But, enough about me. Tell me about you. What really brought you out here?"

"I was a medic for the Consortium," she started. "We were stationed on the old Junos. Most of the civilians had cleared out, and we were left fighting your lot. I was the only one around to patch up his friend...Damon was his name, I think. He died a few days later. We made sure not to leave the Juno sober. From then on, we traded around to stay together."

"Experiences like that really bond you to someone. I'm sorry," he said, voice uncharacteristically somber.

"I still can't believe he's gone. Sometimes, I wake up, expecting him to stroll into camp. But he's never going to. He's up there...floating around in the dark."

"He would never have left you alone down here. You know that. That wasn't who he was."

She nodded, wiping away some tears, "Thank you."

"Come on, let me show you something," Nath stood up and took off. She followed, surprised at how quick he was. She had to run to keep up.

"Where are we going?!" she yelled. The wind picked up and she was nearly knocked off the ridge by her jacket flapping about.

"Just keep going, it's not too far!" he yelled.

She followed him into a valley, then the caves. A strange pink light emanated from within and she soon found herself at a sight she didn't think she would ever see again. Cherry trees. Just like those in her mother's block back home.

"Nath...how?" she whispered, before resting her eyes on the box and cables hiding on the periphery. The hum of the electronics was masked by the audio recreation of rustling leaves. It almost made her forget where she really was. They were, without a doubt in her mind, the most beautiful sight she had seen in years.

"I pulled the navigation cards. Elyna didn't want any part of it...tried to tell her Vauss dying wasn't her fault. Out of deference to her, I connected a power circuit and set it up out here. Greer will want a go at it once I open it up for business. It's much better than the panel he's working out of in their room."

"Absolutely...incredible," she breathed, walking up to the screens, putting her fingers out to touch the near-invisible barrier. He pulled her back to the middle and pressed a button on his link. The trees shifted in the wind, pulsing with color and vibrancy.

"I know I haven't been the best since we met. I was pushy and I joke about everything. It's who I am. It's how I cope," he set his eyes on her. She turned and looked deeply into them for the first time, hidden behind sunken eyelids. He was as tired as she was, filled with the wanting she knew too well. The deep loneliness. It was a look she had seen before, in Nik's eyes. "Akiko, I want you to know how much I care about you. This disaster...this place...it's made bearable by you being here."

She drew close...then drew away.

"It's beautiful, Nath...it really is...but I can't do this again. I'm sorry... I'm just...sorry," she pulled away gently and left. He stood there, fading into the darkness with the cherry trees. She left the cave, heading out onto the ridges, looking down at the valleys. The stars grew brighter overhead.

She wasn't sure how long she had been sitting next to his grave. His plaque from his quarters lay molded in the dirt, covered in the planet's thick grassy moss. Venko, Nikita K. Her fingers traced the engraved letters. It hurt her heart and she couldn't tear her eyes away from it.

"Hey," Ryan spoke to her. It was deep night, now. She could barely see his face as he took a seat on the ground next to her.

"Hey," she replied sullenly.

"Nath told me I might find you up here."

"He knows best," she murmured. She had been crying and choked back tears. He resisted putting his hand on her shoulder.

"I still think about her, all the time."

"You still have Emma, so really...Iris isn't really gone," Akiko said, her voice scratchy and hollow.

"What happened?" Ryan asked timidly. "Not with Nath, I mean...what happened to you and the captain? That's who it was, right?"

Akiko took a deep breath.

"Nikita wanted a life when the war ended. We both did. When they declared the truce, we breathed for the first time in our entire adult lives. Saw what we were...what we wanted. We wanted to be together. I wanted a little girl, just like your Emma. He wanted a boy. Why not both, I said. Reality hadn't set in, yet. Its cold, dream shattering talons, still waiting."

Ryan shifted his legs, leaning in closer. She had gotten quieter.

"We tried. Didn't want to believe the worst...but soon we had no choice but to find out what was going on. Kepler's syndrome. Too much exposure to autonuclear radiation, coupled with repeated hard space to ground transfers. It had damaged my ovaries...along with a host of other benign problems. I was – I *am* – a doctor. I knew what it all meant."

"But there are treatments for that," Ryan whispered.

"There were...but it wasn't good enough for both of us. I got the treatments. We were going to make it work. There was a limited window, but it was a chance. We tried and tried, but it just wouldn't happen. That's when they told us the next problem – Nikita had cellular damage. He was just as much of the problem. All the same radiation plus much more. He had fought too long...since he was old enough to draft and leave home."

"I'm sorry," Ryan whispered.

"The worst of it is I blamed him. All that stress and pain came out and I decided to leave him – two wrongs weren't going to make a right. With the right partners, both of us could make it work. We could have our dreams of making families. I met someone else after, caught up in the moment. I thought I still had time. It was what *I* wanted...and so we tried, but it was too late. My chance was gone. I would never have children...not ones that were mine. He left me when he realized that. He knew I cared more about having a child than being with him."

"You couldn't adopt...not with the Essex laws," Ryan drew his head up. She could feel the sympathy...and the fact that he knew what those laws were made her feel even more for him. Unstable parents couldn't adopt children. There were too little children after that awful war, and the state had its limits. She didn't qualify.

"No, and I was too proud to go find Nik...and we weren't ready to forgive each other, anyway. We both let each other be. I hoped that he had found someone. Now...now I realize how foolish I've been. When he messaged me, I knew – I *knew* that he had suffered the same news I had. When you and Emma came to medical that first time, that's when I asked him. He could never have children, either. We both had our dreams of a better life ripped away...mama called it silent thunder...deadly and devastating, a force unseen and unnoticed but by those who feel it."

"That's a lot to hold in," Ryan mouthed after a long while.

"I don't mean to be dumping this on you...and I had the audacity to call you young...then Iris died, and I had a long few months to reflect on what has happened to you and all the others on this world. They had their futures ripped away from them in an instant, while fate cruelly led you on. Iris shouldn't have died. If there is any fairness in this life, that poor girl should still be with you and her daughter. But...this life is far from fair. We both know that, now." Ryan broke her gaze for a moment.

"He was all you had left. That's why you signed on."

"Yes," she nodded gravely. "We promised ourselves that we would always be there when we needed each other. When the cards were down... that's the only promise that counts. I could not say no to him again...but fate wanted to gut punch me one last time. And I was gullible enough to let it. Nik's dead...and even after all these years, I still can't figure out how to live my life without him."

Ryan drew himself up off the ground. "When my mom died, she left me a lot of debt and a lot of pain to uncover about why my dad left. She had a kid with someone else. He was angry...and he reported her just before he left her. They came and took her daughter – my half-sister – away. When I finally found her...she had been put through the state system, traded between horrible families and jobs. She turned to drugs. I was still holding her hand when the paramedics pronounced her dead."

"Ryan..." Akiko looked up at him. He was holding back his own tears. She felt an urge to hold him. To take the pain. It was all she could do anymore. But even that was too much for her in this moment.

"I wanted to find him and kill him. When mom was gone, I signed up and drifted on the tours, looking for him. I found out that he died just before I joined up this tour. He had married someone rich who donated to all the right causes. They had a lot of good things to say about him in the article. I talked to her. She offered me money to cover all the debts. It was 'the least they could do', she said. I told her I couldn't take it. I signed up for this tour...then this thing with Iris just happened. I felt sorry for her...I wasn't going to let what happened to my mom happen to her."

He paused, drawing a deep breath. "I don't know why we crashed down here, but we're still alive – and that has to count for something." He held out his hand. She shook her head no. She wasn't ready to go just yet.

"I'll be back before the blink...I just...need to be alone for a while."

"Are you sure?" Ryan asked, still holding out his hand.

"I'm sure," she nodded.

Ryan slowly dropped his hand, standing there and trying to judge the reaction on her face. She was thankful he couldn't see her trembling. Her tears fell on the grave. He left her there after a while. The sky grew darker and the stars grew brighter.

"I wish you could be here. I wish I could tell you everything. I did what you asked...saved what little we could. Why did you have to die? Why?!" she cried into his grave.

It started to rain.

Akiko reluctantly slogged her way home. Sunlight whispered on the horizon, threatening to end the night for a brief moment. They were somewhere near the equator of the lopsided world, oscillating between light and dark as the seasons shifted. It was a quaint little planet that doubled as their prison. She suddenly felt like her mother...stuck with people who felt sorry for her.

She pulled the door shut, hanging her sopping wet jacket on a hook next to her locker. After drying off her face and hair, she fell back into her reading chair, looking for solace in her books. None of it excited her. She read the words over and over, but they just went in and out of her head. Angry and sad and hurt, she threw the book at the wall, burying her head in her hands.

Morning was still hours away. Her stomach ached. Akiko slowly opened her door and headed out to the common room. Elyna was out of her room for once. She started to get up, but Akiko urged her not to go. Though physically fine, her eyes were bloodshot. She was obviously sleep deprived.

"You're still having the nightmares," Akiko guessed.

"Blaire should be here...not me," Elyna shook her head, "I can still see her...just lying there."

"You know it's not your fault," Akiko took her hand.

"You don't know anything!" she whispered shrilly, tearing her hand away from Akiko's.

"Elyna, I just want to help," Akiko sighed.

"Ask Zain. She knows. She's hiding something," Elyna said, swallowing the rest of her coffee and disappearing back to her room.

Akiko wasn't sure what to make of that. Zain had problems sure, but they all did. What could she be hiding? Something about her family? There was the case of the stolen drugs...no one had ever come forward, but they had stopped stealing. The Rhali family were drug runners...but Zain didn't seem keen on emulating them.

Honestly, she had suspected Elyna of trying to overdose...but the provisions and stock taken from the Rhineland were smart variants. They could never provide more than max dosage in detected half-life. If Elyna wanted to end her life, it wouldn't be easy for her...she would have to come to bitter terms with it. This wasn't the interaction she needed to end the night with...but it brought reality back down for her. Nath probably didn't want to talk after tonight...but he might know what Elyna was talking about. He seemed to know everything around here.

Nik had spent several months tracing the mysterious overpowering signal from the pod's radio echoes. That meant a lot of walking. It was hard at first, but eventually he could go a whole few days without taking a single tab. It was almost a miracle...until he stepped on his leg the wrong way and was reminded of how painful missing bone and cartilage truly was.

He had to be careful about how he spent the heat on the pod, since the Kilimanjaro had lost all functional power without the latent radiation from the reactor powering the electric batteries. Not that warming up from radiation was a wise decision in any case...but the option was now out of the question.

The link he had found beneath the reactor housing had to belong to Captain Nugyen. There were few other conclusions to draw, as the original content of the locked container was missing – the note had suggested a device with an operating frequency of 200 Hz and a clear warning to avoid turning it on. One logical conclusion was the source of all the noise had to be that device.

It was scattering all signals in and out of the immediate region, but even if he walked beyond the perimeter, he couldn't tell the difference between his signals and anything else – not without carrying the pod with him. He didn't have the technical know-how to deconstruct its radio banks. Only Cole or Nath had that kind of knowledge...he was at a loss.

But – it had to be somewhere nearby. There were cave systems under the tundra, and he had mapped many of them within a fifty-kilometer radius. Bits and pieces of equipment that presumably belonged to the decommissioning crew littered a few of them, giving him false hope. He figured they were looking for the source too...the narrative he was building of what happened didn't make sense.

Nugyen or one of the others had found the message in the log and deployed the device. They then left a clue behind for anyone who came looking for it in the future. Meanwhile, something happened to the crew onboard the Kilimanjaro that caused one of them to kill two of the others – he had never found a weapon. It had to be with Nugyen, which was why he was betting on her as the culprit. People could do crazy things when isolated like this.

He scoured several more cave systems, but his first real clue came when the signal grew in intensity, blasting noise across the limited range of both his link and the one left in the industrial lockbox. It had been tuned to it. Whoever had written the program had also rigged a circuit that fed power to its battery cells via wireless induction – the signal itself was powering it.

Like most of the others he'd delved, the cave entrance was dark and foreboding. He flicked the lights on his suit, casting shadows within. When he stepped inside, he felt strange, almost lightheaded. The oxygen content seemed to tick up – his suit switched over to its filtered levels automatically after a few more seconds.

It went down. None of the others had done that. An itch on the back of his mind told him to abandon this...he was following the orders of someone who may very well have laid a trap to kill the remaining survivors. He stopped, bringing up Fowler's logs again. One of them stood out.

SOURCE: personnel-log-278
RAW: 302925
DIGEST: c769bbb8a3b339159c7bf8639213c17b2b4033b0989
CREATED: 2179-03-23 03:21:58 EC
AUTHOR: Eru Fowler [kil-26]

Suki woke me up again. She's convinced Weston and Barret are planning on stealing supplies and leaving. Her paranoia is starting to get to me. I'm locking these files with my digest just in case she starts using the links. Back before we crashed, she was always calm. Down here...she's losing her mind. I think she's looking for it again. Always seems to be mumbling on and on about it.

[FILE END]

I think she's looking for it again. He read those words. What had she been looking for – the device? The gun she used to kill the others? Of course, you probably wouldn't go mumbling about that. He thought of his own situation – alone for three years. Other than a few nights of crippling anxiety and doubt of his prospects, it hadn't been too harrowing.

But unlike her, he had been in foxholes. Nugyen had likely only ever been exposed to tight corridors on a few ships too small to decommission properly. She wasn't prepared for something like this to happen. Could anyone be, really? The faces of his crew swam in his mind like a fever dream, making him nearly lose his balance.

"What—?" his fingers caught a ledge before he tumbled into the glowing depths below. They looked like crystals, flaring up with his light and dampening just as quickly when he shut off his helmet. It was like they were holding onto the light, absorbing through osmosis. He flicked them on a few more times, watching the effect.

The signal on his link magnified.

"This is it," he said to himself. "This has to be it."

He clambered down the edge, his knee aching at every foothold. Eventually, he reached the bottom. The lights on his suit lit up the shiny black rock, causing it to glow minutely before going out. Each time he shone his light directly, the signal graphs on each link went wild – he had copied the code from the older one to the newer one by hand, in case it died on him.

Then it grew audible. Almost vibrating the rocks – no, it was the other way around...the crystalline rocks were making the signal. A few were broken apart as he neared a dead end. What he found there was not unsurprising...but it was still unsettling.

A body with its arms wrapped around large cylindrical device. He dialed the noise canceling on his helmet to its maximum, but it still came in as a dull roar. He crept closer, looking at the tag on the body's suit.

"Hello, Captain," he smiled, reaching out for the device.

A genuine fear gripped him when the arm grabbed him first.

"Hey!!!" he jerked away. It slumped to the ground, arms rolling apart – like there was no rigor mortis. He stood there, the last thirty-five months replaying in his mind to check if he still had his sanity. This had to be a hallucination. There was no body. There was no crew. There was no captain. He was alone. He was alone.

"Don't...listen to it," a voice told him. It was in his helmet, breaching the noise cancelling. Sometimes the old systems did that.

"Captain Nugyen...Suki?" he asked timidly, waiting for a few seconds. She didn't answer him. It had been a woman's voice...but she didn't sound human. Electric. Static. She didn't sound like anyone at all.

The body wasn't moving now. Its arms were still wrapped around the device – it wasn't alive, it had only moved when he touched it. It hadn't reached its arm out. He had imagined the voice. It was all in his head. Even if he did believe that...this would fuel a whole new set of nightmares. The noise had grown so loud.

An old LED flickered on the device. A slot that fit the size of the old, but uncommon link sat next to it, almost double the width of his link. It had to be experimental when it was still new. Before he could stop himself, he pushed the old link into the slot and the LED went from green to orange, orange to red, red to blue, then off.

The noise stopped.

In those moments, all he could hear was his own breathing and the thumping of his heart. His link reported no noise. The old link had lost all power after he socketed it, stopping its wireless power sink. The other curious thing was the total lack of radiation. His counter had dropped to zero. He didn't remember if it had been reporting before he came down. He felt like it had.

Swallowing his fear, he bent down and wiped the dust off the helmet of the lost captain. Her shadowed, gaunt face lay almost pristine behind it, eyes closed. She was dead and the environment in the cave and her suit had preserved her. He noticed she was holding another link. He took it, pulling himself away from her and the device. When he turned his lights on the rocks, this time the glow did not fade away after he turned off his lights. They lit the entire cave.

An unnatural fear crept over him and he felt an intense urge to leave. The hairs on the back of his neck stood on end, and he didn't look back as he climbed the ledge, adrenaline overcoming any pain he felt in his leg. He walked back to the pod, still playing the moments over and over in his head. Finally, he decided he had to review the log off his link.

In the pod, he took off his suit, breathing heavy as he lay back on one side, flicking through the sensor logs. If there was audio, it had to have recorded that voice. If it wasn't there...he was starting to hear things. If it *was* there...then his link was starting to hear things, too. She couldn't have said something. She couldn't.

The logs were already rolled over. He had taken too long to walk back to the pod. It wasn't a supercomputer – it had limited memory. He cursed at the ceiling, throwing his link at the radio bank. It clinked and clanged against the boxes before coming to rest on the floor of the ship. It now had a crack.

Then he remembered Nugyen's link in the suit pocket. He scrambled to the corner and fished it out, carefully powering it on. The battery was very weak, but still had a charge. A brief flash of the Kilimanjaro's RTOS screens flickered before it died. He would have to recharge it. Its design sat somewhere between the archaic link pads on the old ship and the new one now permanently left in the mysterious signal device. He wasn't going back for it.

It did have a power connector. He found the appropriate adapter from the tech he'd scavenged and brought back from the Kilimanjaro over the years. It took a few tries for it to connect properly – lots of dust and debris in the port – but he finally got a clear charge indicator. He left it on the radio bank, leaning back into his sleeping bags as the pain in his leg started up again.

When he woke up from his involuntary nap, his thoughts returned to the radio. If it was free of the noise now, he could try the longer-range scans. He cleared the bench, pushing all the right dials back to the positions they had been in when he first crashed. The meshing started up, no longer trying to connect to the Kilimanjaro, as its comms had been shut down. He waited.

Nothing seemed to happen for the long few minutes he stared at it. He took a walk outside – it was in a weird stint of mildly cold air, never going warm enough to melt the permafrost. When he came back, the meshing signals still raced across the screen, unable to find anything. He took the dials again, lowering the range slowly, hoping for a connection to something, anything.

Still nothing.

He set the auto-scan and left the pod again, deciding to visit the completely overgrown graves of the old crew and Torv. Their tags were under permafrost now. He wondered what had happened to them – Nugyen didn't have a weapon. He had checked, despite his delirium. It was a mystery that would have to wait until after he got some rest.

Later that night, when he drifted off to sleep, he predictably had a nightmare. Nugyen's body had her eyes open, begging for water from the ghost voice in his helmet. He shook awake, drenched in cold sweat on the sleeping bags. That was when a new train of thought occurred to him. Maybe he had the story wrong.

He reached for her link. It was fully charged. He disconnected it, looking at the RTOS screen again. Nugyen's last logs were listed. Not sure what he would find...he keyed the first.

SOURCE: personnel-log-312
RAW: 303018
DIGEST: f5od14cf00b2c70813a3670dfc57a9015ca8d421987of3ef
CREATED: 2179-03-24 13:35:17 EC
AUTHOR: Suki Nugyen [kil-27]

Fowler was having another episode. He told the others that I was looking for some kind of device, and that I was waking him up every night to tell him about some new conspiracy. He is not sleeping well, and naturally I have no idea what he was talking about. I agreed to placate him, finding the log entry he dug out of the old corrupt files. I had Hunter track down the blueprints. There was a maintenance section under the reactor that sounded like the note's location.

There was a lockbox stuffed in it. Looks like something the colonial militants left behind. Did a bunch of tests while the ship still has power. Still not sure what it is.

[FILE END]

Nik thumbed to the next one.

SOURCE: personnel-log-316
RAW: 303073
DIGEST: 88551c469b20f6ab9a2e6b945d9a091a98cdd8fbb68d69
CREATED: 2179-03-30 01:05:49 EC
AUTHOR: Suki Nugyen [kil-27]

It's an autonuclear frequency generator. I am now convinced that it is the reason we crashed. The navigation computer was having issues before we were told to decommission it. The thing was still *on*. Someone did this to us. It was pumping out low frequencies that the ship couldn't accurately attenuate. The bottom line...we've been irradiated. It's building in our brain tissue. Maybe not today. Maybe not tomorrow. But... eventually, this crash will drive us all insane.

[FILE END]

Nik thumbed to the last one.

SOURCE: personnel-log-318
RAW: 303086
DIGEST: 270d747ada9eb34e49187a933c1c5b0ddaf9e8a281bfec8
CREATED: 2179-04-19 11:32:02 EC
AUTHOR: Suki Nugyen [kil-27]

They're all dead. Fowler killed Weston and Barret. I found Hunter in engineering, pumped full of radiation with no anti-rad boosters. Fowler was sitting in my chair, just staring at the wall when I found him. He had just...died there. His eyes were still open.

I can't turn it off. I've taken the generator into this cave. Left my other link in case someone comes down here looking for it – this thing is not a harmless experiment. It's a weapon.

The rocks here have a naturally occurring wavelength. I was able to tune it to something they'll absorb on the same resonance curve. As it is...I can barely keep my eyes open.

[FILE END]

Nik toggled the view back to the primary screen. The running program was listing a resonant frequency well below 200 Hz. The last input, presumably from Nugyen herself...was 26.23 Hz. He looked up the manual chapter on human harmonics and found that frequency was in the range where it would resonate in the skull.

The rocks had absorbed his light, and they had clearly been absorbing the other parts of the spectrum. There was no radiation down there. If she had matched the resonant frequency of that device to the ones in those rocks...it *was* blocking re-transmission of that spectrum. Emphasis on *was*. The device had canceled it out.

Natural or artificial radio waves that low could be dangerous. They could have effects on people – most body parts vibrated in those same frequencies. It was a highly unusual problem that happened occasionally in older ships...that might be how she got the idea. And now with it off, the rocks could release the radiation.

He pulled his suit on and ran back to the cave.

Nugyen's body was still sitting there with the device clutched in her hands. He felt that strange feeling again as he neared her...like he didn't belong there.

"Don't...listen to it," the voice repeated. He checked his link – it hadn't recorded anything. He flung his body around, flashing the light on the cave walls. The signal-voice echoed.

"Suki?" he asked, throwing all caution to the wind. If he was crazy, he might as well get crazy answers.

"Don't...listen..." the voice oscillated between high and low pitches. His heart beat in his chest as he looked at the body. She wasn't moving...but it was her voice. He knew, somehow. The noise grew more intense – not just in his ears, but in his bones, in his mind. A migraine so severe his nose began to bleed, drops of blood clotting on his helmet.

Nik fell to his knees. He gripped the straps of his helmet, clawing at the magnetic lock. In the panic, he realized why there were no sensor logs – the entire spectrum was being flooded. The sound...it was coming from the walls, blaring the spectrum they had heard over the long years. Her words had been imprinted on the rocks, absorbed as she lay there dying.

His mic and speakers were caught in a deafening feedback loop as they tried to interpret the blended signal. He finally ripped the strap off and threw his helmet, cracking it against the cave wall.

The monstrous noise stopped. His head was throbbing.

"...going to be four this year. Can't believe we've been down here that long." The voice came from so far away...but he knew it better than most. It was Akiko's voice. It had to be.

"...has only gotten more defensive since you had me talk to her last year. She's hiding something. Elyna is right about that."

"...don't know that."

The words were like someone had their hand on a radio dial, twisting it back and forth. He tried to listen, drawing closer to the rocks, almost the color of obsidian now. He felt the warm trickle of blood down his ears. His knees sagged.

He fell, hitting his head on the rock before he blacked out.

Ryan did not agree with Akiko and Nath – Zain, and anyone down here, for that matter – had a right to privacy. They had cornered her in the common room. She was already yelling as Nath went to her quarters. He and Akiko were holding her back before she hurt someone. The others had woken up – it was just after midnight.

"You have no right to go through my stuff!" she screamed.

"That would be true if it *was* your stuff, but we both know it's not," Nath's voice echoed out of her room. He soon came out.

"Is that what I think it is?" Akiko asked, involuntarily releasing the younger woman. Zain pulled her arm out of Ryan's grasp, reaching for it. Ester of all people barred her way.

"Where did you find it?" Ester asked, her expression hard as stone.

"What is it?" Ryan interjected. It was a compact metal box, but Nath was struggling to hold it.

"One of the black boxes on the Rhineland. The only other one I found was destroyed," Nath shot her an accusatory glance.

"Ryan?" a voice spoke. He turned. It was Emma.

"Take her outside," Oliver spoke to Nadia sternly, coming up with her from behind. The older girl knew not to argue when he used that tone.

She looked at Ryan for his ok before scooping up Emma, who started to cry, heading out of the camp.

"What's going on?" Brit asked.

"Zain's been hiding a flight recorder," Elyna told her.

"Why would she do that?" she asked Oliver. He shook his head.

"That's yet to be explained," Nath said loudly, clearing the way to Zain, who had stopped trying to get at it.

"Well, what do you have to say?" Akiko prodded.

"It's not...I..." she stuttered.

"Get it out," Nath urged, narrowing his eyes.

"I...was hiding a shipment. There's a batch of narcotics on the ship. Someone had moved the crate after we left the last stop...I'd been looking for them for a while. It's all there...in the log."

"And you thought *that* was important to hide? Are you mad, girl?" Akiko stood over her. Ryan had never seen her like this. Akiko grabbed Zain by the shoulders. "That log can show us what happened! It could have answers to getting a message out. Why would you hide that? Why would you think that was worth hiding?!" She pulled her hand back, clearly prepping to strike her.

"Akiko," Nath grabbed her hand. "Enough."

"I'm sorry," Akiko broke down, pulling away, "I'm sorry." She retreated to the corner of the common room, filling up a drink.

"She's right," Nath said to Zain, who had hung her head so as not to look at anyone else in the room. Everyone had come out.

"I didn't know...I just...I didn't want you to think less of me," she looked up at Ryan. He didn't know what to say.

"Well, we certainly think less of you now," Nath said unceremoniously, gently dropping the black box on the common room table. It made a heavy sound even with the small drop, echoing violently.

"Everyone go back to sleep," Nath ordered. He and Akiko were still the de facto leaders. If there was punishment to dole out, they would be the ones handling it. They all did as he said.

"Not you," Akiko spoke. Zain froze. "What else are you hiding? What other things do you need to tell us about?"

"Nothing," she said immediately, "I never found the box. I was trying to find it those first few months...but when it never showed up, I assumed it was destroyed in the crash like the rest of the cargo."

"So, you *were* stealing the drugs that first year, because you couldn't find your own batch."

"No – I swear that wasn't me. You tested me – you know I'm not using," Zain defended herself.

"Akiko – you tested *everyone,*" Nath interjected, "Whoever took them hasn't used them yet. I doubt that Zain would be so stupid as to hold that information back now, anyway." Zain looked between Nath and Akiko, fear in her eyes.

Ryan stood there watching all of this unfold.

"So...what happens now?" Ryan finally asked. Zain looked to him, her eyes pleading.

"We find out what's on that black box," Nath said simply, "If nothing's there, no harm done. If *something*'s there...then we may be able to find a way off this world. As for you, Zain...you'll have to live with the outcome."

"I'm going to bed," Akiko sighed.

"Ryan...I..." Zain started, but he raised his hand.

"If we could have sent a message out – if I could have saved her...why would you hide this?" His eyes teared up, then he turned and walked away, back to his room. She stared after him, tears rolling down her cheeks.

"Go to bed, Zain. It's over now. I'll see what we can do and we'll talk about it in the morning," Nath's voice echoed behind him.

Ryan followed Akiko. Nadia had quietly slipped back in, helping Emma to find her way to him. He picked her up, trying to calm her down. She was already rubbing her eyes. He put her to bed, a small one that Camden had helped him build. After she was tucked in, he pulled the light shield across the front of her bed and retreated to his part of the large room, dropping into his own bed.

All he could do was stare at the ceiling for hours as his eyes struggled to stay open. Eventually a sound outside interrupted his reverie. He jumped out of bed, slipping his shoes on. No one else seemed to have heard the noise. Nath was lying on the ground, unconscious. Zain's room was open. She wasn't inside. She and the recorder were gone.

"Nath, can you hear me?" he rolled him over. He was still breathing. There was a bad bruise on his head.

"Nath?!" Akiko shouted. She was wearing her nightclothes, her robe sweeping over the ground as she came to rest next to him.

"I'm going to find her," Ryan resolved.

"Be careful," Akiko nodded, "we don't know what she's capable of."

"What's going on?" Oliver whispered. He must have heard Akiko.

"Zain's gone. She's taken the recorder. I'm going to look for her. You coming?"

"Yeah," he said, without hesitation. The two of them ran off into the night. A slight rain had started – a storm was coming. They yelled for her repeatedly, circling the area. She wasn't there.

"Use the ping map – maybe she still has her link," Oliver said, pointing at his wrist. They both checked. She didn't.

Ryan yelled angrily and swore into the night sky.

The two of them scoured the lake and the surrounding area but there was no sign of her. She was gone. The rain started coming down in earnest and they reluctantly headed back to the camp.

Nath was sitting up now, tended to by Akiko.

"What happened?" Ryan asked.

"What happened," Nath paused to cough, "is that Zain exercises more than I do," he chuckled. "I had just opened the recorder's core and that was when she lunged at me. Not as young as I used to be...so my reflexes were a little slow."

"Are you feeling alright?" Oliver asked worriedly.

"Yes. I've taken my fair share of hits to the head," he smiled weakly, scratching his wound. Akiko pulled his hand away.

"A fair share is a share too many," she shook her head, her expression oddly worrying to Ryan.

"I'll keep watch tonight in case she comes back after the storm. She can't stay out there in this," Oliver volunteered.

"We both will," Ryan nodded.

"Come on, Nath. To bed," Akiko urged.

"Be careful, you two," he eyed them, retreating to his room.

Ryan and Oliver played cards until the rain stopped, trading conversation about Nadia and Emma. After the first year, they had all revealed their birthdays. Oliver had turned 36 last year. His position on the Rhineland was a step toward a government job. They were building smaller fleets after the war, with more advanced ships.

"Nadia will be fourteen in a couple months...I wish Junie could be here to see it. She's not the same kid she was up there."

"I remember one of the other officers telling their kid off for being on the bridge. Said it was her fault."

Oliver laughed, "Yeah. I had to come get her more than once. Always wanted to be places she didn't belong. Doesn't seem to be rubbing off on Emma, thankfully."

"She's a good kid," Ryan agreed.

"What do you think came over Zain? She'd already done the damage. What could she gain by taking it and running away?"

"Maybe she's lost it, man…I don't know, Ryan, I think Akiko's tests were wrong – she may be using somehow."

"Why do you say that?" Ryan was shocked, laying his cards down.

"I've taken some isocaine before the quarterlies she does and sometimes it doesn't even show up."

"If the tests are bad, then anyone could be using."

"Well, they're all those smart meds, anyway. I think the only thing you can OD on down here is radiation," he smiled grimly. "Those storms are getting worse – we should probably all go looking for her when the sun comes up. She might be in a ravine somewhere, if she wasn't careful."

"I hope not," Ryan sagged down in his chair, "I don't want what I said to be the last thing she ever hears out of me."

"We'll find her," Oliver nodded.

"Yeah," Ryan nodded, throwing the cards down. Light was starting to filter in. He stood up and went to the corner, looking for the coffee packages. He fumbled across them. His eyes were very tired.

"Make me one, too," Oliver stood up, stretching.

"Make one for all of us," Akiko yelled across the room. She was already dressed, wearing her jacket. The weather promised to be much cooler after a rain like that. Nath stood at his door, nursing a new bandage on his head. It had bruised spectacularly. Camden and Ester emerged soon after, followed by the kids, then Jin and Halim.

"We'll monitor the radio," Brit said, followed by Nadia, who was holding Emma's hand. Jin and Halim took a seat with Brit at the console on that side of the common room, while she explained the controls. They had never explored the area much, so it figured they would stay behind. The door to Elyna's room stayed shut. She wanted nothing to do with the search effort. Akiko agreed she would probably be less than helpful – even though it was her accusation that caused it.

"Don't go, Ryan!" Emma pleaded. He froze at those words. Her mother had said the same thing to him before Kipp had died. He found it hard to take it as anything other than an omen. He pushed those thoughts away, leaning down, smiling at the small child.

"I'll be back, ok. We just need to go find Zain."

"Is she ok?" Emma asked.

"She will be," he promised. He hated the thought that he might be wrong, but he didn't have time to explain this to her.

"Ryan's gotta go," Nadia took her hand, "but we'll be here with you. Everything's going to be alright."

"Don't go!" she repeated. Her eyes were tearing up. Where had this come from? He could only wonder.

"I won't be long," he pulled her in for a hug, looking into the two different shades of her eyes. At first, he had been alarmed by it, but now he found it a comforting sight.

"Radio if you see anything strange," Nath told Brit and the others. The three of them nodded.

They all split up into the usual pairs – he and Oliver, Akiko and Nath, Ester and Camden. It took most of the day to cover the initial radius, before they expanded out to the main radius. There were no thermal signatures they could see on the scanner and her link was not registering, just like the night before.

"Nothing," he told Oliver, pocketing his link after he sent an acknowledgment back to the others.

"She's going to die out here," Oliver shook his head, "what was she thinking?" The pair stared into the blue-black contrast on the horizon. The sparse clouds seemed to crackle.

"There's one place we haven't checked," Ryan realized. Oliver gave him a quizzical look before his face turned pale.

"If she went in there, then she *is* dead."

"We didn't use the other caves because they get flooded too easily and the metal ore inside the Rhineland is a target for that insane lightning that comes off those storms. If she knows anything about ships – and she does, being who she is – then she knows they're internally grounded to runoff coils. It would technically be safe in there."

"Except for the 800 Lievs of autonuclear radiation...radio the others. Safe or not, it's a sure bet she felt she had no other choice," Oliver sighed.

Ryan signaled the others. A couple hours later, the six of them stood in front of the Rhineland. Dusk had started, leaving them in a strange mist. It was foreboding and did nothing to help his thoughts from earlier – this was how it had happened last time. He suddenly didn't want to go inside.

"Thermal's picking up nothing past the shielding. We're going to have go in," Nath observed.

"This is not a good idea," Akiko told him sternly.

"If we go in as two groups, we can cover more ground quicker. Three and three. One-hour exposure, right?" Nath asked.

"Yes," Akiko said, pulling out her kit and dolling out the extra boosters – they had each taken some before heading to the crash site.

"Let's get this over with," Camden shuddered.

"Oliver has the next best medical training to me," Akiko said, "I think you need to go with Camden and Ester. Ryan can come with us." They all nodded and started inside.

Ryan fell in step behind Akiko and Nath as they delved once again into the mammoth skeleton of the Rhineland. Its dust had finally settled. Strange splotches covered the decks and wall plating. Akiko guessed they were a mold growth resistant to or mutated by the radiation the reactor.

"Wait, that can't be right," Nath said, backtracking. They were in the substructure under the mining section. He was pointing his scanner at the reactor section in the rear.

"What is it?" Akiko asked, her voice filled with worry.

"The reactor's thermal mass...it's doubled in size. It's not following the model I plotted. I don't see how that's possible," he fumbled with his scanner, a more compact piece of equipment than the first one had cobbled together out of pod parts.

"Meaning what?" Ryan's voice was strained.

"It means that we don't have an hour...among other more pressing concerns. We need to find Zain and get out of here, *now*," he urged. Akiko radioed the others. They were scaling the bridge, looking for any thermal mass the size of a human.

"Where would she go?" Ryan asked them. He asked Camden, too, but she messaged him back that she already checked their usual meeting spots.

"What about crew quarters?" Akiko asked Nath.

"Hers were blocked," he confirmed, "and there's no heat signature up there that I can see on the scan."

"What about food stores? There weren't any rations gone from the packs," Ryan suggested.

"Both kitchens are out of reach," he shook his head.

"What was his name...Lancing? What about his lab?" Akiko snapped her fingers. Nath raised his head, shifting his eyes around the substructure. He pointed toward the direction of the lab.

"It's still reachable. Couldn't scan it. If his stores are unlocked..." he trailed off. "Tell the others to get out of the ship. If she's not in Lancing's, we're not going to find her in time."

They ran for the lab. There was no one inside. They wrenched open the lab door, realizing that if it wasn't already open, then Zain hadn't come this way. But...they did find a crate inside that looked very out of place. Akiko popped its seal. There were unmarked canisters packed to the brim.

"This has to be her drugs. Unbelievable," she shook her head as she unsealed one and inserted a test strip.

"We don't have time for a narcotics raid, Akiko," Nath warned, his usual sarcasm overpowered by uncharacteristic anxiety.

"I've got what I need. Let's go."

They were all back out in front of the ship a few minutes later, hurrying away from the crashed ship. Akiko was waving a scanner of her own over each of them, hurriedly injecting a booster shot moments after the results popped on the screen.

"That was far too close," she scolded Nath.

"Well I wasn't going to know it had gotten worse before we went in, now was I?" he shot back.

"You're right...I'm sorry," Akiko put her hand on his shoulder. He nodded and she removed it.

"So, what's wrong? You didn't really explain that part," Ester asked. She probably had a better idea than the rest of them, but she usually gave the others a benefit of a doubt that they had no clue.

"The Rhineland's reactor is an old Aamed-Fletcher autonuclear series. It was stable when we crashed – with adequate cooling it should have stayed that way. I checked the growth levels both when we first crashed and then I checked just now. The problem is – despite no significant loss of cooling mass – its growth is not slowing down."

"It's going to blow up?!" Camden interjected.

"No...well, not in that way. It's a controlled fusion reactor. Growth and contraction are both normal...but only if it's being fed by something. Cole was always warning me about the network lines. They get degraded when it throws out too much power. That's why he kept frying the net backups."

"Is that why the network went down? Maybe the reactor was having issues before we crashed," Ester speculated.

"That's not out of the question...I'll have to do a lot of research. We're safe for the moment, but long term – we can't stay here."

"He's right. We don't have many anti-rad boosters left, and the ones I can synthesize won't be enough for this kind of thing," Akiko warned.

"Outside the region is just desert. If we leave, we won't be protected from the storms," Ryan pointed out.

"Exactly," Nath nodded grimly, "which is why we need to start planning – but we're safe for now, with the current numbers. Let me do some research tonight and we'll reconvene in the morning."

They arrived back at their camp a little after midnight. Nath immediately locked himself in his room, asking for quiet. Oliver quickly explained the situation to Brit, Jin, and Halim, who had only seen Nath's initial warning over the radio. They already knew that Zain was still somewhere out there...though the chances of her survival were dropping. Emma was asleep in Nadia's arms, waiting by the radio. Ryan picked her up gently and headed to their room.

Her sleepy eyes opened as he laid in her bed. She smiled when she saw him, reaching out her arms again. He leaned in and gave her a strong hug, kissing her on the cheek.

"Don't go," she begged, voice weak with sleep.

"I won't," he promised. She drifted back off.

Zain was gone. It was going to be next to impossible to figure out where she had ended up, especially if she was dead. With no body heat to find on a scanner and no traditional bacteria to make things decay, she could lay in a ravine forever and they would never find her. He got in bed, but he couldn't sleep. His thoughts of Zain dulled as the other problem of leaving the region took priority. What were they going to do?

He left his room, quietly shutting the door. Nath was shouting to himself behind his door, audible even through the soundproofing. He did that when he was working on particularly hard projects. Everyone else had gone in for the night, leaving the common room empty. It wasn't very inviting to stay there with Nath's noise, so he trudged on past and headed to the workshops.

To his surprise, Elyna was seated at the pieces of the old cockpit they had pulled from the derelict ship. She was absently flicking the dials, rising slightly when she noticed him walking into her field of view. Her normally sullen face wore a different expression tonight. Almost...determination. A glow in her eyes he hadn't seen since they landed.

"You heard about what we found?" he asked. She nodded.

"And...you didn't find Zain?" she asked, hesitant.

"No. We didn't," he nodded, taking a seat across from her in a rolling lab chair.

"I shouldn't have said anything...she never would have left."

"Why do you think she did?"

"You don't know about the Rhalis, do you?" Elyna turned her head, as if judging him for the first time. They had talked here and there, but never held any long conversations in the four years they had been marooned. Hearing her voice was odd.

"Just that they're a drug runner family."

"They're not just *a* drug runner family. They're *the* drug runner family. They own all the major arteries for pharma production and distribution, selling to governments, independents and space mafia alike."

"She talked about it, but not much. Why was she on the Rhineland?"

"Well being female puts her at a disadvantage – after the war, most of the runner families were down a lot of members, so to protect their interests, they all agreed to biolock all their possession code, like old medieval royalty. Control of the family can't pass to an XX, only an XY. If she lost a shipment...well, she's better off dead."

"You mean she doesn't *want* to send a message out?"

"I heard her crying through the walls before we got the soundproofing done. I was the only other one still up. She saw me and we started talking that night. She's still angry with herself. If there's a chance of getting a message out and leaving...they'll ruin her."

"But we can't leave anyway. No matter how many messages we send. Nath and Akiko both said it's too expensive to send a ship. The most they could do is trade messages. No one would have a chance to come and hurt her. No one would need to know. Why would she think we can leave?"

"Me," Elyna hung her head and closed her eyes.

"You?" Ryan leaned down, looking into her eyes. "Why? How?"

For the next hour, Ryan listened to her plan. She was a pilot, after all. She had the training. All they lacked was the parts. He agreed with her that they should wait until Nath presented his own findings. Whatever they were going to do, they needed to decide on it soon and start executing. The Rhineland wasn't going to give them a choice.

Nik could feel himself wake up a while before he found the strength to open his eyes. For the first few seconds, he found the headache unbearable, but it soon grew more tolerable. The small cave was still alight with sound and energy, flooding his link with radio noise. He crawled over to the old captain's body and pulled the device free from her vicelike grip. It weighed less than he would have imagined, somewhere around ten kilograms or so.

He grabbed hold of the old link and ripped it out. The device's light sprang back to life, quieting the pulsing screams and glowing light on the rocks. His head just had a dull ache now, like he had only bruised it. His legs felt like jelly as he stood up, but they soon came to rest. Partially scared to leave, but unsure of what would happen if he stayed, he heaved the device on his shoulder and started out. He left his helmet behind – it was shattered. Now useless.

The walk back to the pod was easier than he thought, even carrying the extra weight. He laid the device down on one of the crash seats and took a seat in the opposite one next to the radio. It was going mad with all the noise. He shut it off to calm the warnings.

He pulled off the suit, emptying the pockets to find the old link. It was alive again, but the running data card had been fried. He threw it on the radio then leaned back. His stomach rumbled, making him realize how hungry he was. He tore open a couple days' worth of the old Kilimanjaro rations and wolfed them down.

Satisfied, he crawled into the covers and slipped into a dream, seeing flashes of Akiko and their old friends, drinking and hiking through the far reaches of deep space. They were in the hinterlands, walking the trails. On the broken Junos, climbing the falls. Running through the orbitals, looking for candy and souvenirs. He could almost taste the old earth chocolate. Nothing like it anywhere else.

When he finally woke up, he realized his alarm hadn't done it – the sun had. Its warmth swallowed him like a forgotten blanket, making him feel for a single instant that he was back in his quarters, in front of the radiator. The thought floated away, but the heat remained. He shut the pod's heat off, walking outside.

Dew glistened on the tundra. The first layer of permafrost had begun to melt. He climbed to the top of the small hill where the graves lay beneath. The world stretched out to the horizon. He could see the Kilimanjaro in the distance, crowded by the cave systems surrounding it.

Turning around, he saw the tundra stretch away, dropping into the valleys he had sworn off traversing after the first few months. The world was brand new. His lank hair and long beard draped onto his torn, blood-spotted shirt. The flashlights and the pod's dim running lights had never been this bright.

Quietly, he sank down to his knees and just sat there on the hill for hours. The sun didn't go away. It hung just above the horizon, a stark blue white jewel. He looked over at Torv's rusted suit tag, suddenly getting an idea. Facing it now, while he could see the sun...it might finally be bearable.

He went back into the pod, grabbing the link and the old data card from Torv's link. It didn't take much to interface them. It was old, but unlike the wired pads that littered the Kilimanjaro, it had the right pins and the right firmware. He imagined it was like the links and syncs on the Rhineland – only the officers got the better hardware. Nugyen had come well equipped on her mission. He retreated to the hill, wanting to be next to his grave when he viewed it.

Torv's link lit up. The old screen showed the Rhineland RTOS, all its screens as fresh as they had been when they left. Static modules like this carried the operating system with it. Two files were pinned to the corner. He tapped the first. It was a video. He watched Torv's pixelated face fill the screen, mouthing wordlessly. He stopped it, finding the audio toggle on the side. The old speaker was just barely audible, distorting his voice.

"Nik, I don't really know how much time I have left...we're running out of heat and air, so I'll try my best to explain all this," he paused, breathing hard before continuing, "The mining corps wanted you gone after your second tour. The numbers were very clear – statistically you wouldn't live through a third tour, much less a fourth. Others with your...[the audio briefly cut out]...of cellular damage are usually in home care, learning to deal with the pain of just walking to the fridge – let alone living up in space, commanding a ship. I knew this when they gave me the assignment, which brings me to my next point – whether you've guessed it or not, I'm a field agent for the transfer regime."

Nik felt his knees give way as he landed back on the hill, his heart beating faster and faster.

"I was assigned to the Rhineland to track down a post-war asset. It's not clear who's flag they fly under – both the Consortium and the colonials kept spies after the truce. They kept their intelligence active well after the war ended. Pretty common for them to slip people in and out of deep space, to keep eyes on old caches. All we knew from the message we intercepted is that they were boarding the Rhineland for the whole tour –

took me a month to dig through the ship's logs after the corps agreed to sit me with you. I admit, I don't have much experience commanding mining vessels...my credentials took time to fake, and they were hungry to get rid of you, so it was an easy sell, to my management and the corps. I realize now, that was very optimistic."

Nik couldn't help but look at the grave with a new perspective. He turned back to the link, focused fully on the younger man's voice.

"I combed through the personnel docs as much as I could, but nothing came up...so I pushed a few of the suspects off the ship at our last dry dock. Changing the mining rates was cold...but it was one of the only levers my management could pull without tipping them off. I hope you'll forgive me – what is it you said? 'Mining's still mining, be it ore or ice.' Well...I think you'll admit that those miners were the real winners in all this." Torv stopped to cough, violently. He eventually calmed down.

"So that brings us to the crash – I'm not the one who pulled the trigger, but I may as well have. When I was crawling through the coolant ducts, I finally found the device that had forwarded the message – explaining the logistics of it involves a whole lesson on quantum tunneling. I don't entirely understand it and I won't get into it. Bottom line is that trying to tap it was my mistake. They knew I'd found it. From that point, we were on borrowed time."

Nik struggled to remember those last events. Cole had praised Torv for going through the ducts and taking initiative. He and Nath seen a movie. It felt like a lifetime ago.

"There was an explosive in the outer ring – found its trigger when I was detaching the bridge on my side. It could have been put there yesterday or when the ship was built – hard to tell. The reason I found the signal device at all was because of some irregular readings in the navigation network. I tried to warn Vauss as soon as I figured out what happened. Guess she got the message, since I can see the other few pods that made it out angling down with the ship."

"This planet we're crashing onto has to be an old cache. Maybe you'll know who's – you planted some yourself, back in the day. It's partly why I believed you were left in charge this long. Your biorom still has all the old opcodes. That's the real reason they're phasing you and the other cross-classers out. You're dangerous to keep in space – and the new regime isn't big on trust."

"If there's a cache here...and I'm literally betting my life that there is... you're the only one who can get to it aside from the one who crashed the ship. Due to the way they fast tracked me and my lack of unabridged identity, I was never properly propagated into the command opcodes." He stopped to cough again. His voice was getting lower and he was on the verge of onset asphyxiation.

"I modified the pod trajectory the best I could to get us down there. Hard to do that while spinning off the outer ring at the same time. Hopefully it's enough. Whoever did this, they don't care how many people they have to kill to get at what's down there. If we're lucky, they died in the crash...but I don't think that fate would be so kind."

Torv had twisted the camera over to Nik's own body, in the crash seat. Nik could only sigh in disgust at the frail man he was. He hadn't seen any of this – not by a mile. He had let the entire crew down. The voices in the cave might not have been hallucinations after all. His only hope was that Torv was right – that some pods had indeed made it down with them. It was a tepid hope...but now it was all he had.

Torv had turned the camera back, laughing to himself, giddy with loss of oxygen, "You may be wondering why I don't think it's you. After all, you have the opcodes, the motivation, and command. You were at the top of my list...the day we were in medical, and you were ready to pass out from the pain in your leg – you told me to keep that girl on the ship. Keep her with her baby. Even I started to doubt myself...keeping her on the ship solved a lot of problems. No unnecessary calls to the corps. No extra stops. I spent weeks racking my brain for reasons why you would agree to work for the government again, but I couldn't rule you out. In the end, I told myself to assume the worst, like I do for everyone."

"If I could handle all this on my own, I'd have left you up in space...but the simple truth is that I couldn't bring myself to do it. When I saw you limping to the other bridge, ready to disconnect the outer ring – you couldn't survive that. You wouldn't be out there if you had set off the explosive. I was wrong – you were vindicated and I was almost relieved to see you. You were there to save your ship. I realized my mistake could be salvaged. We could figure this out together. But that's where my luck ended. One little crack..."

Nik watched as he held up a helmet – his helmet.

"Only one of us is going to make it down. You've got the opcodes stitched into you, not me...so the choice is simple." His breaths became shallower, his face growing paler by the second.

"I know it's not ideal. Maybe you'll be dead when we hit the ground anyway, and this will be some story they read a hundred years from now when they find us...but if not, this is on you now, Nik. Everything you need to know is in the other file. It's more than I have any right to ask of you...but I have faith that you'll know what to do."

The video blanked out.

He stared at it for several minutes. He didn't know what to say.

The other file hung ominously in the file directory. He clicked on it. A digital spindle of diagrams and dossiers flooded out of the hidden archive. Analyzing them would take a while. He shut off the link, holding it in his hand and staring back at the sun.

For a moment, he had been content. A small, fleeting feeling that everything was going to be ok...and he had to ruin it. He should have just crushed the data card. What use was it to keep anyway? He pulled his arm back, ready to throw the link, but just as quickly lowered it.

In his heart, he couldn't ignore this. What kind of person would lack so much of a conscience that they could do all this? He already knew the why. The reason didn't matter. It was the *who* that mattered to him now. They were after something on this planet – probably the strange frequency generator. Maybe other things. Torv had been right...back then they had buried things all over the place when they got wind of a possible ceasefire – they had no idea it would turn into legitimate peace talks.

But now it didn't matter. He stood up, realizing for the first time that day that his leg no longer had any pain. The thought was so startling he dropped the link, barely catching it before it hit the ground. His reflexes were better, too. He had a sudden urge to see himself. Something was wrong. It had to be.

He tore back into the pod, grabbing a bottle of the distilled frost, pouring it onto an upturned crate facing the sun. The water shimmered in the light. He stood over the top of it. What he saw frightened him...not because it was a face he didn't know – but rather a face he knew all too well. Past the graying fringes were the familiar black tones of his hair growing at his scalp and the scarred, but unwrinkled skin of his younger self.

A small part of him knew that this had been happening to him ever since he landed. The pain in his leg always grew worse under gravity, not better. Having never had a need to look at his reflection, he wasn't likely to *see* a difference in his body other than the weight loss that accompanied the spartan ration diet.

Something was wrong with this planet. Or right. He had no way to understand. Suki had tried to warn him, in her own way. It made him wonder if the perpetrator of the crash knew about the natural radiation down here. The Kilimanjaro was an old ship...but the Coalition and the Consortium had lived long lives before they came to blows. Someone could have scanned for it.

His mind raced. Whether by providence or sheer luck, he could cross the tundra with the sun. Somewhere on this world, Akiko and Nath – the only friends he had left – were in danger. All he had to do was find where the pods had landed. The mesh network could breach the natural noise – it found some bandwidth to communicate with the Kilimanjaro when he shut off the generator. With it active again, that was going to impossible.

But impossible seemed to be working in his favor these days. The last four years of studying signal analysis and theory out of the manuals and sparse material in his own pad culminated in one last guess. If he was wrong...he might never find them. He stopped cold, realizing it had really been over four years. For all he knew...those were echoes in the cave. They could be dead. But, if he was right...

No. They weren't dead. Not until he saw their bodies. No more guesses. No more mistakes. His mind was made up. He popped the rusted screws on the pod's radio box, jerking it out of the small metal cage. It took an hour to rearrange the cards like the notes on his articles suggested. Once finished, he flipped the power switch.

Instead of the mesh dots, directional signal strength pointed toward the strongest waves it could find – pointing directly at the generator. He pushed his link into the slot, keying in the signals it could safely ignore. The digital compass slowly tilted its needle toward the direction of the Kilimanjaro. He thumbed down the paper manual he'd stuck on the pod's dash. A list of comms bands was written in red. It had taken a year to find that red pen. Then another year to nail down all the comm bands leaking out of the ship. All that work hadn't been for nothing, after all.

He input the bands, watching the needle slowly but surely move away from the ancient ship. It seemed to waver in many directions, aimless. His fingers twisted the analog knob slowly, clicking the sensitivity higher and higher. The needle's pixels shifted and finally stood still, pointing toward a spot just to the left of the sun.

"There you are," Nik breathed. The signal strength to distance calculation placed it somewhere between fifteen and twenty-two hundred kilometers away.

Leaving the pod was a daunting prospect. He took everything he could pack – enough food stores for three months, water ripper, the thinnest environment tent, and lastly the frequency generator. Whatever it was doing...he was afraid to just leave it behind. Not to mention it could be a bargaining chip for the militant that had stranded them all here. It could still save some lives.

He hadn't been this weighed down in...years. Not since he had still worn the uniform. The math behind the walk time was fuzzy, but he knew that the storms would keep him grounded at some point. If he could just do 25 kilometers a day, that would be enough that he wouldn't burn out on the way there.

He used one of the tools to cut his hair short and get rid of most of his beard. Its loss was like letting go of a weight he had carried for ages. It made him feel scared, yet emboldened. Wasn't this what everyone wanted...to be young again? Some part of him had wished for this, but his soul was still the same age – and it was still weighed down. Torv had faith in him and now he felt he had to earn it. He had a job to do...and he was being given the tools to do it.

The Kilimanjaro lay in ruins to the right and the impassable valleys to his left, with the sun streaking nearer to the old ship between them. Torv's grave and those of Nugyen's crew were still buried under the hill. Before he left, he knew he had one last rite to perform. He returned to the cave, carrying the generator strapped to his back. Nugyen's body had finally started to decay.

He carried her to the hill with the others, digging a fresh grave. She had done what she could for her crew...but it hadn't been enough. Her loss would have to be his gain. He lowered her inside, leaving her suit intact as he covered her up. The last respect he paid was to stand her link atop the mound. He whispered the only words his mind could conjure.

A poem his mother had once told him, the day before she died.

Space is not as cold as the darkest soul
Nor the sun as hot as the most vengeful heart
Give me strength to face these demons
And reckless courage to route my fear

Nik pulled his pack together and left the six of them behind.

Akiko had forgiven Zain in her heart, but the poor girl had never returned. They had looked for days. Unless she had been hiding food – which was unlikely, given that Camden had double checked her records over the years – she didn't have long out there alone. It had been a month, and they had been forced to write her off. The truth was...had she not run off, they would never have gone into the Rhineland and discovered what was coming. In the end, she had helped after all.

A new focus had driven the rest of them from their usual grind – even Elyna had weighed in. The plan, after all, was half her idea – much to Nath's chagrin. The scans told them that they were surrounded by desert. Coupled with the storms, that made them nearly impassable. There was only really one option – crossing them with momentum.

Nath had announced his version of the plan after locking himself in his room for a few days following Zain's exodus. The old ship they found could be resurrected, with the right fuel mixture. It couldn't make it into space, but it was good enough to get across the desert. That was going to be enough, until today.

Today they had taken new scans. With a better calculation for growth, it was clear that the fusion reaction in the Rhineland was being aided and abetted by some unseen energy. Bottom line – nowhere was going to safe. It would start affecting the atmosphere if not stopped. The storms had already started to get worse.

"So why not use it?" Elyna had suggested, backed by Ryan. The two of them had become more acquainted in the past few weeks. It made her happy to see the depressed woman regain herself.

"What are you on about?" Nath asked.

"The biggest problem to accelerating is the fuel you have to use to do it – when the indie ship crashed, they burned it all."

"The Rhineland was powered by a reactor – we can't just shove it into the back of that indie and ride off into the sunset. Even if we could fit it, we'll all be irradiated."

"Then use the reactor's *energy*. We have a way to harness it. You turned it off when we first got here."

"The superconductor cell? You're kidding," Nath laughed.

"You said you didn't train to be an engineer – well I did, before I transferred to be a pilot. I know it can work," Elyna eyes locked with his, daring him to find a way to shoot him down. Akiko had smiled when he couldn't, fussing about scenarios under his breath that he talked himself out of before being convinced.

"Charging it will be incredibly dangerous. It's a one-shot – we charge, we hit afterburn."

"Wait," Ester interrupted, "what do you mean by afterburn? You're not talking about crossing the desert, are you? You're talking about leaving the *planet*."

"Yes," Elyna nodded.

"We can synthesize fuel for blueshift from the supplies we have on hand. In the end, she's right – gaining altitude is the only real problem. If we can get up there...we can go home."

"What do you need?" Halim asked, his thick accent startling most of the room – none of them save for maybe Jin had heard him speak before now. His question hung in the still air, waiting for an answer.

"Chaladiom," Nath replied finally, "6 percent ought to do it."

"How soon?" Jin chimed in.

"At the reactor's current rate..." Nath paused, reluctant to put words to the truth he knew, "we're talking weeks, not months. I've got the ores Ryan's been able to pull, but I'll need to condense them back to usable materials for the blueshift formula."

"Then we don't waste any more time," Halim nodded toward Jin and the two of them returned to their room. Minutes later they re-emerged wearing their old suits. Ryan joined them soon after, kissing Emma goodbye and leaving her with Nadia.

Akiko joined the others as they laid out the plan – the navigation equipment on the old ship wasn't going cut it. The control circuits and all the old comms hardware was dead. But – the Rhineland's wasn't. Nath and Elyna would handle piecing it together inside the small ship, but they would need help locating control cards.

That meant diving into the Rhineland one last time. She knew the drugs wouldn't flush fusion radiation that fast. They would only be able to go in for minutes at a time and break for days after. It was a long process, but Camden and Ester volunteered – they had been exposed the least, up to this point.

Weeks passed and anxiety was running high. Ryan, Jin, and Halim worked day and night, joined by Camden and occasionally Ester, when they weren't scavenging net cards from the ship's exposed terminals. Oliver and Brit had focused on plotting the weather and making paths for the charging optics, mostly to occupy Nadia and Emma.

The two girls were nearly inseparable. It made her think of Khiti and their days in Sydney, playing cards and voxel games while waiting for mom to get home from the circuit. Emma was going to be five before too long. Planning a birthday party in the middle of all this seemed like a foolish thing...but they needed to ease the tension somehow.

Eventually she found herself alone in the camp, going over the numbers on stores and logistics – without Zain, it had become a bit of a chore, which she had reluctantly taken on. She kept expecting Oliver or Brit to radio and say they found her body...but nothing. Nath had regretted her loss and was shouldering more blame, though he dared not say it. He had been hard on himself after the initial crash. Losing another one of their number had stifled his good humor. She could see it, taking it out on his machines and occasionally Elyna...though she proved far tougher than Akiko would have thought for someone who stayed locked in their room for the better part of the last five years.

She ran the water till over her hands, washing her face and drying off. In the mirror, she could barely recognize herself. That was when it hit her. The picture of her and Nik pinned to the wall...she had to take a double take of herself and the picture. The rest of them had exhibited signs of healthy regression. Virgin air was known to help with that, purity in place of the chemically treated atmosphere most people usually breathed.

But *this* much? She could still see the lines, but her skin had tightened. Her old muscles had returned, hiding the bones and sinew on her arms. The more she stared, the harder her heart began to pound. A crashing noise startled her. Nath cursing at the table came next – he often crashed into it on the way to his room, though he never wanted to move it. He hated to change things.

"Nath?" she called to him, emerging from her room.

"Yeah...what's up?" he turned at his door, holding his foot, rubbing the sole. She could see it in him, too. Younger. There was no other way to describe it.

"Do you feel...different?" she asked.

"Like what? Sick? Pale? Throwing up blood? No, I don't have rad sickness, Akiko. You can see that," he waved her away, retreating back into his room. She followed him to his door.

"No...I mean, since we landed. Do you feel...better?"

He stopped, turning to her. He went to his door, motioning her inside and shutting it behind them.

"I don't feel old, if that's what you're getting at," he said, his voice having taken on a conspiring tone.

"My hands used to ache from storms – arthritis and nerve pain, usually. They used to do it all the time for the first few months...but now I can't remember when I stopped feeling it. Gravity used to make it settle down, but not disappear completely," Akiko said.

"From all the ground I've covered around here...I've had cuts and wounds go away in hours that used to take days to fade."

"Why didn't you say anything?" Akiko sighed in retort.

"I just figured we all felt it. All the terrible fortune we've been dealt down here, and we get one good thing in return? Didn't need saying, I guess," Nath flopped down in his chair. His room was plastered in diagrams and stray pieces of abstract art – he liked to paint in his spare time. When he let himself *have* spare time.

"It's not natural," Akiko shook her head, taking a seat on his bed, staring down at her hands, still finding the scars.

"It's natural *here*. Some of the old boys back home would be all over this place." He smiled, looking up at his ceiling. She could tell he missed his friends – he barely ever talked about them. His family had abandoned him.

The Rhineland and his short time between tours was all he had. "Nik would have been into this, too..." he shook his head, trying to shake away the sentiment. She could sympathize.

"Do you really think we can leave this place?" she asked him as direct as she could, emptying her sincerity in one go.

He noticed the seriousness in her tone, sitting back up and taking a long look at a few diagrams on the wall – they pictured several methods for tying the modern nav network into the ancient ship's control hardware.

"Yes," he said at last, "I do."

"What happens if we don't trigger it in time? If we're too late?" she whispered, almost afraid to pose it audibly.

"Well...that's your department, I would think. Either you treat the onset rad sickness or..." he pulled the old gun out from under his desk, hitting its actuator, "...we take the easy way out." He clicked the trigger, emptying a small hiss of wind at his forehead.

The easy way out. Rad sickness was painful. It did horrible things to the body. She didn't want to think about it. Not just for what it would do to herself, but she couldn't bear to see it happen to others. Not again.

"Then we won't be late. We can't be," Akiko stood up, resolute. He nodded in silent agreement as she opened the door. "Nathaniel...when we get off this world, let's visit some real cherry trees." She could see the beginnings of his smile as she shut the door.

The weeks passed slow for some, fast for others. It seemed to never be enough time for Nath and Elyna, who spent more and more hours integrating components and writing software for the newer parts to talk to the old ship. Luckily its airlock seals were still intact, even with Nath having busted the pressure lock. Replacing it was the first thing he had done. There were no vacuum suits left intact and they did not have the equipment to make and test new ones. It was their only safety.

Ryan said the weeks dragged on and on – but he felt good being with his old mining crew. Halim missed Kipp, finally letting others into his struggles – they had joined together before the tour started. At night, Ryan would read to Emma and help her with some of the educational exercises they disguised as games – that had been Jin's idea.

The little girl was very bright. Akiko spent a lot of time with her and Nadia, once Camden and Ester had collected all the cards they could off the Rhineland. The two of them split to help the others, Ester with the nav hardware, Camden with the mining.

"What's this?" Akiko pointed at the pad. Emma stared at it, screwing up her face and narrowing her little eyes. It always made Akiko laugh when she did that. Unlike Ryan, she preferred the direct approach to education – though she tried to be as nice about it as she could. Child development wasn't required medical training.

"'O'," she finally said.

"Great job – and this?" she held up a capital B.

"'B'," Emma said confidently.

"And this?" she held up a picture of a cow.

"Zebra," she said after a few seconds, frowning.

"Oh, really?" Akiko grinned, pulling the pad around to look. "I don't think that's a zebra. It doesn't have stripes."

"Oh, oh, oh – it's a cow!" Emma grinned.

"Very good. I think that's enough for today," she laid the pad down, getting up from the table to stretch.

"Akiko...can I ask you something?" Emma asked.

"Anything," Akiko told her, leaning back down.

"Sometimes I hear you crying...Ryan says you cry because you miss someone. He does it, too sometimes. I asked Nadia...and she said that she was missing some people too."

Akiko sat back down. "You want to know who we miss?" she held her breath. Was it normal for a four-year-old to ask this?

"Ryan said that Zain is missing, too. I just thought...if we find them, you don't have to cry anymore."

"It's not all the same," Akiko paused, taking the little girl's hand and tracing lines in her palm.

"What do you mean?" Emma cocked her head to one side.

"Zain is *missing*. Though we miss her too...we don't know where she is. We know where the others are. They're not missing. We just *miss* them because they're not here."

"I don't get it," Emma turned her head back.

"Tell me about it, kid," Nath propped the latest piece of old hardware on the table.

"What's *that*?" Emma leaned in, looking at the shiny black cubes packed into the interior.

"*This* is a poly-fusible carbon nanotube matrix."

"A hippopotamus doesn't look like that," she shook her head.

"And cows don't look like zebras," Nath smiled at her, laying the sheet of cubes down in front of her.

"It's so shiny," Emma's eyes widened, the insult going way over her head. Akiko glared at Nath, but he just shook his head in turn.

"What does it do?" Akiko asked, looking at it herself.

"It's the Galileo's old runtime computer – that was its name, based on the stamping plates we found in the inner hull."

"What's a galley-leo?" Emma asked, pronouncing it slowly. She had focused on what he said this time.

"Galileo Galilei lived a long time ago and figured out a bunch of things about the stars. They used to name ships after famous people."

"Can this help us?" Akiko wondered, "or is it dead?"

"It's the whole key to getting us out of here."

"Emma, no!" Akiko shouted. She tipped the sheet and it fell off the table. Rather than be appalled, Nath was cackling.

"I didn't mean to!" Emma started crying.

"It's ok, it's ok," Nath rushed to her side, picking up the small sheet and laying the cubes back in place. "Don't you worry your pretty little head. These are some of the strongest things in the universe. You couldn't break them if you tried."

"Still...Emma, you need to be careful with things that aren't *yours*," Akiko scolded her. She wiped her tears out of her eyes.

"It's alright," Nath put his hand on her shoulder, "you didn't damage anything." She eventually smiled when he put the pieces back together, good as new.

"Did you get it working?" Ester asked, breathing hard, followed soon after by Camden, Ryan, Jin, and Halim. They were all covered in dirt and sweat.

"Mostly," Elyna said, coming up behind them. She was wearing glasses, pulled from her trunk they'd scavenged off the ship. "The voxel displays are all cracked. We'll have to be careful to map the old I/O shell. The matrix is hardened against cosmic radiation and deep acceleration stresses."

"Are *we* hardened against that?" Jin asked. His voice was hoarse.

"We will be," Akiko promised. She had spent the rest of her time synthesizing the drug packs and panels they would need to survive the one-month trip to the nearest inhabited Juno. It was going to be very close quarters, but they would make do. It seemed too good to be true...but no one was virally sick. Hopefully that luck would hold long enough to let them make it back to civilization.

She had used Zain's stash to build the deep space panels – she had been giving Emma hers in small doses, to build up her tolerance for the drug. It pained her to give her injections...but if she didn't, she would stand a good chance of dying up there. Blueshift was one of the first long range autonuclear fuels. Despite improvements, it remained a dangerous way to travel – but it was all they had.

"We can try a charging circuit by next week, once the optic shielding has set," Nath informed them. He headed off toward the old makeshift cockpit. Akiko had volunteered to help Elyna move some of the voxel panels from the cave that were unusable in space. She was still uncomfortable around them, with the memory of that night when they crashed still simmering with complex emotions.

"Ryan, you got a minute?" Akiko asked, as they all dispersed.

"Yeah," he nodded, "let me take a shower first."

Nadia absconded with Emma after he was redressed. He pushed the door closed when Akiko nodded at him to do so.

"What is it?" he asked, "you figure out what to do for her birthday?" Akiko hated this...hated to ruin his happy mood.

"No...it's not that. I need to talk to you. About something I found when I was looking through the sample of Zain's drugs."

"Ok...what did you find?" Ryan asked, leaning against her back wall, stretching his legs. He looked haggard but determined.

"That's just it. There was nothing strictly illegal about it...I mean, sure in combination you could make some opiates and even some decent pharma cocktails – but no more than you could make given any average supply of medicine panels."

"Maybe she was just hoarding for when she could get back on the market for herself. How much would it go for?"

"You might be right...it would certainly get her a leg up. More than she would make on a single tour, that's for sure. It was a pretty sizable crate of pharma."

"But not enough to go crazy over?"

"No? Yes? I don't know. It was her dream, and she knew we would probably kill it. But now...I just wish she was on that ship with us. She doesn't deserve to be left down here."

"You know the odds. Six weeks now. Even if she did take food, she's not showing up on the scans."

"You think she went into the desert?" Akiko looked at the pictures, some of them hard prints of Zain, on the days when they tried to forget their troubles down here. Lots of movie nights. Lots of spirited game nights, too. Her laugh was a distant memory now.

"We did our best to find her, Akiko," Ryan came over, putting his hand on her shoulder, "it's not your fault she's gone."

"I blamed her. She could see that."

"If she comes back, she comes back. Otherwise, I don't think she can survive out there. Not forever."

"What makes you so sure?" Akiko asked suddenly. "I mean, when is the last time you were sick, or injured, or just cut your finger? Do you even remember?"

"Yeah, I cut my fingers all the time. See," he pulled his hand up, pausing to find the cut and his expression turning from a smirk to a neutral annoyance...and finally a frown.

"You can't find it, can you?" she asked, shaking her head.

"I cut it on the lasing miter. It's...somewhere," he dropped his hand, looking at her for an explanation.

"This planet is different. I don't know what to call it. It's like it's...new. But somehow...also old."

"Like a house someone bought then never moved into," Ryan whispered, staring off at the ceiling.

"It may sound crazy...but I think this place is trying to help us – trying to heal us."

"While it's trying to kill us," Ryan said somberly.

"I think there's a chance she's still alive. I feel it, in here," Akiko patted her chest above the heart.

Nik had crossed the tundra as it quickly turned to desert, pausing when the abrupt storms raged overhead, sloshing water on his environment tent and occasionally burying him in a mild form of quicksand. Wrestling out of it took a lot of his strength, but he always managed to find it again. The brace around his leg was itching, his knee tight and constructed...but not in anywhere near the pain it had been when he first landed.

He had to be crossing the planet's equator. Its orbit around the blue sun had no bearing on its axis. That was why he had stayed in the dark for so long. It spun on the same side that pointed to the sun, only occasionally drifting as it had when it woke him. The never-ending light dwindled as he drifted, bringing him back into the night cycle that soon gave way to a blinding day. Quint had seemingly landed them on the thin line that circled the planet. He had never pegged her for being that great of a pilot – she was still green from her last tour...but he had to admit, she was good.

When he stopped for the night, he always made sure to mark stars, rocks, and what little landmarks he had before he slept, drawing a giant line on his pad where the radio pointed. Sometimes he found it hard to sleep, with Torv's files quickly occupying every corner of his mind. He had watched the video many more times, looking for any possible hints.

Torv's list had been narrowed down to nine people that were still on the ship when they left the last dock. When he first opened the list, he balked at them all – certainly none of them would be capable of this. In the back of his mind, he wondered if it had all been an elaborate lie. That maybe Torv was the madman. That this was all a nightmare and he could finally wake up now that he knew the monster was dead. He wished for that each time he slept.

But no man he had known would die for a lie. Torv *had* been there, disconnecting the other bridge. He knew as well as Nik had that their chances of survival after disconnecting the outer ring were next to none. The only thing that he had on him was his youth – and now that Nik had seen the video – his arrogance. He assumed he could figure all of this out on his own. Or rather, he and his management had assumed as much. Surely, if they knew that this could happen, the transfer regime would have grounded them.

The nine people (other than himself, as he was also on the list) were crewman he had personally recruited and put his trust in. To think that one of them was a murderer…it was hard to stomach. Torv had known he would feel this way. He had read his file, after all. The dead man knew more than most men did about his checkered past. He had stopped for the night, deciding to read the list again. Torv had whittled his intel and notes down to single paragraphs on each. Quaint little words for what was now such a large accusation.

Lisle Etta Plothman
Mining Forman, Deep Space, 1ˢᵗ Class
Probability C+

On Rhineland for 2 ½ tours. Dedicated to his staff. Did not leave with downshifts in mining wages – loyalty to Venko probable factor. Did not serve in the transfer war. Supply chain officer for mining corps before coming aboard. Net history and communication logs suggest colonial leanings and connections to militant groups.

Justice Zachariah Lancing
STEM Corps, Deep Space, Ph.D. Forensics Analysis
Probability C-

On Rhineland 3 tours. Incredibly talented scientist. Thesis on extra-atmospheric food growth engines is impressive work for being twenty when he wrote it, with no prior spatial exposure. Served Consortium for one year at end of transfer war. Declined post on inner core ships – penchant for exploration likely factor. Net history and communication logs show minor abuse of illegal market trade and non-standard tech.

Axel Tipton Polard
STEM Corps, Inner Space, Masters Hydroponics Development
Probability B-

On Rhineland 1 tour. Born after transfer war. If recruited by prior regime intelligence, there is no record of it. Relatively light net history other than mild curiosity in growing custom strains of hallucinogenic drugs. Low wages for position, comparable to other deep-space ships. Access to many restricted sections of the Rhineland. Explicit retention of inner space designation implies no long-term commitment, raising probability.

Junice Bolynn Lowe
STEM Corps, Deep Space, Masters Hydroponics Monitoring
Probability B

On Rhineland 1 ½ tours. Ten years old at end of transfer war. Parents known defectors from colonial militia. Divorced, 6 years. Child, eight years, Nadia Lowe. Socialite. Shares curiosity with Polard; drug tests minor positive more than once in regular testing. Access to restricted areas. Relationship with lead deck officer Oliver Tam may be more than idle romance. Net and communications activity questionable, but not conclusive.

Zainaneme Ferrier Rhali
Mining Corps, Deep Space, Quartermaster
Probability A-

On Rhineland 1 tour. Middle child of prominent runner family Rhali. Older brother killed by illegal skirmish with other families in line of business. Biolock on cryptographic possession prevents passage to female DNA profile. Younger brother set to inherit the family business. Tension pushed her to adopt career outside the family. Net and communications activity littered with thinly veiled references to illicit activity. Quietly notified agents in TROI of missing shipments in inner space. Deemed grade A in part due to unrestricted access to most core systems on Rhineland, allowing lateral movement. Motivations uncertain.

Kipp Mickey Euler
Miner, Deep Space, 2nd Class
Probability C

First tour on Rhineland. Special hire by Venko, by all accounts. Kipp's father served with him in the war, posthumously awarded honors. Laughably little personal background. Despite late addition and already low wages, he is the only miner to stay aboard despite the obvious dip in wages and qualification for higher wages aboard the ice miner, albeit a shorter period than 5 years. Seems too obvious, but mining access gives access to exhaust and cooling ducts. Fun fact – he has a chinchilla hidden in his locker.

Akiko Rai
Medical Corps, Inner Space, M.D. Extraplanetary Medicine
Probability A

First tour on Rhineland. Replacement for last minute departure of medical officer Aiden Getty. Association to Venko is too close to ignore. Deep ties to Consortium military and political spectrum, though those have appeared to evaporate after she used her credit to try and get higher up on the state adoption approval lists. Troubled medical career. Many agencies disavowed her after a high-profile relationship ended badly and the political machine did its due diligence in burning her. Next to no unusual net traffic outside her line of work. Motivation for joining Rhineland appears to be personal appeal from Venko. More information needed.

Elyna Hayden Quint
Flight Corps, Deep Space, Pilot, Probationary
Probability C+

First tour on Rhineland. Born three years before war's end. Affluent parents donated to Consortium war efforts and propaganda. Failed out of private engineering school. Official record states lack of emotional and intellectual engagement. Pursued new career in extraplanetary naval piloting. Last minute adjustment placed her on Rhineland. Possible involvement by family contacts. Suspicious communications and net activity around hiding investments.

Sebastian Wycliffe Cole
Mining Corps, Deep Space, Autonuclear Engineer
Probability A+

On Rhineland 3 1/2 tours. Served in colonial militia armored corps. Several hundred verified kills in group. Highly opinionated on recent increase in transfer regime anti-propaganda. Net traffic routed through paid networking tunnels, decryption still pending after leaving dock. Immediate and unrestricted access to every part of the Rhineland. Highly trusted and respected by Venko, despite serving on opposite sides of the war. Personal dislike of my declared transfer status suggests he is smarter than I gave him credit.

[FILE END]

That was all of them. Whoever was still alive down here would have to answer to him, one way or the other. There were 198 people on the

Rhineland, and if even one of them had died, he would still go after the one responsible. It was *his* ship. *His* responsibility. Torv should have trusted him...but it was too late now.

According to his link, he was closing in. It was somewhere between 700 and 900 kilometers now. Walk. Eat. Read. Sleep. Repeat. Every night he slung the frequency generator to the ground, seeing its ever-present pulsing light. From what he had gleaned of its internals, it was powered by an autonuclear battery, its tiny rods capable of blasting the same noise until well after he died, and his bones crumbled away.

Sometimes he heard things. Voices in the rocks and the wind. He told himself it was repeated spectrum from the battery. Hoped it was. They didn't say anything he could understand. It could also be the effect of the generator on his brain – prolonged exposure to the radio waves could only be wreaking havoc on his brain cells, like it had the others.

Except one day he heard a voice he *could* understand. He had to strain to see the spec of black in the distance. It was a large crop of rocks, sinking in the tundra-soaked swampy desert. It took another half hour to reach it, by which time the voice had died back to the dull whisper he usually heard from the rocks. Then he heard a moan, much more distinct.

He dropped his pack on a dry rock that was jutting out of the ground near the front, rushing to the rear. The sound grew louder the closer he drew to the middle of the rocks, shaded from the storms and the weather. Someone was curled up on the ground below the jutting rocks, clothes torn and bloodied.

"Zain...?" he called hoarsely, coughing until his voice returned.

"Who...?" she lifted her head up, moaning in pain as she pulled back. She pulled a sharp tool out from beneath her, waving it in front of him. She promptly dropped it and fell backward, barely able to keep her eyes tracking on him.

"Zain...it's me. It's Nik," he said. She just stared.

"I'm...hallucinating," she fell back on the rock.

Nik caught her before she hit her head. The shiny surface of the rocks was the same as it had been in the cave where Nugyen had cornered herself. He could already see the telltale glow beneath their surface, now that his generator was in range. He waited with her until nightfall, giving her something from his pack. Her legs were paralyzed.

"Where...am I?" she asked, twisting to see him.

"I don't know, honestly," Nik smiled at her. Half of him wanted to grab hold of her excitedly and relate how happy he was to find someone else... but thanks to Torv, that feeling had been muted to a dull observation. She was on the list. It could be her.

"Captain...?" she widened her eyes, struggling to keep them open for long. She blacked out a few more times. Sores, cuts, and bruises covered her body, not to mention the sunburn. He avoided that with his hood.

It was hours before she could finally stay conscious enough for him to feed her something. She ate it but could barely keep it down. The Kilimanjaro rations turned her stomach. He fed her some of the pod rations, but they fared little better. After a while, she recovered enough that she could rest her head on the rock, her eyes open and her breath wheezing. Her outlook was not good.

"Zain," Nik began, "I need to know what happened."

"What...happened?" she closed her eyes, tears starting to form on the edge of her eyelids. He reached forward and dried them with a towel he pulled from his kit.

"Do you know why we're on this planet – a planet we can *breathe* on? Are we here because of you?"

"No. Not me," she shook her head.

"Then who?" he demanded.

She looked at him for a long moment, opening her mouth but saying nothing. Her head had a very large gash and she seemed to have suffered repeated heat strokes.

"I tried...to tell them."

Nik got on his knees, looking her in the eyes.

"Tell them what?" he asked.

"How did I...get out here?" she looked away.

"Zain, focus," Nik waved at her. Her eyes darted back.

"The ship. It crashed," she closed her eyes. He waved again.

"What happened before the crash?"

"I...was hiding it. I'm so sorry, Captain. I didn't..."

"What were you hiding? What do you mean?" Nik tried to recall Torv's notes. She didn't mean drugs, did she?

"Justice...said he would hide them. As long as he...got some. It was so...stupid," she finished, closing her eyes. She was hanging by threads.

"Listen. I'm not talking about drugs, or whatever you were stashing on the ship – I'm talking about what caused the crash. Do you know what caused the crash?"

She lifted her hand, pointing weakly to her only surviving pocket on the pants she was wearing. He pulled it inside out, finding a small data card that looked like it had come out of her link.

"Nik...I didn't know," her face was panicked. She shook her head, her eyes drifting down as her head slowly slumped to her chest. She was gone.

"Zain..." he sighed, pulling her eyelids closed.

He ejected Torv's card from the old link, having manually copied its contents to his own after some creative thinking over the last few weeks. A fragmented RTOS flashed up, but it wasn't from the Rhineland. If he was reading it right, it was from one of its distributed flight recorders. The content was a raw binary mess, and the old link was struggling to process it. He had a moral dilemma while he sat there – what was on this chip would dictate how he had to handle her body. She could be hiding more.

After a long, awkward and irreverent half hour, the files finally loaded. It was footage from the terminals on the Rhineland, directly prior to the crash – it was black box data. That meant she had dug it out of the Rhineland sometime in the past five years. There were precious few *good* reasons she would have black box data cards. Removing them from the recorder was likely to damage them. The digital distortion on the files made them difficult to watch. He focused all his attention on the tiny screen while ignoring the corpse of his old quartermaster next to him.

"...data lines are getting feedback," Cole was speaking to the terminal. His pockmarked face was sprinkled with missing pixels, but it was his engineer, panicked. "Nath, we've lost navigation."

Nath's voice was alarmed on the other end, "What?! Ok, ok...I'm patching the feed. Can you still control the reactor?"

"For now."

The file ended. He clicked the next in the timeline.

"Vauss, are you still in control of the helm? I can't reach Nik. His terminal access and half the ship are invisible on the RTOS." It was the much livelier voice of Mikhail Torv.

"Yes...barely. I can only see your terminal and the hot link to engineering. Cole says his end is nonresponsive. What did we hit?" Blaire Vauss's voice was calm, but the layer of panic was evident – it was always a risk in her job. Remaining in control was vital, since one could never fully rely on the autopilot cards.

"I don't know yet. I only had this session open because I was checking on some feedback in the nav protocols. From what I can tell, it's spread across the Rhineland's whole network. Sensors are going insane. I'm still seeing systems go down on my end. Wait – I see it now...I think the outer ring's been hit. Vauss – trigger the emergency comms." The surprise in his voice was understated. He had clearly not expected this, not then.

"Done," Vauss answered.

Torv's session ended, leaving only the image of Vauss as she focused all her attention on the nav array. He skipped ahead.

"...Ester, get over here!" Nath was yelling. She was clearly in disarray, not fully grasping what was going on. Her hands were shaking in the bottom of the link's static, pixelated viewport. He came over and grabbed her by the shoulders, pulling her toward the pod. The screen then went dark, though it was still recording. The feedback. It was the first time he put two and two together – was it the noise? Was it another frequency generator...or the planet?

Zain's face came up next. She was in the crew quarters, trying to get through the mining section. Her expression was fearful but determined. It wasn't clear why she was using the terminal. He rewound the timeline scrubber, looking for any associated data. The terminal command list popped up.

No...she wasn't trying to get through it. She was trying to close it. She kept checking over her shoulder. That was when Camden Senia came along with a miner in tow. He looked like one of the new hires. Torv had vetted those...hopefully he hadn't brought any new trouble aboard. If they caused this...well, Torv was already dead.

"Zain, the section is blocked off. We can't get to the rest of them!" Camden shouted. Zain jerked her hands away from the terminal, a horrified expression on her face.

"Where's – where's the nearest pod?" she recovered. Camden craned her neck to see the small emergency tick lines on the hull.

They left the terminal. He couldn't figure out what she had been doing. Was she trying to read the message? That had to be it. He rewound a couple more times, eventually getting the black box ID from the footage and comparing to the command dump.

It was raw text, but he eventually found it.

"We're crashing. I don't know how. Something hit us. The containment broke on the seals and I tried to lock it in the mining section. If you can find us – I've tagged our nav coordinates. Oh god – I think—"

That was where it ended. The message had been intercepted. No one was coming to find her. Torv had no time to decrypt it before trying to head off the outer ring's damage.

Zain wasn't innocent...but she wasn't wholly guilty. Whatever she was hiding, she had assumed the miners weren't locked in. That meant most of them...if not all of them...were dead. The bodies he had seen floating inside were because she had prematurely locked the door and started a decompression sequence.

It was her quantum transceiver that Torv had found in the ducts, probably the same used by runners and smugglers. Logically it made sense – they did regular power analysis and the cooling systems sucked down a lot of wattage at irregular intervals. It was a good place to hide it. She couldn't exactly stick it in her quarters. He stopped the playback. There would be time later tonight.

For now, he had one more body to bury.

He used the multi tool he brought with him to dig a spot near the shaded outcropping, where she wouldn't resurface if a hard rain came in. The day he had hired her, she had told him that she was running away from her family. He had known that about her already. None of that had been news to him. The thought she would put her own baggage above the lives of others...that was unexpected. He clearly hadn't judged her well. All of this was on his shoulders. The rest of her story would stay buried with her.

He looked at her face, one last time.

The tattoo around her eye was marred by a cut that dug deep into her skin. He used some setting gel from the kit to keep her eyes closed before lowering her into the grave. None of the people he had put in the ground on this world were his first. Not even the war was responsible for that.

"What we do in this life, we need not carry into the next," he said softly, reaching down to close her fingers and hold her hand before covering the grave. He didn't linger long. Whatever she had been running from...he was running to.

When he stopped later that night, the old link was still burning through the footage. Few terminals had anything but darkness in the video files. The network outage had spread until there were only two terminals left active: navigation and the engineering core.

"...are you up here? Why aren't you in a pod?!" he had fallen asleep, jerking his head up. Vauss was yelling at someone on the tiny screen. Groggy, he rubbed his eyes and refocused.

His attention snapped to the screen – the terminal shook. He remembered that moment – he had radioed the bridge. The network was down, but the radio backend wasn't. It had been silent...but why if Vauss was there?

"...why are you—" she was cut short, thrown across the array by the sudden gravity shift. Elyna gripped the controls, silencing the radio. He sat up in the tent, scrubbing back the footage.

"Why aren't you in a pod?!" Vauss yelled. Suddenly, Elyna ripped her from the controls. The ship shook as a result.

"...why are you—" Vauss threw Elyna against the side of the panel. She turned and threw Vauss into the holographic nav array, but she managed to pick herself up, shoving Elyna into the array herself. A nasty wound on her side showed in the pixelated footage. Elyna pulled a knife from her pocket and jammed it into Blaire's ribcage, shoving her off into the edge of the panel, slicing her head open. The older woman fell to the floor, no longer moving.

Elyna bent down, pulled the knife out, then stumbled over to the controls. He could hear his own voice. "Bridge? Report!" She ignored it, tearing open the field kit, rubbing the gel on her wounded side. Once she finished wiping the blood off her hands, she retook the controls.

"Captain?" She unmuted the radio.

He knew the rest...and now he knew what Zain had been trying to tell him. Whatever had happened, she was simply trying to hide what she had done. She didn't realize what else had happened before the crash – she had just assumed it was an accident. Her actions had no doubt killed several miners who could have used the extra time to make it to a pod. It was wrong, and it was tragic...but it was over. They were gone. Zain was gone.

Elyna Quint was his focus now.

Akiko was not overly fond of birthday parties. As a kid, she hated every one of hers. But for her sister Khiti, she would always go with her mom to find her a special present. For some reason, she felt compelled to do the same for Emma. Most of them opted not to care about their birthdays, but they had made a fuss over the two children. Nadia had gotten her fair share of custom voxel games from Jin and Halim, though she hadn't gotten to play them with the nav screens being repurposed for their flight.

What do you get a five-year-old? In the past years, she had found some unique toy to print, but every scrap of material was being put through the need/toss list that Camden, Elyna, and Nath had drawn up. Every *metal* material, that is. They had made her clothes and tried to customize them, but now that they were leaving, there was no longer any need to store the synthetic leathers.

A jacket. That was perfect. The one she had was an old one of Nadia's they had dug from the wreckage. While she checked the others for exposure and shored up everyone's dosage for pre-flight, she had taken to mapping out the pieces. Emma's favorite color was somewhere between purple and blue – she had a hard time telling the difference on occasion. She had a bit of color blindness and retinal damage, particularly from the blinking sunlight. When they made it off this world, she would have to get her checked.

Indigo was what she decided on, dying the last couple of rolls that would cover all the pieces. The others were watching a movie while she worked on it. Emma was sitting in Ryan's lap, laughing at the screen. They hadn't needed the projector's parts, and it was the only real relaxation they could get while they prepared.

She could see it from the table, the bright characters and colors flashing across the set. It was an animated film. Nath and Elyna had gone to bed – they were not necessarily socialites. Camden, Ester, Kipp, and Halim were in chairs next to Ryan and Emma. Oliver, Brit, and Nadia were huddled on a makeshift couch. It was a nice little moment. She secretly took a picture with her link.

While she took the picture, her link flickered. It was strange. She shook the small device, watching the same block of pixels. It had been ages since they had a real mesh radio connection, but that was what that part of the screen was meant to show – it was, as Nath had explained many times, a "real-time" device. Its inputs, outputs and radios were designed to handle constant polling.

It had to be a fluke. As the storms grew more frequent, so did little things like this. Systems going down with a sudden power strike, loss of cables – you name it. On the one hand, the planet had rejuvenated them… on the other, it was as Ryan had so aptly said – "trying to kill us."

The movie ended and they all drifted to bed. She did, too. Her dreams were filled with odd pictures of cartoon versions of herself and the others. When she woke up, it was storming outside. They opted to stay in. She worked more on Emma's jacket. It was a slow day otherwise. Elyna and Nath were working on the final tweaks for the cockpit, before they integrated the panels in the old ship. Ryan was sleeping in.

Nadia tapped her on the shoulder.

"Akiko?" she asked, coughing slightly.

"Hey...cough still bothering you?" she asked. A nasty storm cold had taken her down for a couple days. It was unusual in light of the otherwise enhanced health they all enjoyed. Brit was the last one to have one, last year. It was important she knock it out quickly.

"A little bit. Almost done with it," she smiled weakly. "I wanted to ask you something."

"Alright," she laid the jacket down.

Nadia looked around for someone, before turning back. "Emma and I were talking about Oliver and Brit, since she heard them say they wanted a baby. I uh...told her the basics. She asked me where her mom and dad were."

"What did you tell her?" Akiko sighed, taking off her pair of glasses and rubbing her eyes. She put them back on, then pulled them back off, noticing she could see slightly better without them.

"I said that her mom wasn't here...and that Ryan was her dad," Nadia said quickly, "I'm sorry. I panicked."

"What did she say? Where is she now?" Akiko stood up, looking around for the little girl.

"I left her in the shop with Nath and Elyna. She started asking more questions and I didn't know what to do...so I came up here."

"Ok. It's fine. I'll go talk to her. Thanks for letting me know," Akiko smiled at her, heading down to the shop.

Nath and Elyna were having an argument. Emma was in the corner, with her hands over her ears. She wasn't crying, thankfully. She didn't often cry, anyway – just when others were fighting. It was a very pleasant part of her young personality. When Akiko entered, Nath and Elyna realized they were being loud. She bent down and took her hands away from her ears, taking her hand and pulling her along. They walked out of the camp, where the storm was slowly calming down as dusk settled in for the night.

"It's so pretty," Emma pointed. The sky had an aurora.

"She was pretty, your mom," Akiko said after a while.

"Nadia told you..." Emma looked at her; those striking eyes.

"It's ok to want to know."

"Nadia said she was gone. When is she coming back? I want to meet her!" Emma beamed. Akiko put her arm around her.

"I know this hard for you to understand....your mother is dead, Emma. She isn't coming back." She wrestled with whether to wake Ryan. They had agreed to share the burden of raising her. He had not wanted to do this, but he did not forbid her from it. He just didn't know if there would ever be a good time. In the end, she settled on letting him sleep. Seeing Iris was painful for him. The rain had started to die. It was time for her to deal with this. There was never going to be a right way or a good time.

"Are we going to die?" Emma asked.

"No, we're not going to die," Akiko said, pulling her into her arms.

"So, I'll never get to meet her," she frowned.

"No. I'm sorry," Akiko whispered. They were both silent for a minute. "But I can take you to her."

Akiko went back and found both hers and Nadia's old jacket, shifting it over the child's shoulders and pulling on her own. They went out in the rain. The aurora lit the way. At the gravesites, Emma held onto Akiko's hand as they tread over the footsteps others had left over the years. Iris's grave was near the end. A flower was drawn next to her name on the small metal plate stone set in the earth.

"F...r...i..e..d...rich," Emma pronounced. They had taught her English since everyone spoke it here. Akiko occasionally tried to teach her some

Japanese phrases. "She's down there?" she pointed under the ground. She had seen enough movies to know what a grave was.

"Yes. Her name was Iris. When you were born, her heart stopped...and she died."

"Why did it stop?" she asked.

Akiko wasn't sure how to say this.

"It took a lot of her strength to make sure you could be in the world. She just didn't have enough of it left over for herself. I tried everything I could to save her...but in the end, there was nothing anyone could do."

"I wanted to meet her," Emma nodded, sitting down on the ground, pulling up some of the small grass and spreading it over the grave. Akiko knew she couldn't quite understand, just yet. But she did know.

"Your mom loved you. She's the one who named you. She wanted to be with you – and she would have loved to meet you, too."

"But what about my dad? Nadia says everyone has a mom and dad. She said Ryan was...but he already told me...he said he wasn't."

"Is that why you're upset – you thought Nadia lied to you?" Akiko asked, taking a seat next to her. She looked over the way, seeing the grass covering the empty ground below Nik's grave plate.

"Yes," she mumbled, burying her face in her knees.

Akiko sighed. "Ryan *is* your dad," she said, pulling the child into her arms, hugging her. "No one can replace your parents...but Ryan was with your mom before you were born, and he was the one who's taken care of you after. He chose to be your dad."

"Does that mean you're my mom?" she looked up at her. Akiko paused, then shook her head.

"No...and I know it's not easy to understand. We all knew your mom. It's not easy to replace someone you know. We didn't know your real dad. Ryan is the only one we have ever known. I'm sorry for confusing you."

"Ryan's my dad," she whispered, looking up as the rain began to start again. A few drops hit her face.

"Let's go back before we get too wet," Akiko pulled her up as she stood up, pulling the jacket over her shoulders. The new one would fit her much better. Hand in hand, they went back to the camp, watching a few strikes of lightning glaze the sky with harsh blue, green and white light. Dusk was setting in by then.

"Akiko," Nath said pointedly, standing by the fridge. She let Emma go. Ryan was playing a game with Jin on the projector.

"What is it?" she asked Nath, pulling a cup off the shelf and filling it with the reconstituted coffee mix. He nodded at her to follow him to his room. She poured water in the cup and followed.

"We think we've got the old controls mapped to the modern nav software," he explained, closing the door behind him. "Which is good, because we have less than a week before we're going to get stuck between a couple problems."

"What do you mean? The storms?" she guessed.

"The autonuclear resonance is increasing its effect on the wild shifts in the weather. These storms are going to get more violent and more frequent. So...not only do we need to get out of the atmosphere before the radioactivity starts to cook us, but now we have to escape before the storms fry us in the process."

"It's like this place knows what we're doing," she shook her head.

"Well, we stabbed it with a giant knife and never pulled the blade out," he nodded at an image of the Rhineland wreckage.

"How does one ship do this? I've never read about anything like this."

"I have, but nothing that affects a whole planet. Old colonial landers used to set off all sort of atmospheric powder kegs. Like stirring up dust in the attic when opening the door."

"I think we need to call a meeting, then," she raised her head. He nodded in agreement.

An hour later, everyone but Nadia and Emma were in the shop with the old cockpit pieces, temporarily connected to the nav frame. Nath and Elyna were standing in front of it. Akiko could hear the distant whispering of Emma and Nadia. They were probably trying to watch and listen.

"We're ready to integrate this into the old ship. Thanks to the rest of you, we've got the charging network and the fuel mix ready. We need to run some flight diagnostics that we couldn't do without the old cabin connected, but other than that...we're essentially ready to fly. That's the good news," Nath nodded.

"The bad news..." Elyna started, "is that the storms are getting a lot worse. We need to take off before this valley becomes a new front and we're stuck here."

"And if we're stuck here...we die from the radiation," Halim said, his tone ever serious.

"Yes," Nath nodded, "but we can be connected and finished with the diagnostics in four days. That will be enough to charge up the superconductor and clean the old reservoir to prep the fuel mix."

"While they integrate this thing," Ryan pointed at the cockpit, "the rest of us need to finish the supply stacks we'll need for the next month while we make it to the nearest Juno. Weight shouldn't be too much of a problem. Just space."

"I'll be making the final dosages for the radiation exposure we'll face out there," Akiko took her part, "and work on checking the air ratios on the remaining masks we have, in case we run low on air or have a vacuum leak. It'll be tight...but we can make it."

"What about the old ship's comms?" Ester asked, "do we have any way of radioing for help once we're in space?"

"They're the slow band," Nath shook his head, "We'll be at the Juno before they can refract toward the larger arrays that will pick them up."

"And everyone *can* fit inside this ship? I mean...thirty days is a long time," Camden noted, concern and awkward implications evident in her voice.

"There's a toilet on it. Cramped, but good enough. Forgoing showers is necessary," Ryan chuckled. They all had a laugh.

"Thirty days is enough to pay for getting back to civilization," Elyna smirked at Camden. She finally nodded.

"Anything else we need to do?" Brit asked. She and Oliver had remained quiet up to this point.

"I suppose any last things you want to take from the Rhineland's wreckage before we go are still on the table," Nath scratched his chin. Akiko knew now that he had never liked having a beard.

"I wouldn't," Akiko spoke up quickly, "the levels are too high to be reversible in the time left. Going in there might be fatal at this point." Nath made a gesture, mumbling "of course" to himself. He seemed embarrassed.

"Can we fit the projector in the ship?" Nadia asked, hiding behind one of the crates. Emma wasn't far behind her.

"You know, that's not a bad idea," Nath smiled. Normally, he would have been annoyed at their interruption – they were usually evicted from their meetings because they couldn't stop talking.

"Takes too much power," Jin said. "But...we can take some of the voxel screens we're not using. They sip power. Could pull the video cards out of the projector and stick them in a less power-hungry box."

"Sounds like a plan," Nath smiled. Everyone nodded in turn.

Akiko helped where she could. The next couple of days went by in a blur. They had made a clean path to the old ship from the camp. It was about ten kilometers. Between the whole group, they got the parts there in record time. Nath and Elyna set to work integrating it, sleeping in the cabin of the ship, since it was now shielded from their upgrades over the past few weeks.

She finally finished the jacket. It wasn't going to be Emma's birthday until they were in space, but part of her wanted to give it to her now. She was hiding her nervousness – she didn't understand what was going on, and Nadia could only explain so much to her. Ryan and Akiko sat down with her on the third day of final preparation and explained everything.

"We're never coming back here?" she looked around the room.

"It's not safe here, Emma," Ryan told her.

"Everyone is coming with us – no one's getting left behind. Nadia and Oliver and Jin – everyone. This is just a place. I know it's been the only home you've ever known...but home is with us. It's going to be alright," Akiko took her hand, glancing at her own in comparison to Emma's. The startling realization of her missing age lines had worn off by now. She still found it hard to believe the change that overcome her...or anyone here.

"Ok. If you're there with me," she ran forward and hugged Akiko, then pulled away and hugged Ryan.

"We'll be there," he hugged her back. "Don't worry."

Nadia and Oliver helped Jin disassemble the old projector. It was a complex piece of machinery, and even Akiko found the innards of it fascinating. So many mirrors and net cards. It reminded her of a miniature fun house she had seen when her mom and Khiti had gone to an old-world fair when she was kid.

Nath had stopped in the camp, presumably for the last time – he was packing up his room while Elyna ran the diagnostics. She had packed hers up the day before. Akiko closed the door, seeing him tossing things in the corner and occasionally tossing something in the crate he was using for his stuff. They hadn't been able to pull his trunk out of the Rhineland. His room was blocked like Zain's.

He had stopped. He was holding a picture.

"I didn't think you liked pictures. You always poke fun at mine," she laughed, taking a seat next to him. He handed her the picture. It was one of Nik and the first command crew. There were people she didn't know – Getty was most likely the one with the medical jacket. Cole was standing there, too, with the same hardened look on his face. There was Nath, standing near Nik, with a wry smile. Nik was leaning on his good leg.

"I'm glad he had friends out here," she put her hand on Nath's arm. He didn't move away.

"I'm sorry you found him just to lose him again," Nath said, his arm trembling a little where he held the picture. Like herself, his age lines seemed to have evaporated. His graying hair was invisible now. "I'm sorry you got stuck down here. I'll apologize for him, since he's gone. I know he would have hated himself for that."

"I imagine that by now I would have solved that old storm cold epidemic and been placed in a boring old hospital above a planet I never visit. Wouldn't have gotten to know you or Ryan or all the others down here. Or Emma, of course," she smiled, a rare genuine one she felt inside.

"You know they're going to try and take her, don't you?" he turned to her, his eyes on the verge of tears.

"I do," she said, "but they won't."

He smiled then. "I believe you." Then she kissed him. He held it.

"Are you going to be ok?" she asked, looking into his eyes. He was no longer an old man. The vision of Nik's younger self bubbled up and she did the best she could to repress it.

"Once we're away from this world," he breathed, "then I'll let myself feel something again."

20
REAL PLAN

Elyna hated her last name. Hated her family. Hated this world. All she had ever wanted to do was be an engineer. They need pilots, her father had told her. People on the front lines. Front lines of what? A war they wouldn't let die. They had made sure she failed out of school, despite her talent. Threatened her and changed her records.

They had all the money. What was she going to do? She could never go to the transfer regime – my parents are megalomaniacs who are plotting with the colonials to start another war. Yeah, they'd say, hers and every other rich set of colonial parents. Take a number. Her friends had warned her. Some of them had tried to come clean and she never saw them again. In the end...she became a pilot.

She lulled herself into thinking that this career could be her new dream now. Her parents didn't run her life. They had no sway over what she could do. That worked for a time. But then...the message came. Sign up for this tour. Go to these coordinates. She tried to contact her parents. They were unusually mute – do what the message says. Don't ask questions. In her mind, she could see the gun pointed at her mother and father as they typed it out. She contemplated not going...but without her parent's money, her career aspirations – her life – would be as bad off as Zain's.

242

Her training was decent. No one suspected anything. She had found the transceiver in the cooling ducts when Nath gave her the tour of the nav system traces. Nathaniel Royce – he believed he was a renaissance man. In many ways that was true, but he was blinded by his own ego that she often found insufferable. To be trapped on this world with him of all people. Someone hated her.

Nothing had gone as planned. Someone had found the transceiver she "borrowed" and she was forced to prematurely start the sequence. There had been no time to discretely get rid of Vauss. They were crashing too soon, and she did what she had to do to land them here. Blaire had put up more of a fight than she thought the woman could. Elyna would have bled out if the doctor hadn't shown up.

Akiko. Venko had pulled her aboard last minute. She was the kind that focused on solving people. Applying consistent pressure, like on a wound, but not too hard. More than once, she thought about confiding in her. She had been in a depression for much of their time down here, just not for the reasons Akiko assumed.

Nothing stopped the dreams of pods floating in space, with only frozen bodies inside. There had been no time for any of them to get a good vector during the crash. The images went in and out of her head. She dulled them with drugs while she tried to destroy any evidence. She managed to copy and digitally shred the first recorder before it was found by Nath. She snuck out several times to find the second, but then Zain had found it first.

She waited for the inevitable conclusion, ready to give up or run or something...but nothing happened. Zain hadn't opened the recorder – she'd simply hidden it to hide her own sins. According to the first recorder, she had stowed some of her family's drug stores on ship – stolen them, as it turned out. When Nath started to dissect the second, it left her little time to act before she and Zain would both be implicated.

Zain's drugs were unique. The ones she had left with Lancing were modified military blue packs. Hallucinogenic scripts mixed with top grade opiates. She found them in Lancing's lab on one of her secret trips, replacing them with the regular stores she'd stolen off Akiko's initial stashes then re-welding the door shut.

While they were focused on Zain that night, Elyna had laced her drink with a large dose of the blue packs. It wasn't long before her paranoia made her attack Nath, knocking him unconscious and fleeing the camp. It had been a good improvisation...except Zain had also taken the recorder. It was hardened physically, but still vulnerable, and even gave off some faint signatures...it was one of the things she had learned in her training. She needed to get it and hide it somewhere no one could get to it. There wasn't much time before the others would notice, so she followed Zain to the edge of the desert that night.

Even drugged, Zain was still dangerous. Elyna disguised herself as a miner with one of the suits from the ship, hoping she would simply see her as another hallucination. It worked well enough, helping to lure her to an outcropping where she shoved her off, taking the recorder and leaving her there as the storms erupted overhead.

With little time to make it back before the others started searching, Elyna took the recorder back to the Rhineland, loaded up on an anti-rad dose, then hid it in the substructure, where it was masked by the dying reactor's noise. That was when she learned about the radiation growth. She had guessed at that herself, but without the scanning equipment that Nath kept in his room, finding out for sure was impossible.

It was rough getting back in the storm – then rougher avoiding the others before she could get back in her room, but she was skilled and she was able to slip in without even Nadia noticing. No one seemed to suspect her – and even felt sorry for her when she regretted telling them about

Zain once she ended up missing. She told Ryan about her plan to escape. He liked it, so she found her in with the group and the possibility of finally leaving this planet became real. Her luck had finally shifted back.

And now it was done. They were all grouped around the table together, sharing stories and airing their thoughts and anxiety of what they were going to try. The nav system was building the autopilot vectors...not that they would be much help, if the front came when they thought it would. That was why she was accelerating her plans. Lifting off with that many people and the weight was too risky if they waited too long.

It wasn't killing them, she decided. At least not directly. She filled the water reservoir with the last batch of the blue packs. It was difficult to modify its form – but she had learned from Zain's mistakes. According to the footage on the first recorder, the drug had broken its vacuum seal and become an aerosol. It flooded the mining section before it was vacuumed out. None of those poor people in there had a chance, between the aerated drug and the ship crashing.

They were all drinking it now. In a short while they would start to be overwhelmed. Out of the corner of her eye, Ryan was leaving the camp, with Emma in tow. Her mind raced. How could she have predicted the child? She left quietly, following behind.

"You sure you want to do this?" Ryan asked her. The little girl said a feeble yes. He held her hand and they climbed the ridge near the lake. They were heading for the graveyard. She crept close behind, watching as they neared the grave of her mother. A handmade artificial flower was in her hand. When she went to place it, the little girl fell back, dropping the flower. Then she started convulsing.

"Emma!?" Ryan yelled, dropping to the ground. He yelled for help, but Elyna knew no one would be coming. He turned, relieved as Elyna walked up, fear in his eyes.

"Help me get her back to camp!" he shouted, turning back to Emma.

Elyna took the metal bar from behind her back and hit him across the head, violently. Ryan fell next to Emma, who had gone just as still, fallen atop her mother's grave. They would want one of the children. Nadia was the obvious choice. The other one, Brit's son, had died on impact. She had tweaked the emergency comms to get to them first. Ryan and Iris were near Nadia on the Rhineland, finding a pod before the vectors were unusable. But Emma...she knew they would want her. The effects of radiation on a world like this were important to them.

The superconductor had collected enough of the radiation to build a signature. But a piece of machinery was one thing...what it did in humans was another. On adults, it reversed cell damage. Akiko had figured that out in the last year, though it should have been obvious. On children...who knew what it could do. Nadia had gotten sick. She was no better than any of the others.

But Emma had never once been sick. Or cut. Or anything. She was a true wonder. It was her decision now...but she knew they would want the girl. She picked her up, then started making her way toward the old starship. By the time she made it, dusk had set in and the old site's floodlights had pulsed on. The charging network reported to her link that it was nearly complete. She lay Emma on the table in their small workshop off to the side, taking a quick scan using one of the Rhineland's more advanced tools she'd hidden away. She hoped that all her guessing was right...if she killed a child, too...

No damage. Just an overzealous immune response.

"You are one incredible girl," she smiled at the child.

Next came the relatively straightforward portion. The nav system was reporting 60% completion on vectors. The weather watching network showed the storm front encroaching. Another hour, she decided. They had stacked the supplies in the ship. Thirty days would be more than enough for just her and Emma. She wasn't sure what story she would use when she woke up. Her mind was already trying to concoct a tragedy. In the end...she was just a child. She didn't have to *tell* her anything.

Her own nervousness came out as she waited. No one radioed. No one was saying anything. The bands were silent. By now they would all be strung out or unconscious. She clicked her link, increasing the precision of the charger. It was very slow. Trying to map the old superconductor battery to the link's OS was easy work for Nath, and easier work for her once he was done.

It was finally in the range she needed. She turned the ignition. It warped the vessel's metal as the sudden surge of power heated up wires that hadn't been used in decades. Some things popped. A computer core was offline. Not unexpected, but not necessarily a welcome sign either. She traced it. Pulled the carbon core. It had a few fried cubes...which didn't bode well. The superconducting battery was a marvel of colonial engineering. A long time ago, it was their long-term plan for expansion. Her family was well entrenched in the colonial network. They had told her all about the old tech. It was part of why she wanted to be an engineer. Part of why she had not refused this placement. She could fix this.

She took the cubes and headed out to the table. Emma was still laying there, her breathing slow but stable. A box of carbon cubes was still in the shelf – Nath hadn't moved them into the ship. Lazy old idiot. Well... young now. That was the most annoying part. She hadn't gotten much "younger", herself. She wasn't a biologist. Maybe it just made old people less old. Maybe they'd tell her later.

"Was this your plan?" a voice asked. She pulled the gun from her pocket, stolen from Nath's room. Finding the energy pack and the slicer for the metal ammo block took a whole two years.

"I know you're here," the voice said again. She turned away from the table. It didn't surprise her who stood there...just annoyed her.

"You *really* should have drank your tea," she pointed the gun at Nath.

"I'm *really* not into military-grade sweeteners," he threw his cup near her. It crashed and shattered on the ground. She tightened her fingers. Shooting him would be easy. She really wanted to shut him up...but she wanted to know what else he knew. He might not be alone. She looked at her link. It showed no one else...in fact, it didn't show him.

"What do you want?" she asked, gesturing with the gun.

"I want to know the plan. The whole plan. Before you shoot me. Like all the villains do in the good movies."

"This isn't a movie. I'm not going to give you a monologue," she pulled the trigger. It didn't fire. She looked up at him, watching as he hit a button on his link and a wave of pain erupted out of her side. She looked down, seeing a mess of blood and charred clothing clinging to her chest. Her strength evaporated and she fell to the ground. He walked up to her, kneeling to look her directly in the face. She could barely make him out through the pain, finding it increasingly difficult to breathe.

He stood up, grabbing a large box hidden on the table next to Emma. When he came back, he held it in front of her. Her vision swam but she could tell it was the business end of the laser sink that Ryan had pulled from the Rhineland. It was still smoking. She felt a deep sense of violation and disgust mixed with fear as she tried desperately to pick herself up, but everything had gone horribly numb...and cold.

"I think you've gotten our roles confused," Nath bent down to her level. His eyes were frighteningly calm. "You were just going to leave them *all* down here, stranded? Didn't they teach you any better than that? Or were you too busy looking for mum and dad's approval that you forgot to stay aware of your surroundings?" He dropped the laser on the ground, its soft thud barely registering in her dimming senses. He pulled the gun from her hands as he stood up, towering in the swimming space above her.

Elyna stopped breathing as the world slip away.

21

DARK STORM

Akiko raced into the rain as it started pouring, trying to place Ryan's signal. It was gone. Nothing was pinging. She searched and searched, feeling her stomach turn. She stopped near the lake, vomiting into it when she couldn't handle it. Something had been in the drinks. She and Nath had decided to make tea instead of just plain water. The others were yelling and fighting, hiding in their rooms.

Ryan and Emma were gone. She ran to the top of the ridge, trying to place where she had heard someone yell. There was a dark mass laying on the graveside. She ran, finding Ryan unconscious. Emma was nowhere to be found. Adrenaline coursing through her veins, she pulled Ryan's body up and started back. The storm was buffeting, blowing against her. She turned into the old camp. A few lights and a couple crates were all that had been left there.

She put him on top of the crates, leaning down and making sure he was still breathing. He was. A large square bruise on the back of his head and deep clean cut told her enough – he had been attacked. Someone had followed him up here and done this. And now they had Emma. Hopefully Ryan hadn't had a drink tonight...if he did, when he woke up, he'd be like the others, now. Losing their minds.

Outside, the lightning lit the sky with volley after volley. Rain blew into the mouth of the cave. She did what she could, trying to wake him. He finally stirred, raising his fist before seeing it was her. He relaxed, sighing and letting his head drop. She caught him before he banged his head into the crates.

"You're likely concussed. How are you feeling?" she asked.

"Sick...but still here," he nodded.

"Did you drink anything tonight?" He shook his head no.

"What happened? Who did this to you?"

"Elyna," he said, raising his head up. "I have no idea why."

"She might have been affected by what was in the drinks. The others... they've gone insane. I heard you yell and went to find you."

"Emma!" he said, pulling his feet to the ground. She held him down. He had a look of fear in his eyes. "Where is she?!"

"She wasn't with you. Elyna may have taken her...we need to find her – but the links are all dead. I think the network got hit with lightning again."

"We have to get back to the camp. Maybe she's there," he said, trying to get up again. He managed it this time. He looked outside, his expression dropping when he saw the extreme rain. He gritted his teeth and walked over to Akiko.

"We'll manage," she said, tearing a piece of her shirt and wrapping it around his head. The two of them ventured back into the night. It was dangerous, lightning strikes hitting the ridges, coming near them a couple times on their way to the new camp. He paused once to steady himself.

Once there, the situation had only improved slightly...instead of yelling and fighting, there was silence. Jin and Halim were collapsed on the floor near the projector. They searched the whole camp, forcing open any closed doors. Everyone was unconscious. Camden and Ester had been barricaded in part of the shops. Oliver and Brit were in separate rooms.

"Emma isn't here. Neither is Nath, Elyna, or Nadia," she noted. They searched again, finding nothing. Ryan searched outside while Akiko tried to wake the others. They didn't stir. She told Ryan to sit before he raced out into the storm. She quickly dressed and taped a waterproof patch to the back of his head, discarding the old piece of her shirt, then gave him a panel of anti-concussion meds to control the nausea and headache.

"Help me get them all in here," she said. Together they put the other six of them in the seating area where the projector used to be. She tested them. Whatever was in the drink had run its course, leaving only the fallout now. She didn't feel well herself, if she was honest – but she also wasn't going mad.

"They have to be at the old ship. Why would they go anywhere else?" Ryan suggested. She had no better ideas. They found their thicker hooded jackets and put them on, then hurried that way. It was a dangerous trip, as the storm had grown even worse. The lightning never stopped. The sky was a blinding strobe.

Around an hour and a half later, they reached the ship. The world grew silent the closer they came to the worksite, where they noticed the lightning rods were redirecting the powerful storm. It still made a significant amount of noise, but the energy was being channeled into the ship's superconductor – Nath's idea, since it was essentially the perfect protection.

"Emma?!" Ryan shouted. No one answered.

"Nath?! Nadia!? Elyna!?" Akiko shouted after him.

"In here!" Nath yelled. They saw him under the workshop, out of the rain. They ducked inside. Emma was on a table.

"Emma," Ryan hurried to her, sighing in relief. Akiko did, too. She wasn't moving, but she was still breathing. Nath was standing by, forlorn.

"Are you feeling alright? I think something got in the water," Akiko told him.

"That makes sense now...I didn't drink my tea when all the shouting started. I saw Elyna and followed her when I saw her leaving the ridge carrying Emma. I had gone out because I thought you yelled, Ryan – sorry I didn't stop," he apologized. "The radio is out. Thought I could message back to have the others check on you...but I couldn't. Then the others at camp were already acting strange. I juggled all the options... figured you'd want me to look for Emma."

"It's fine, thanks for going after her...is she alright, Akiko? I know she had something to drink tonight," he held the little girl's arm. Akiko noticed the advanced scanner on the table.

"Where did this come from?" she asked Nath.

"I don't know, but Elyna was scanning her with it," Nath picked it up and handed it to her.

"It's a full bio-scanner. Thought it was strange I never found it in the wreckage," she turned it on, seeing the scans. Someone had already used it to check on Emma.

"Where's Elyna?" Ryan looked around the clearing.

Nath shook his head, "I confronted her. She was scanning Emma with that thing and she ran off. Was rambling about Zain and a host of other nonsense. Finding her is going to be hard, if not impossible."

"Emma's...fine," Akiko said with a note of relief, pulling the scanner to her face. "Just a crazy overreaction from her immune system. According to this...there are traces of hallucinogens and even opiates in her system. It could have killed her...but she's just...fine. If this is what's in the others... we're lucky no one is dead."

"Where would she have gotten those from?" Nath asked.

"I thought it was strange that the stashed crate in Lancing's lab didn't have any real narcotics. The labels on the sides, I recognize them now – blue mil packs...someone replaced them."

"Elyna," Ryan tightened his fists.

"But why," Akiko shook her head, not sure what to make of it, "and where would she go? The ship is her only way off this world."

The storm surged, sending sheets of rain across the ground. One of the lightning pylons arced brilliantly a hundred meters away. The three of them moved to the edge, trying to see the damage. A large part of the grass had ignited on the ridge in the background.

"We don't have any time left," Nath warned, "we need to leave now. Can we get the others here in time?"

"They're all knocked out back at the camp – except Nadia. I was hoping she was here with you. Have you seen her? And what about Elyna?" Akiko turned to him, "do we go after her?"

"You said it yourself – the ship is her only way off. She's bound to come back. Which..." Nath trailed off, heading into the ship then returning with the control circuit for the computer matrix. "There. Now we just have to keep an eye out for her. Three against one ought to be good odds."

Ryan and Akiko nodded in agreement.

Akiko looked out into the mist of the clearing, "Hopefully whatever kept Emma from getting hurt is helping Nadia...but she may be roaming outside. We have to find her...and what if Elyna finds her first?"

"We don't have time, Akiko," Nath said harshly. She turned to him, a pained look in her eyes. He shook his head, "I want to find her as much as you do, but this is down to logistics. I'm sorry – but look," he gestured at the sky, "this is it. We need to get everyone to the ship that we can. We search for Nadia or we get the others. This storm is not going away."

"Let's get the others," she said, shaking her head angrily.

The three of them ran back to the camp. The others were still unconscious. They would have to take them in pairs of three. Two more trips. Six more hours. More really, since they had to drag them there. Akiko hated the cold calculus of it all...but Nath was right. They tore the cots and wrapped their feet, so they could be dragged. It was rough going, but it was all they had. They took Jin, Halim, and Camden first. It took a little more than three hours. The trio were all sore, and they were over their estimated time.

With those three stowed in the ship, they headed back, sloshing through the mud that grew into a slurry on their fresh path. The pylons were placed at equal distances from their camp to the ship, catching the lightning as it grew in intensity. Akiko was having a horrible flashback. She had spent too much time in trenches.

Oliver, Brit, and Ester were next. They spent the next three and a half hours haggardly dragging them to the old ship. Slips and falls were hard to avoid, and they all were covered in mud. Eventually they had all of them that they could find, minus poor Nadia. Akiko knew her heart couldn't bear to lose another child. She had to go looking for her.

"Get the ship ready, Nath," she nodded to him, "I'm going to find Nadia." Nath nodded in grim understanding. Ryan shook his head and started to follow but she turned him back.

"Emma needs you, Ryan. Nadia needs a doctor. If I don't make it back... tell her I love her. I love you, too," she smiled.

"You won't find her on your own in time. I'm going with you," Ryan shook his head vigorously, but she grabbed his arm.

"I'll be back in time," she reassured him, despite her warning, "help Nath get ready." Ryan suddenly put his arms around her, and she hugged him back. She realized then that if she had a son...he'd be about Ryan's age. It was the warmest thought she could conjure. She pushed him away.

The night grew perilous as she ran back. The sky overhead oscillated between pitch black and blinding green and blue light. It lit the way between the pylons. She started yelling for Nadia. There was no answer. She tried to think of all the places the girl could be. She remembered her filling her bottle more than once and was likely on the hallucinogens... where would she have gone? She made it back to the camp, her legs aching but managing to stay standing. Her reinvigorated strength was starting to fail. She could feel the quiver in her calves and the soreness in all her limbs.

Then light pierced the sky, illuminating a silhouette standing atop the ridge. It was Nadia's. She bolted for her, watching her try to make it across the ridge as lightning singed the world. Fires seemed to be popping up everywhere. The fourteen-year-old saw her between the flashes, slipping in the ridge's mud. Akiko ran toward her, trying to grab onto her.

"Get away from me!" she shouted.

"It's me, Nadia! It's Akiko," she shouted back.

"Where's my mom? What did you do to her!?" the girl shouted back. "You killed her. You all killed her!" She was delirious. She threw her arm out, punching and scratching Akiko's arm, getting too close to the edge.

"Take my hand!" she shouted. But the girl slipped, falling into the lake. Akiko was horrified. She didn't hesitate, leaping down in after her. The freezing water enveloped her like a cloud and the pain from smacking into the surface surged through her knees. The girl was sinking. She grabbed at her, pulling her to the surface.

Lightning struck the water's edge. The gap between the sound and the explosion of rock was frightening. Silent destruction then thundering aftershock. She felt herself sinking now. Whatever she did, she didn't let go of Nadia. The girl had stopped struggling. It grew darker as the surface overtook her. The lights switched between brilliant white and muted green. Orange fires licked the edges of the lake.

She felt someone grab her. Her strength was gone. The gritty shore scratched her face next. The form dove back into the water, pulling Nadia over next to her. She felt herself being pulled out of the rain. She knew they were in the old cave. The figure returned a moment later carrying Nadia, placing her on the crates.

"Akiko, you still with me?" the voice asked. She didn't answer. They grabbed her wrist. She couldn't say anything. It occurred to her that the drugs may have finally kicked in – she was seeing Nik's face. As if he had pulled them from the water. She knew that's where they still were, drowning, at the bottom of the lake.

"Akiko?" he shook her. It was Nik's voice. She had been granted her last wish, after all. She'd get to see him one last time.

"Akiko!?" he yelled. It was strange. He looked just like he did in the picture. Black hair, square face. Dark eyes.

"Come on, wake up!" he yelled. She felt a needle push beneath her skin, bringing the world back to clarity.

"Nikita?" she said feebly.

"I'm here," he held her, "I'm here."

Ryan watched Akiko go, his heart wrenching in his chest. He was torn. He didn't know what to feel. He didn't want to leave Emma...she'd be fine, he told himself. Oliver and Brit had essentially adopted that girl...he knew if they were awake, they'd be out there, too. They would probably have wanted to be left behind – but Akiko was right. Even if they found Nadia, the ship still needed to be prepped if they wanted a chance to leave and they were out of time. Nath's voice tore him from his thoughts.

"Mainer," he snapped, "help me!"

He turned, seeing what he meant. The charging network was going crazy. The superconducting battery could handle the current – but the cables couldn't.

"Release the clamps!" he yelled. Ryan did what he said, pulling the charging cables off, creating an arc flash that nearly took his arm off. Nath pointed to the next one. It was tedious work, made harder by the raging winds and the whipping rain.

They spent the next hour pulling them off. Some of them were already melted. One had fused. He raced over to the toolbox, opening it and nearly having a heart attack. Elyna Quint's body was stuffed inside. A large part of her right side was missing...as if something had burned through it.

Nath had disconnected the last cable on his own, using a tool he'd already extracted from the box. Ryan's hands were clammy as he tried to close the box. His mind raced. The body was too fresh. Nath had to know. He saw the blood on the ground. Was this what happened to Zain?

"I got it, don't worry about getting the tool," Nath told him, waving him back over. Had he seen him open it?

Ryan nodded, unsure of what to do. His first thought was Emma – she was still lying on the workbench. They hadn't put her in the ship yet. He had to do something about Nath...but what? He floated over to the workshop, looking for anything he could find. Any tool. Any object. There was an omnitool tucked in the corner. He took it.

"Don't," Nath warned, pushing what Ryan knew to be the barrel of a gun into his back.

"Don't hurt her, please," Ryan pleaded, dropping it. He turned, putting himself between Nath and Emma.

"I won't hurt her," Nath said with absolution. "And I won't hurt you either. Not unless you force me."

"Why did you kill her? You...you used the laser, didn't you?" he realized, trying not to picture the terrible damage that had been inflicted on Elyna.

"You saw what she was willing to do – totally sober, I might add – or have you already forgotten the concussion she *just* gave you? Here, take this," he threw him an injector. It was marked with a drug name he didn't recognize. He didn't move to pick it up.

"What is it?" he asked.

"Something to keep you from becoming a problem – don't worry, it's not more narcotics. I've already given the reversals to the others. I don't plan to spend the next month in a floating asylum."

"No," Ryan said, throwing the injector on the table. He had likely given it to Emma, too. That was why she was ok when Akiko had checked.

"In case you haven't noticed, Ryan, we need to leave. Take it. Now," Nath ordered. He held the gun steady, pointed straight at his heart. Ryan knew he had no choice. He picked up the injector, pushing it into his skin. His legs soon felt weak. Nath lowered the weapon.

"Why are you doing this? We...trusted you," his mouth started to slacken as he fell back against the shop table, sliding his back down the edge, looking up at Nath.

"As you should. You all would have died much sooner if I didn't put a stopgap in the Rhineland core. We would have been irradiated a month after we landed if I hadn't."

"Where's...Zain?" he asked, putting two and two together.

"Elyna thought she killed her at the edge of the desert after she drugged her and let her attack me. She was too far gone to know which way to go. Last I saw before I disabled her link, she was heading *into* the desert. Probably for the best that she didn't make her way back. After that, I would have found it much harder to be kind."

Nath picked up Emma, taking her into the ship. Ryan tried to move, but nothing worked. Not a single large muscle. He soon came back, putting a piece of machinery on the table. It looked strange.

"Don't mind me, Ryan. Keep asking your questions. We've got a little time before I can clear the comms for us to leave."

Ryan could barely see him working on the machine. He wondered where Akiko had gone. She would be hours away...if the storm hadn't killed her.

"Akiko will come back," he tried, though he didn't sound at all intimidating. Nath knew it was an empty threat.

"No, she won't. She shouldn't have left," Nath said, nodding at the path back to camp that lay behind Ryan. "Those pylons are disabled, now." The distant sound of thunder increased, no longer deafened by the dampers set into the machines beyond the ridge.

"Why don't you just kill me or leave me here?" Ryan asked. "If you've killed Zain and Elyna...and now Akiko. How are you going to keep me from telling the others?"

"I didn't kill Zain, but I know you don't care for the nuance. Thanks to Nik and Torv, you are Emma's legal guardian. I need you – or your body at least – to prove it. Along with the records I pulled from the Rhineland computer before we crashed. Without you, the transfer regime will take her as soon as we set foot in port. When we signal to land, there will be agents on that Juno."

"I'll tell them what's happened. I won't let you take her," Ryan pleaded, not sure if he could even stand up to Nath, let alone them.

"Don't misunderstand me – if you tell the others on the ship, and if you tell the authorities, they will quarantine all of us, and Emma will be shipped somewhere you will never find her. You know this better than anyone. You had a hard time finding your own sister, right?"

"How do you know that?" he sputtered, eyes wide.

"I know a lot about everyone, Ryan. It's my job."

Ryan stared at him, a new panic setting in. "What...are you?"

"Dangerous," Nath leaned down, his voice lacking any hint of his usual sarcasm. He put his arms around Ryan and picked him up, his brute strength far greater than he had shown in their stay on this planet. Ryan watched the strange sky warp in and out of its colors. He wondered if dawn was hiding behind the storm.

Nath placed him in one of the makeshift crash seats they had repurposed from their old pods. He headed to the front of the aircraft. Ryan looked closely at the others, looking for any sign of movement. There was none. Emma was in the seat next to him. His anger was roused at the sight of her. This murderer had been alone with her. This man – this friend – they had all trusted.

"I didn't mean for things to happen this way, Ryan. I want you to understand that. We should never have crashed so fast, only slowed into orbit, with plenty of time to get off...but something went wrong up there. Something I had no way to anticipate."

"What are you talking about?" Ryan asked, confused. Nath had carried the piece of technology back in with him, setting it down on top of the console. It was shaped like a large metal cylinder. A link was shoved in its slot at the top.

"Elyna triggered a transceiver signal that sent a command interrupt to the Rhineland navigation computer. What she didn't know is that this generator could intercept that signal. The loop started a cascade feedback that repeated the command hundreds of times and burned out the data and power lines in the outer ring, rupturing the conduits. The Rhineland was dead in space the moment she pressed that button."

"Elyna...crashed the ship? For this...battery?" Ryan looked at it, trying to imagine how such an innocuous piece of technology could have destroyed a giant mining ship.

"We used to hide tech on planets like this...leaving frequency generators – ones like these," he pointed at the cylinder, "that would let us know where to look. Except...the ship that was sent here had the same problem as the Rhineland. They crashed too fast. A scout was sent to find out what happened, but they fell to ground, too. This gun," he patted the weapon on the dash, "was in the hand of the last colonial who charted this world."

Ryan remembered the body Nath and Akiko had found. Nath had known exactly who it was – probably how he found it anyway.

"The battery...it's colonial?"

"Yes," Nath confirmed, "and ironically it was probably carried here by this ship. Back then, they didn't know much about energy distribution and containment. The knowledge to rework it for lift and thrust wouldn't come until later. This ship was probably built in a dry dock. Never been inside an atmosphere."

"So why come after it when all the others crashed?" Ryan wondered. A tingling in his fingers gave him a burst of hope. He tried to move them, but he soon realized it was just the breeze against his nerves, which were almost totally blocked.

"I have my reasons," Nath turned, hitting more keys on the link attached to the frequency generator, "but if you're looking for the reason Elyna's superiors fed her, it has to do with the sun's interaction with the radiation on this planet. It doesn't behave the way it should. Gets under your skin, but instead of tearing you apart, it stitches you back together. To a point, of course."

"You knew what was happening to us?"

Nath nodded, "We called it cyan sky, from the colors it makes during the blink. I won't pretend to know all the details – in truth, no one does. The 'air' here isn't really air. This atmosphere is a trapped cloud of natural autonuclear particulates. When sunlight hits it, the propagation bends contrary to our knowledge of physics. The process creates oxygen, nitrogen and all the molecules necessary for life – all without true photosynthesis or other 'natural' processes...at least as *we* know them."

Nath talked like he was teaching one of his lessons back in the cave. He lived for this. Ryan found it revolting. It started to make him sick.

"I remember the first time I saw the sky blink, when I finally understood even half of what it was doing...the effect was as beautiful as it is unsettling. Very few mysteries still exist in our little corner of the universe, a result of the needs war and survival have thrust upon us. But this planet is special – there's only one other world like it in all of known space...just not like this. Not anymore." Nath stopped talking and his eyes seemed to gloss over, his hands slowing down at the controls.

Ryan had seen that look on him – he was lost in a memory. He watched him at the console while he kept fighting his growing fatigue. Nath had known. He had known a lot of things.

"What happened to the other world?" Ryan finally asked.

"The war happened. We nuked it so much no one could tell where the smoke ended and the clouds began. Totally unbreathable. But this place – you've seen what it's done to you, and you weren't born here. Emma...she's only ever breathed this air. The radiation should have killed her when she was born, just like it killed Iris, but it didn't. She's a walking miracle."

"You want to study her," Ryan realized, his voice heightened with a fresh concern. He tried as hard as he could to flex his muscles, but he was totally immobile.

"Everyone will, and that's why what happens after we get back to civilization is up to you," he turned around, walking to stand in front him. "If you tell them what happened here, the state will take Emma and it won't take them long to figure out what she is. They will lock her away and dissect her. If you keep all of this to yourself, you can both walk away from this disaster. I can document her condition and once they have the data, they won't ever need to know about her. After that, I will leave you alone and you both can live a normal life. I know it's not a good choice – but it's the only one you have. You can't protect her or the others by fighting me on this. Believe me."

Nath injected him with another dose of the tranquilizer, putting him down completely. The implications of his plans for Emma rushed through his mind, filling his head with nightmarish scenarios. Ryan fought the drugs as much as his body could let him, but he wasn't strong enough.

He had never been strong enough.

Nik looked into Akiko's eyes, his heart turning over in his chest as she focused on him. Like him, she had grown younger. Her contacts were gone, leaving her navy-blue eyes. She stood up, looking at him over and over until finally leaning into him and wrapping her arms tight around his chest, shuddering between tears. After a long moment, she let go and her gaze turned to Nadia. She rushed to her.

"She's fine. No water in her lungs. Just dazed," he told her. She was breathing. Nik was right. He had saved them both.

"We have to get to the ship!" she turned back to him. "If they haven't taken off yet, we may still have a chance. We fixed an old ship. Attached a battery to it. Elyna and Nath think that it can get us airborne. They think we can escape the atmosphere."

"Wait, wait. Backup – Elyna had this plan?" Nik frowned. She nodded and he related everything he now knew about what had happened, including Zain's alibi and finding her in the desert.

"Elyna...she killed poor Vauss," Akiko's eyes strayed to the ground. "I just took her at her word...the ship was shaking." Nik quickly showed her the footage to prove he wasn't lying. She was still in disbelief. This all seemed like a dream.

"If she's with the others, they're in danger," he warned.

"Then we have to go, now!" she said, standing to her feet. He stood too, handing her the pack off his back so he could pick up Nadia. She saw the device, asking what it was.

"I think it's a colonial homing signal," he explained, "but it's interacting with the natural signals on this planet. The captain of the ship I landed near was dead...but she looked as young as us. I don't know what's going on here...but it's not natural."

"Or it is," Akiko nodded in memory. "Just not to us."

"The embedded link in this generator has data they want, either way. I was going to use it as a bargaining chip, depending on what I found out here...but now it looks like we'll just have to see where the night takes us," he shook his head, pulling his hood over his head and trying to shield Nadia's face as best he could. They took off into the blinding storm.

As they crossed under the ridge to the new camp, Akiko noticed the path was no longer lit. She suggested they duck into the camp. It was totally dark inside. Akiko gasped when the walls began to glow.

"It's the generator," Nik said quickly, "the rocks are absorbing the signals...mixing with the resonance."

"Put her down here," Akiko urged. He put Nadia on the table. "If the path is out...we'll have to find another way there," Nik said, looking up at the skylights. The glass had cracked, leaking water into the room.

"The network is out, too. You think she disabled it?" Akiko asked.

"Maybe," Nik mumbled, unconvinced.

A roar and a light that sounded nothing like lightning flashed overhead. Nik ran out of the camp, looking at the sky. It was clear that the unmistakable running lights of a ship were gliding over toward the ridge, near where Akiko said the Rhineland was. He went back inside, watching the radio box he had adapted slowly move its signal to follow the ship –

Elyna had another frequency generator, but she wasn't lifting off yet. She had stopped.

"What is she doing?!" Akiko asked, heading outside to see her touch down in the distance.

"She must need something on the Rhineland," Nik guessed.

"The radiation levels are too high for humans," Akiko warned. "We need to hurry over there."

"We both can't if we're carrying her," Nik nodded at Nadia.

"Akiko..." Nadia mumbled, as if in answer to their silent prayer.

"Nadia!" Akiko went back to her. She slowly stood up. Despite the storm outside, the planet's usual regenerative energy seemed to be at work. It should have taken a few hours more to wake her.

"Who...who's that?" she backed away, as Nik turned.

"Oh good, you can see him, too," Akiko said aloud. Nik smiled.

"Yeah...but who is he?" she asked sharply.

Akiko grabbed her arm, taking some readings, "It's the captain. He crashed on the other side of the equator. He followed our signals to find us. He saved us from drowning in the lake."

"The captain...but he's old...and you said he was dead," she turned back to him, squinting her eyes. Nik remembered the first time he had seen her, having taken her back to her mom. Finally, her eyes went wide and she stood up, walking toward him.

"It really is you..." she looked into his eyes, and he knelt down.

"Looks like you took the right stop this time," he said. She grinned, then started to tear up. He came close and held her. She started to sob uncontrollably, more than Akiko had seen her do in years.

"It's ok," Nik said softly, "Everything's going to be ok." He pulled back and looked Nadia in the eyes. She had stopped crying. He looked to Akiko. She nodded then started to look around the empty camp.

"We can't go in and around the Rhineland without anti-rad boosters. Anything more than fifteen minutes and we're risking permanent damage. I'll go get what I have left," Akiko rushed to her room.

"What is wrong with the walls?" Nadia looked around, "I didn't know they glowed in the dark."

"Lot of secrets on this planet. We'll explain later," Nik promised. Akiko returned, asking for help. The three of them went back to her room, pulling down some of the plating to give more light. He quickly spotted his trunk in the corner.

"You dug this out of the wreckage?" he asked. Akiko nodded.

"Never could open it."

"I moved a few blocks," he said, going over to it. She watched him key in the sequence, popping the lock.

"Here," Akiko pulled Nadia over to her, injecting the booster. She did the same to herself and finally to Nik. She pocketed the others, cinching her jacket shut.

Nik dug his mementos out, tossing most of them on the floor. He finally just dumped his whole trunk. He pulled off his worn jacket and threw it aside, pulling on his old naval jacket that had never fit after he grew out of it. It seemed to be snug now. At the bottom, he dug out a dense little box, handing it to Akiko.

"What's this?" she asked.

"Open it," he insisted. She did. Inside were three pieces of a rifle. She knew it all too well, pulling them out and connecting the old metal links with muscle memory.

"Well good thing you never opened *that*," Nadia joked. Nik traded a glance with Akiko, and they both smiled at the morbid thought.

"And...this," Nik grabbed a small folder, pulling out a single picture.

"I knew you had it," she smiled at him.

Suddenly the memory of her shared kiss with Nath floated into her thoughts. This would be tough to navigate, if they managed to make it back to the ship – it was, though, the very least of her worries. The picture was of the two of them, on their first leave together. Akiko knew they both were sharing the memory.

"Let's get going," he nodded.

The three of them crossed the terrain, quicker now that Nadia had recovered. Rain and lightning cascaded around them. Near the Rhineland, Akiko immediately noticed a change in the atmosphere. The crashed ship's running lights were active.

"I thought you said the network was dead," Nik turned to her.

"It was," she said, "Nath said it was overloaded."

"Elyna's not *that* smart, is she, Akiko?" Nadia asked her. Akiko noticed the scared look on her face – worry for their shared family. She felt it too.

"Nath said she took off after he caught her. Maybe we're wrong. Maybe Nath went ahead and took off so she couldn't come back. All you really know is where the frequency generator is, right?" she turned to Nik. He nodded, hesitant. She knew the look in his eyes. He knew something wasn't right.

"Look," Nik pointed. The ship was next to the connection in the rear substructure. It was shielded from radiation better than a human body was, so anyone inside should be ok, at least for now. "Let's go."

"Another dose," Akiko warned. She dosed herself then Nadia. Nik took an injector and hit the actuator, tossing it.

"Wait," Nik stopped, pulling up his pants near his bad knee. She could tell he was still stiff on his leg when they made their way here. It was only now that she realized it wasn't because he was still wounded – it was because he still had the brace. He grimaced as he tore it off, leaving it on the ground. A few bleeding depressions on his knee were all that was left.

The cartilage had grown back. He looked at Akiko as he pulled the leg of his dark jeans back down.

She could only see the soldier she had once known. Unchanged. Unburdened of the horror that war had hoisted on his shoulders. He was even wearing the same jacket. The moment passed, but she felt emboldened. This was it. This was their end run. Whatever waited for them, they were as prepared as they could be to face it.

"Nadia, once we're at the ship and we make sure Elyna is not inside, you get in and lock the door. You still remember how to do that, right?" Akiko asked. They all had practiced. She nodded in affirmation. The three of them took off.

As they crossed the wreckage, Nik became increasingly unsettled at the parts of the ship lighting up and turning off. Elyna was inside, messing with the terminals. He had already toggled his old link, but it was not able to connect – she had disabled them. They finally reached the ship, where they found it sealed, but not locked.

The transparent metal windows at the front gave them a view of the inside. Everyone was there except for Nath, Elyna...and Emma. Akiko heaved the door open. She and Nadia went inside while Nik stayed outside, standing guard with the rifle. After a minute, he knocked on the door for a status report.

"Ryan's been tranquilized," she warned. "The rest of them are all still recovering from the drug cocktail."

"Then we need to find Nath, Elyna, and Iris's girl," Nik summed up. Akiko and Nadia came back out.

"You stay here," Akiko told Nadia, "and when this number," she pointed at the advanced scanner, which now held Ryan's vitals, "when it gets to this point, give him this. It will wake him up. Tell him where we are and how long we've been in there. This will directly link to Nik – to the captain's radio. Ok?" Akiko handed her the scanner and her own link, which they had ad hoc synced. Nadia nodded, carrying the scanner back inside and shutting the door.

"I don't like this," Nik shook his head as they both started inside the Rhineland. Every few seconds, the running lights flashed in and out, casting them in a strobe light.

"There," Akiko pointed at the radio box – it was directing them to the reactor core.

"The levels are lower," Nik noticed, pointing at the indicator. "It must be the battery on that ship...it's drinking the radiation."

"Why would they hide that kind of technology here – we didn't have it during the war? Did we?" Akiko raised her eyebrows.

"No. We didn't," Nik confirmed.

The two of them headed for the reactor. They split up once they reached the access corridor. It was already open. He gave Akiko the rifle so she could take the high ground while he took the direct path. She was the better shot between the two of them. The feeling in Nik's stomach grew worse as he crossed the threshold.

Nath was typing on the main access terminal. Cole's radiation ravaged body lay unceremoniously next to him. Emma's small body was leaning against the railing, still unconscious. Akiko saw him first.

"Nath, where's Elyna?" Akiko asked.

"Dead," he said simply. He did not turn around.

"What are you doing, Nath?" Nik asked.

Nath stopped typing on the console, then slowly turned around.

"Torv really missed the forest for the trees...huh, Nik?" Nath sighed. Nik did not like his tone in the slightest.

"You crashed the ship," Nik put voice to his fear, "Why?"

"You think you're the only one they wanted off the Rhineland?"

"That is no excuse to murder 198 people," Nik replied coldly.

"I didn't intend to crash like this, but with Elyna pulling the trigger early and Torv looking in all the right places, my hand was forced. I did what I had to do."

"And the others? Why did they have to die?"

"Collateral damage. Zain and Elyna both sabotaged our way off this world by trying to hide their guilt, but only one of them had remorse. Elyna was going to leave us all behind. I couldn't let that happen."

"Collateral damage," Nik repeated, his voice void of emotion.

"You understand, Nik. The cost of our actions. They ordered you to bomb your father's Juno. They gave you a ship, but it wasn't a home."

"His Juno wasn't home either. But it was still wrong," Nik said softly.

"You're not innocent either, Akiko," Nath looked up. She held the rifle on his face. "Overdosing those dying children on anti-rad panels. You were young, and it was war, but you made that choice for them."

"No, I'm not innocent," she sighed wearily, eyes welling up with tears, "Watching children suffer is enough to break anyone." She wiped them away with the back of her hand.

"You decrypted Torv's data," Nik discerned.

"Surprisingly difficult to do, actually," Nath nodded. "He was using methods I didn't think the transfer regime knew yet. Shows what I know. Been out of the game a while now," he paused, looking between them. "We all make hard choices," he nodded gravely, "And we make new ones to atone for our mistakes. I tried to make it work here."

"I thought I knew you," Nik shook his head, exhausted, "but all these people are dead because I didn't pay enough attention. Why does the corps want to get rid of you?"

"Oh, not the corps. They couldn't care less if I took up air on the Rhineland or not. No, the Coalition wants me off. Or what's left of it. A war no one remembers, you said? I wish that was true. War is a state of mind. It never ends for them. Peace is a state of mind, too. For me, I made my choice. I was content to live in the latter. But then they took that choice away. After my family got irreparably irradiated by recon priming? After my friends were all incinerated by the first wave bombings? After all the years of my *life* I sacrificed for them? No. They don't get to throw me away. Not like the two of you."

"Recon priming? First wave bombings?" Akiko's brow furrowed, "That was before the war...over 50 years ago." She shifted her rifle slightly.

"You remember what I told you? I got stuck on a moon. Well, that was half right. It was a planet. Much like this one. Already half irradiated. We were testing it for a new variant of these generators," he motioned to the frequency generator sitting behind him and the one Nik himself was still carrying. "But one day they found us, and started shelling without warning. My team was incinerated. All except for me."

"You said they found you a few months later," she recalled.

"They did. But it wasn't months – it was decades. The war had passed me by. I was given a new identity, seeing how I was younger than I was when I left. They realized too late what they had found and started looking for more planets...but then the war ended. When the transfer regime got its claws on their books, they started consolidating. I agreed to disassociate and join the mining corps. Burned my older accounts. My profile doesn't look suspicious to someone like Torv because I was never in it. No serial number. Even my DNA had changed."

"Why now? What do they care what happens to you?" Akiko leaned down, trying hard to not to relax her grip.

"The first rule of being an asset is asset *control*. You don't get to make your own choices. The second rule is die young. I bent the rules. Go to ground, they said. Settle down. Live out your life. I agreed. In a way."

"So, when the opportunity to land yourself on another one of these planets came, you took it?" Nik guessed.

"Nothing's ever that simple…but yes," Nath nodded.

"What do you gain out of this? What do you want with Emma?" Akiko questioned, moving a little closer and lining up the sights. Nath tracked her with his eyes, flicking between the two of them.

"The battery isn't enough for them. Emma was born here. Where the first planet healed me of some childhood injuries and put the cancer from the bombing into remission – this world may have made her invincible. Even without boosters, she's flushing the radiation. I had to get proof before I head back. It's the only way to make them see their mistake."

"You're not leaving with that little girl," Nik shook his head.

"Sorry, Nik. But I am," Nath narrowed his eyes at Nik, clicking his link. The reactor room went dark.

Akiko fired as the lights went out, but she missed. She dared not fire again in case she hit Emma.

Nik felt the gut punch before he saw it but recovered quickly enough. The walls of the Rhineland reactor housing began to glow with latent Cherenkov radiation and the effects of the generators. He realized in that moment that the rocks of this world must be highly radioactive. Nath found him again, grappling and throwing him against the railing.

Nik fought back, steadying himself and finding the old combat stances. Hook, counter, grapple. Struggle. Throw. Hook. Hook. Counter. The two of them fought while Akiko struggled to get a fix on Nath. She fired a couple times, narrowly hitting him in the shoulder. He staggered, the wound stopping after a few moments.

Akiko rushed down to the lower level while Nik continued to get pummeled. When she had a clear shot, she fired at Nath until the rifle jammed, knocking him to the floor. He lay there, bleeding out. Eventually he stopped breathing altogether. Akiko bent down and felt for his pulse. She sighed, shaking her head.

Nik sighed too, rubbing his shoulders, breathing hard. He nodded, pulling the link off Nath's wrist then heading to the terminal while Akiko rushed to Emma, picking her up and injecting her with a booster shot – regardless of whether what Nath said was true or not, she was not going to take any chances with her life.

"What was he doing?" she asked, carrying the five-year-old in her arms. She was relieved that Emma was still breathing.

"The network is locked. He was trying to pull the data from the core. I'm assuming it's something his people wanted."

"Who were his people, really?" she looked back at him, disgusted. She didn't know what to think of him...he had helped them so much in the last five years. Was it really all for this? Was this who he really was?

"Could be the Coalition, like he said. Could even be the transfer regime and he didn't know it. They're all fighting for control. I stopped paying attention a long time ago."

"We both did," Akiko smiled weakly. Nik lowered his head, taking a moment to build out the opcodes on his link. It completed in seconds, authorizing the deletion, erasing Nath's data.

"All of this is my fault..." he sighed, bending down to look at Sebastian's horribly burned body, gently reaching over to grab his link.

"No, it isn't. But it's over now," Akiko put her hand on his shoulder, "Let's get off this planet." He turned to her, seeing the tears and resilience in her eyes, bathed in the cool blue of the reactor. He nodded in agreement and the pair stood up.

They left the reactor behind, telling Nadia they were on their way. Ryan had yet to wake up. Back at the ship, they put Emma back in one of the crash seats while Nik investigated the cockpit. Akiko went to shut the door. Nadia screamed as Akiko was violently pulled out of the ship. Nik snapped his head in their direction, rushing the door and throwing himself at whatever lay beyond it.

Nath had survived the gunshots, landing underneath Nik as they toppled to the ground. The two renewed their previous fight in the sloshing mud. Akiko was struggling to recover a few meters away. She pulled an injector from her pocket, tossing it near Nik. He saw it, but before he could reach it, Nath threw him violently against the side of the old ship, cracking one of his ribs. Akiko scrambled to try and get at the injector again, but a gust of wind blew her off her feet, throwing sheets of rain across her face.

Lightning sizzled near them, terminating at the rod still pinned to the side of the old ship. The rear of the ship glowed with the sudden influx of power. Nik had an idea. Crude. But necessary. He ran for a long, thin piece of shrapnel nearby. Nath followed him, his eyes bloodshot, filled with rage. Nik picked up the piece of metal, rushing for the side of the ship. Before Nath could get to him, he used it to snap the lightning rod off the side. It fell to the ground.

Akiko had reached the injector, slipping in behind Nath and jabbing it into his shoulder. Half his body on that side went limp, but he still knocked Nik to the ground. She threw a hard hook to his chest, but he blocked it, shoving her to the ground. He staggered from the drugs, but was able to recover, steeling himself solidly in the mud, against the gusting wind.

Nik pulled his sleeves down over his hands and grabbed the shrapnel. Nath tried to hit him again, but he had trouble with dead weight of his one side. Nik jabbed the metal length into the battery compartment on the old ship. It sparked, telling him it had connected. Nath realized what he was doing, picking up the lightning rod himself and glaring at Nik as he bore down on him, the pointed end ready to pierce his chest.

Akiko found the injector and jabbed it in his leg. It gave him little pause. He flipped the rod and smacked her with the other end, slicing her up the arm and chest, dropping it. He jerked around, picking up another piece of shrapnel and taking his position back above Nik, vapor pouring out of his mouth with every breath. Nik locked eyes with Nath, ready for the end.

A shot rang out, followed by several more. Nik's eyes flicked over to see Nadia holding the old pistol in two hands. Ryan stumbled out as soon as she started firing, grabbing the broken rod next to Akiko and flipping it to the sharpest point where it snapped off. He stabbed it deep into Nath's shoulder blade; he wailed in pain.

Nik picked himself off the ground, ramming into Nath's side and sending him near the rear of the ship. A pulse of blinding electricity arced from the shrapnel to the rod, followed by a thundering crack that echoed across the valley. The metal on both sides was scorched and nearly incinerated. Nath lay on the ground, half his body violently burned by the rush of superconducting current.

Nik's ears were numb and still ringing in the wake of the electric explosion. He slowly regained his hearing as he helped Akiko off the ground. Nadia was supporting Ryan. A few more moments passed before he could hear Nath's wheezing. He turned, walking toward him, kneeling next to him in the mud. The rain was mixing with the other man's blood, streaming down his face. The two men simply stared at each other between the flashes of lightning.

Nath turned to the ship. Emma was rubbing her eyes, standing next to Akiko, who was taping up her wounds and tending to Ryan at the same time. He stood there, looking toward Nath, a blank look in eyes. Nath slowly turned back to Nik, one eye still visible beneath his marred face.

"You can hide her...but they'll find you," he coughed hoarsely.

"No more hiding," Nik shook his head, putting a hand on his shoulder.

"For what it's worth...more should have survived the crash...but Elyna was a little too fast for me," Nath grumbled, his voice garbled with blood. He seemed almost ashamed to admit it. Nik reached down and took Nath's good hand, feeling the strength leaving him.

"I've buried too many people on this planet, Nath. You didn't need to add any more."

"Sorry...to inconvenience you...captain," Nath smiled, his head drifting to the right, rain pouring down his motionless face. This time, he was truly gone. Nik closed his eyes, taking a long breath before opening them again. He finally let go of Nath's hand.

Nik got up off the ground, looking over at the others. Akiko had laid her hand on Nadia's shoulder, whispering something to calm her down. She had taken the gun from the teenager, but she was still shaking. Ryan was holding Emma. He slowly pushed past them, heading to the cockpit. The storm would be in full force within minutes. Fires raged on the plains above the Rhineland wreckage.

"We have a problem," he announced, though he already knew that. It was a calculated risk...but Nath had been relentless.

"It's drained," Akiko realized. They all had come back inside the ship. All of them looked to Nik for guidance. He put his hands on the pilot's chair, toggling a few of the controls.

"Not completely...just enough to keep us from gaining lift."

"You said it was gaining energy from the reactor – can't we just wait for it to charge up again?" she suggested.

"There's not enough from the passive reaction – that's how we could even *be* in the reactor," Nik shook his head.

"And an active reaction?" Ryan let go of Emma. Nik had already jumped to this conclusion. He could see the same thought in the younger man's eyes.

"We need to be in the air. But yes...I think it would be enough," Nik nodded. He stood up, pulling off his jacket, covered in blood and dirt from the fight. Ryan walked to the front of the ship. Akiko followed behind.

"No," Ryan told Nik, blocking his path.

"I need to do this," Nik said, adamant.

"You're a pilot. I'm not," Ryan replied, unhesitating.

"It has autopilot cards," Nik gestured to the cockpit.

"Would you trust them?" Ryan stared deep into Nik's eyes. When Nik couldn't meet his, he knew the answer.

"What are you talking about?" Akiko stepped between them.

"We can restart the Rhineland reactor. The active reaction will supply enough radiation for the superconductor to gain lift."

"*Restart* the thing that's creating this storm without even being turned on? Are you insane?" she shifted her glance between them.

"It can work, Akiko. That's not the problem. The problem is that restarting it is normally accomplished from a line feed to the bridge – a feed that no longer exists."

"You mean it's back down there – *in* the reactor?" she realized.

"Yes," Nik nodded, staring at Ryan.

"Then I'll go," she said, trying to shut them down.

"Akiko, I don't know enough medicine to treat anything that might go wrong between here and the Juno. I can't pilot. I'm useless to you up there. And–" Ryan gestured to the others unconscious in the small ship, "I don't think there are any other takers."

"You're her *father*," Akiko said, grabbing him by the shoulders. He slowly took her hands and pulled them back down, holding them.

"Ryan, you can't go. I'll go. I'll do it," Nadia spoke up. The three adults turned to look at her, watching as Emma grabbed her hand. She looked down at the younger girl. Nadia was no longer shaking.

"None of us would ever forgive ourselves, Nadia. I'm sorry," Ryan looked her in the eyes, smiling grimly, "It's not going to be you." He put his hand on Nadia's shoulder, squeezing it before turning to Nik, who disconnected his link and handed it to Ryan.

"Scuttle protocol. Forces a restart and raw output. It's already coded. Just plug it in...that's all it needs."

"Ryan," Akiko hugged him, kissing his cheek.

"Take care of her," he whispered.

"As long as my heart's still beating," she whispered back.

"This should be me," Nik held out his hand. Ryan took it, holding it but finding himself not wanting to let go. Nik could see the tears building in his eyes and he slowly pulled him into his arms, embracing him. Ryan was close enough to feel the beating of the older man's heart. It brought up a surge of emotion he'd left buried for too long. He leaned into him, shaking his head to dispel the tears.

Nik searched their options several times over in his head while he held him. Ryan was trembling slightly as reality started taking hold, but either way, he was right – it had to be him. The day Nik had gone to war was one of the easiest goodbyes he had ever made – since he had never made one. This was different – Ryan was leaving someone behind. When the war ended, Nik had no home. There was nothing left. His mother and father were gone. He had no brothers or sisters. No chance to say goodbye.

That pain overshadowed so much of his life, and the bleed into this moment was almost too much for him. He had barely known the younger man, and the painful tears he saw in both Ryan and Akiko's eyes told him how much he had missed out on, stuck on the dark side of this world. The moment grew heavier while they stood there, and they both knew every second took away from their odds. Nik felt like he was saying goodbye to something greater, while being given a chance he didn't deserve.

Slowly, he let go, patting Ryan gently on the shoulders.

"I'm sorry," Nik spoke softly, his eyes red.

Ryan could only look at him between tears, unable to speak. It was dawning on him what he was doing. What he *had* to do.

"Please don't go, Ryan," Nadia ran forward and hugged him, "Without you and Iris, I wouldn't be alive...please stay with us. Please don't go." Ryan held her, looking at the young girl he and Iris had picked out of the corridor in the chaos not so long ago. It was hard to believe that this was goodbye...he would miss this part of Emma's life, too. The thought made his heart hurt.

Emma was standing wide-eyed beside Nadia, looking up at Ryan as he turned to leave. He pulled off his jacket and leaned down, wrapping it around her. She had started to cry.

"Don't go, daddy," she said finally, throwing her arms around him. He grasped her tightly, tears running down his face.

"I love you...so much," Ryan held her. The rest of the cabin stayed quiet while the sobs of the little girl filled it. He thought of Iris in the long span of that moment, hoping what he was doing was right and not just abandoning her daughter to some new unseen danger. It was, he imagined, what a father should feel. He sighed deeply, whispering into her ear, "And that's why I have to go."

Akiko took hold of Emma, picking her up.

Ryan stopped at the exit to the old ship, hanging onto the latch, looking at each one of them in turn. He looked at Emma one last time, smiling as best he could through the tears, then turned to leave.

After a long minute, Nik reached out and pulled the door shut.

Ryan found his way to the reactor easily enough, listening to the sounds of cracking thunder and thrashing metal outside its hull. The body of the Rhineland's engineer lay next to the access terminal, marred by severe radiation, but he had no time to dwell on him. He shoved Nik's link into the open alcove. The heavy pause as the terminal screen scrolled made his heart skip several beats.

A startling vibration and heavy rumbling in the massive machinery answered his unspoken question. The reactor's heat refraction system opened overhead, cascading down rain and light as immense heat built up on his skin. His knees gave way and he collapsed back onto the railing, looking up at the sky. The Galileo screamed across it, gaining speed as Nik piloted the craft through the storm and into the upper atmosphere.

The storm overhead grew into one blinding flash of light as the lightning converged and surged down on the Rhineland, focusing on the reactor. He felt the hairs on his skin rise with the raw electric current, breathing in the fresh ozone and closing his eyes as the green light pulsed in rhythm with the blue light of the reactor.

His last thought was of Iris and Emma.

(*)

Nik felt the rush of endorphins as the muscle memory surged through his brain, pushing the toggles and modules that guided them away from the planet. He looked down, watching the reaction between the planet and the Rhineland grow in intensity, giving way to the horizon as they finally crossed it. The false sun of the fusion reaction touched the true sun at its crest, a stark contrast between natural and artificial beauty.

(*)

Akiko had wrapped Emma in her arms, securing her in the seat with her as they lifted off from the world that had been their home for the last five years. She had lost a son. The little girl had lost her mother before she ever knew her and now, she had lost the only father she had ever known.

All their plans, though made by those who meant them harm, had come together. There were no leaks. No loss of oxygen. They had all the power they needed. She watched Nik at the controls, focused and in his element. It brought much needed joy in a moment of such pain...she didn't know how to feel.

She just held Emma tighter, watching the sunrise.

Akiko laid the book down when Nik walked in. She could hear the gate closing in the backyard, followed soon after by Emma's increasingly familiar laughter and a dog trying to bark. The sly look on Nik's face was all she needed to see to know they were keeping the dog. She looked out the back window. It was a small basenji puppy, which explained the strange sound – its bark was more like a yodel. Emma fell on the grass and it was crawling on top of her. She couldn't stop laughing as it kept trying to climb on top of her.

"Did you find anything?" she asked. It had been a few months since they had left the strange world behind.

"Not much. Iris and Ryan have no immediate family left. Still no results from genetic matching. The doctor says they may never match, with what happened on that planet," Nik took a seat, rubbing his eyes. He was certainly tired, but she knew he had finally been resting better.

"Did you talk to Euler's mother?" Akiko asked hesitantly.

"Yes. She was still heartbroken, but grateful for the closure."

It was one of many things he had been obligated to do, some far more pleasant than others. When they made it to the Juno, Oliver and Brit had asked him to marry them before everyone parted ways. He had, his authority as captain having been temporarily reinstated by a friend in the transfer registrar. Once the ceremony was over, he and Akiko both agreed it was also time, asking their friend to do the same for them. Later that night, they too were married with the other survivors in attendance as witnesses. It was the last time any of them had seen one another.

The next day, everyone left on the transport routes. Oliver and Brit took Nadia with them to Sol. Camden and Ester went home to their families, who had been shocked to learn of their survival. Jin and Halim left for the rig depot in Wycliffe, to cash out their special severance, vowing never to set foot on mining ships again.

The mining corps had already declared the Rhineland a loss, so there was little left to close on the rest of the crew that had not survived. Since they had deleted the data on the Rhineland network, there were no records they had saved and nothing Nik or the others could add once they had been debriefed by the registrar.

Weeks later, he and Akiko had been called on to testify in a closed hearing involving the fates of Torv, Nath, Elyna and Zain. On the way to the Juno, they had all debated about what they would tell the authorities. In the end, they agreed to be honest and forward about events, no matter how it all shook out, believing it was the only way to find some peace and closure. Fear and secrecy is what led to the crash, killing so many of their friends and family. Nik feared for everyone – Emma most of all – but it was time for the truth. The others had their statements taken, relieved of being part of the official proceedings.

The hearing and connected investigation was swiftly concluded. Elyna's parents had been found dead three years prior. A cell inside the colonial militants had been arrested and charged. The Rhalis had already declared Zain dead and Torv's messages to the enforcement system had landed them in several investigations involving their roles in unsanctioned drug trafficking. They had given TROI all their records on their activities in exchange for continued licenses to operate in the transfer routes. Torv's file had been officially closed, thanks to Nik's testimony and data from his link. That left Nath. He had been convinced that one of the governments would take Emma, should the truth of the planet become known.

Torv's superior was at the hearing, joined by the intelligence and operations adjutant for the Coalition Provisional Minister. In addition to the frequency generators and the battery, they were also very aware of these planets – and Nath's history with them. While the science was still unclear, the effects were fully isolated to the worlds themselves. Their medical officers had scanned all the survivors and concluded what Akiko had already begun to suspect – they were becoming as normal as anyone else, albeit much younger, which they had seen even in their brief time back. Even Emma had gotten a cold soon after they landed.

Their final conversation and ruling was not lengthy, but they left Nik and Akiko with assurances that no government would be coming for her – or any of them. If someone wanted to pick up this research, they would have to do it firsthand; though this disaster had proven the risk far outweighed the reward. On the more personal question of their request to be Emma's guardians, they were given a timeline of three months to verify no other claims on her could be made. Both had been ready for a fight, but it was more than they could have hoped for, so they complied.

"Oliver called. He and Brit gained guardianship over Nadia. It wasn't an easy conversation. Her father wanted to cede to the state, but in the end, with her age, Junie's will made it Nadia's choice," Akiko smiled.

Nik nodded, shifting the pad on the table. "I guess we should get that settled, too. The deadline was three days ago. I'm done waiting. No one's made any claims against us."

"So, what do we put down?" Akiko shifted the pad so she could see it.

"What do you think of that?" Nik motioned toward the last one. It was a small, hastily written obituary. She frowned, until she saw the last section. Her frown began to soften.

"Ryan Mainer was reported as part of the tragic loss of the MCV Rhineland during its eighth tour of duty…" she read, skipping to the end, "…he was preceded in death by his father Clint Winstead, mother Trisha Mainer, and his estranged sister, Emma Mainer. He will be remembered alongside the rest of the Rhineland crew at plot 107 of the Aurora memorial habitat for those lost in service of humanity into deep space."

"It was the name of his sister," Akiko looked at Nik. They both looked at each other, tears in their eyes.

They finished filling out the rest of the forms, signing and sending them over the Juno's net. Nik had already done the prep work for establishing Emma's records, and he had used the last of his weight in the registrar to close the rest of the records for the Rhineland's survivors, giving them room to breathe and find a way to pick up their lives again.

"While you were gone, I had a long discussion with my friend in the medical corps. Emma is essentially green across the board, other than some minor vitamin deficiencies – which is to be expected. She also showed me the actuarial rates on our radiation exposure inside the reactor…she said she wasn't at all worried. Compared to what we looked like after we were discharged, this was nothing. I had her run some extra tests though…and she found this," Akiko pushed the pad over to him.

Nik picked the pad up and switched his glance between it and her. He put his glasses on, then pulled them off, squinting at the results. She just stared at him, waiting for him to stop reading.

"Is this real?" he finally asked. Outside, Emma had rolled over again with the dog. He looked out at her. She wouldn't be alone growing up. And for them…a dead dream had been brought back to life. Nik suddenly leaped over the counter and kissed Akiko, picking her up and landing lopsided in the chair.

"You're amazing, Rai," he grinned through tears, wrapping his arms around her and looking down at her chest. She did the same, then turned to see the little girl with her dog out the window.

"I hope she doesn't mind someone else," Akiko looked longingly out at Emma as she and the dog rolled at the same time.

"She's got us...and he will, too," Nik twisted in the chair, so they were watching out the window together. He closed his eyes, freezing the moment in his mind, holding it there as the sun warmed his face, hoping it would never end.

Rane Eden is a software engineer by trade who is passionate about faith, writing, coding, science fiction, art, video games and board games. He started dreaming up worlds in his head when he was 5 years old and never stopped. One of his greatest joys is making tabletop role-playing systems from scratch and playing them with friends. He lives in Tennessee.

TYPOGRAPHY

Reenie Beanie	TITLE
IM FELL Double Pica	BODY
Arcon	TABLE OF CONTENTS HEADINGS PAGE NUMBERS
Nova Round	COPYRIGHT PAGE COVER SUMMARY
Share Tech Mono	COVER COPYRIGHT
Monofett	SITE URL